JAYNE ANN KRENTZ

THE VANISHING

piatkus

PIATKUS

First published in the United States in 2020 by Berkley,
An imprint of Penguin Random House LLC, New York
First published in Great Britain in 2020 by Piatkus

1 3 5 7 9 10 8 6 4 2

A CIP catalogue record for this book
is available from the British Library.

ISBN 978-0-349-42441-5

Printed and bound in Great Britain by Clays Ltd, Elcograf S.p.A.

Papers used by Piatkus are from well-managed forests
and other responsible sources.

MIX
Paper from
responsible sources
FSC® C104740

Piatkus
An imprint of
Little, Brown Book Group
Carmelite House
50 Victoria Embankment
London EC4Y 0DZ

An Hachette UK Company
www.hachette.co.uk

www.littlebrown.co.uk

To Frank, as always, with love.

THE
VANISHING

CHAPTER 1

Fogg Lake, fifteen years earlier . . .

C atalina Lark saw the murder take place about four seconds before it happened. Maybe five seconds. She was still getting used to the ominous visions. They always caught her off guard.

She'd had flashes of bizarre scenes for the past couple of years, but a few months ago, shortly after her sixteenth birthday, they had started occurring more frequently. She was trying to convince herself that the visions were merely hallucinations. Tonight, at least, she had a reasonable explanation for the murky vision. She and her best friend, Olivia LeClair, were deep inside the vast cave system surrounding Fogg Lake. Everyone in town knew that those who went into the Fogg Lake caverns often experienced hallucinations and other inexplicable sensations. That was, of course, why every self-respecting teen in the small community made it a point to sneak out of the house and spend a night in the caves at least once before graduating from the one-room high school. The adults didn't approve, but Catalina had heard some of them refer to it as a local "rite of passage." Most of them had done the same thing when they were in their teens.

Tonight was the night that she and Olivia had decided to brave the caves. They had brought sleeping bags, a camp lantern and a couple of flashlights. Their day packs were crammed with bottled water and snacks. An underground river ran through the caves, surfacing in various caverns before it vanished again into the rocky depths. The water was clear and safe to drink, but it was dangerous to get too close to the edge. The wet, slippery rocks were treacherous and the current in the river was strong.

They had heard the two men arrive just as they were trying to decide where to set up camp.

The sounds of footsteps and low voices had echoed in the underground labyrinth. She and Olivia had turned off the camp lantern, grabbed their sleeping bags and rushed to hide in one of the many side tunnels.

They had been startled when the two men—strangers—showed up with a camp lantern and a large black case.

The small community of Fogg Lake didn't get a lot of visitors, nor did it welcome the few who did manage to find their way into town. Most kids are taught to be wary of strangers, but in Fogg Lake, parents took that instruction to extremes. Catalina and Olivia had been raised with a degree of caution that bordered on paranoia, which was why it did not occur to either of them to reveal their presence to the two men. Instead, acting on their ingrained training, they had retreated deeper into the narrow side tunnel. Once safely concealed in the darkness, they had gone very still, hardly daring to breathe. *Like baby rabbits confronted by a snake,* Catalina thought. The analogy was annoying.

The two men had not quarreled. There had been no demands, no violent threats; just some tense, muffled conversation. The shorter of the pair was middle-aged and a little overweight. He wore black-framed glasses and looked like an engineer or a scientist.

His companion was younger—midtwenties, Catalina decided—lean and fit. His head was shaved. He was the one who had carried the black case into the cavern.

Both men were dressed for a trek in the woods.

A short time ago the man with the glasses had opened the case and removed what appeared to be a sophisticated lab instrument. Catalina could have told him he was wasting his time. Computers, cell phones and other high-tech devices did not work well in the vicinity of Fogg Lake, if they worked at all.

The man with the glasses was clearly frustrated by whatever he saw on the screen of his fancy instrument. He leaned over the device to tap some keys. That was when Catalina got a dark vision of Shaved Head reaching into a zippered pocket on the side of his pack. She saw him take out a syringe, yank off the plastic cap and plunge the needle into the other man's neck.

Catalina was still struggling with the vision when reality struck, disorienting and shocking all her senses.

Shaved Head took the syringe out of his pack, removed the cap and stabbed the needle into his companion's neck.

The doomed man cried out and sank to his knees. His aura weakened rapidly. He gazed up at his assailant in disbelief and confusion.

"What?" he managed. Then understanding descended. "You stupid bastard. You don't understand how my invention works. It's tuned to my frequencies and only mine. I'm the only one who can activate it. You'll never find what you're looking for without me."

The killer waited. His aura did not blaze with rage or with the spikes that indicated mental instability. The energy around him was hot but all Catalina could detect was satisfaction and maybe a sense of anticipation. She wasn't sure of her reading, though. Olivia was better at interpreting auras.

The man who had set up the odd instrument grunted and collapsed on the floor of the cavern. Shaved Head crouched beside him and began to search the dying man's pockets.

"Why?" the victim managed in a voice that was thick with the effects of whatever had been in the syringe.

"You served your purpose," the killer said. "You're no longer needed."

"Stupid, stupid fool," the victim muttered.

In the next second his failing aura sputtered and died.

Catalina blinked a few times in a desperate attempt to suppress the images—she was getting better at it, even though the visions were becoming stronger—but the horrible scene did not disappear. The man who had fallen to the floor of the cavern was very real and very dead. His attacker casually checked for a pulse.

Catalina looked at Olivia, who was trying to shrink into the shadows on the opposite side of the narrow tunnel. Olivia's aura was ablaze with shock and panic. So much for the faint hope that what had just gone down in the cavern was nothing more than a particularly powerful hallucination. They had both witnessed a murder.

The sound of movement in the cavern made Catalina turn her attention to Shaved Head. He was on his feet now. The body of his companion was draped over one shoulder. He walked to the edge of the river and dropped his victim into the water.

He watched for a moment, probably making certain that the current carried off the evidence of his crime. When he was satisfied, he went back to the device the victim had set up and started to tap the keys.

He stopped suddenly, his attention caught by something he saw in the shadows of a nearby boulder. His aura flared.

A terrifying vision began to unfold but Catalina did not need it to warn her that she and Olivia were in mortal danger. Common sense was more than enough to kick off a wave of panic.

For a beat, an unnerving hush gripped the cavern. In the echoing stillness only the soft murmur of the underground river could be heard. Catalina held her breath. She knew Olivia was doing the same. She also knew they had both just realized that in their hurry to hide they had left the lantern behind.

Shaved Head saw the lantern, grabbed it and spun around on his heel, searching the shadows of the cavern. Catalina knew he couldn't see them from where he presently stood, but if he began a methodical search it was only a matter of time before he found them.

Shaved Head dropped the lantern and once again reached into his pack. This time he took out a gun.

With a flashlight gripped in one hand and the pistol in the other, he started to examine the side tunnels one by one. Catalina knew that if she and Olivia did not move, they would be doomed.

She looked at Olivia again and sensed that her friend had come to the same conclusion. They had no choice but to retreat deeper into the tunnel in which they were hiding.

———————

The man with the gun continued to prowl the vast cavern, pausing to spear the beam of his flashlight into every side passage.

Catalina switched on her own flashlight. The killer would surely see the glare, but he was still on the far side of the cavern. It would take him a couple of minutes to cross the big chamber to the tunnel where she and Olivia were hiding because of the curve in the underground river. He would have to circle around it. If they moved fast they could be out of sight in seconds. He would hear their footsteps for some time because the cavern was an echo chamber, but it would take him a while to locate the right tunnel.

"Stop," Shaved Head shouted. "Police. I won't hurt you. I'm an undercover cop working for the Feds. I'm here to protect you. That man was a killer, a danger to your community. I was sent to stop him."

A couple of kids from a town on the outside might have bought that story, Catalina thought. But Shaved Head had picked the wrong teens to try to fool. Fogg Lake youth were raised to be suspicious of outsiders in general. It seemed like a good idea to double down on that concept when you had just watched one stranger kill another stranger.

———————

They plunged deeper into the tunnel and rounded a corner, and suddenly the passageway was transformed into a hall of mirrors. *At least,* Catalina thought, *that's how I see them.* She blinked hard but her vision didn't change. She did not know exactly how things appeared to Olivia, but judging from the way her friend clutched her hand, the visions were just as frightening.

"You'll get lost," the killer shouted. His voice echoed down the tunnel. "You'll die in there. Come out. I promise you'll be safe. Trust me. I'm a cop."

Catalina and Olivia kept going. They rounded another curve in the cramped passageway and scrambled to a halt at the sight of the storm of energy—intense swirls of light that Catalina could both sense and see—that barred their way.

"What is it?" Olivia whispered.

"I don't know," Catalina said. "But he's still coming. We've got no choice. We're going to have to go through it."

"You might as well come out," the killer said. "Just a matter of time before I find you."

His voice was more distant now but he had not given up the chase.

Catalina studied the strange storm. "It looks like one of those pictures of giant hurricanes taken from a satellite. There's sort of an eye in the center."

"We'll aim for that," Olivia said. "Ready?"

"Ready."

They tightened their grip on each other's hands and hurtled

forward, straight into the core of the vortex of fierce energy. They dove through it.

Catalina struggled to deal with the onslaught of visions, but she was overwhelmed. She fell into the darkness.

———————

She opened her eyes some time later to find herself sprawled on the floor of a cavern that was illuminated in an eerie ultraviolet radiance. Beside her, Olivia stirred and levered herself to a sitting position. She looked around, dazed.

"Where are we?" she whispered.

"I don't know."

Catalina sat up and surveyed their surroundings. Wonder and dread welled up inside her. She had never seen anything like the cavern chamber in which she and Olivia found themselves. She knew Olivia was just as mystified as she was.

The violent energy storm still seethed at the entrance. The chamber was filled with currents, too, but they were not nearly as violent as those that formed the gate. Hallucinations danced in the paranormal shadows, but they were manageable. Catalina could not entirely suppress them but they did not overwhelm her senses.

She listened closely. There was no sound from the tunnel on the other side. Either the killer had abandoned the hunt or else he had become disoriented and lost. For the moment, it seemed she and Olivia were safe.

The ultraviolet light seeping out of the cavern walls sparked and flashed on shards of some reflective material scattered around the chamber. Olivia picked up one of the jagged slivers and cautiously wiped off the grime.

"It looks like a piece of a mirror," she said.

Portions of the walls were paneled in the same material. Large rocky formations projected down from the ceiling and thrust up out of the floor.

"Stalactites and stalagmites," Catalina said.

She got to her feet and went to the nearest formation jutting upward from the mirrored floor. She wiped away a thick accumulation of dirt, exposing a small area of the crystal underneath. The gem-like stone sparked with the colors of dark fire.

"I think the creep with the gun gave up," Olivia whispered.

"He may have decided that he couldn't follow us, but what if he decides that all he has to do is go back to the main cavern and wait for us to come out?" Catalina said in the same low tones.

"In that case I guess we're stuck in here until morning," Olivia said.

"If he waits that long he'll be in for a shock, because if we're not home before breakfast, the whole town will be out searching for us. The caves are the first place they'll look."

"It's going to be a long night," Olivia said. "But I think we're safe in here. It's weird, though, isn't it? The rocky things hanging down from the ceiling look like crystal chandeliers that someone hasn't dusted in a very long time."

Catalina touched one of the broken mirrors on the walls. "Like a ballroom that was once lit up with paranormal light and music."

Olivia shuddered. "The devil's ballroom."

Their low-tech, old-fashioned mechanical watches were not affected by the energy in the atmosphere. The night seemed endless but eventually they realized that dawn had arrived.

"He'll be gone now," Catalina said. "The whole town will be out searching for us. He won't dare hang around. We have to go back the way we came, though. That means another trip through that minia-ture hurricane."

Olivia studied the energy gate with a thoughtful expression. Catalina knew that she was viewing it with her new senses.

"Hmm," Olivia said. She went forward cautiously. Her hair lifted in response to the energy in the atmosphere. "I don't think it's going to be as scary to get through from this side."

"Why not?"

"I don't know. It's as if it was made to keep people out but not lock them inside."

Olivia held out her hand. Catalina grabbed it. Together they hurled themselves into the storm—and emerged without incident on the other side.

They found the currents of energy that had led them to the Dev-il's Ballroom and followed them back out. They stumbled out of the maze and into the cavern where the murder had occurred. One of the search parties arrived at about the same time.

There was no sign of the killer.

That was the good news.

The really bad news was that there was no evidence of the mur-der. The body had vanished into the river. The device that the two men had set up in the main cavern had disappeared. There was no indication that anyone other than Catalina and Olivia had been in the caves during the night.

———————

Later that afternoon, Catalina met Olivia at their favorite place on the edge of the lake. They sat on the rocks and contemplated the gray mist that hung over the water. Some of the old-timers in town claimed that before the Incident, the lake had not been perpetually shrouded in fog, but neither Catalina nor Olivia could recall a time when sunlight had sparkled on the water.

The gray mist on Fogg Lake was omnipresent, night and day, regardless of the time of year. It made boating a treacherous business. Navigation instruments didn't work. A few people in town had small boats with outboard motors, and some had rowboats, but they only went fishing in the summer, when the fog retreated somewhat. And even on the brightest, sunniest day of the year, boaters were careful to stay within eyesight of the shoreline. If you got lost in the fog, odds were that you would never find your way back. You would spend whatever was left of your life drifting in the mist.

The fog got heavier at night. It slowly enveloped the town and shrouded the narrow, winding road that led down the mountain to the main highway. No one with any sense tried to drive in or out of Fogg Lake after dark.

"It wasn't one of your visions, was it?" Olivia said. "We both saw that guy with the shaved head murder the man with the glasses. I'll never be able to forget the way the dying man's aura sort of flickered and then just . . . disappeared. It was as if someone had blown out a candle."

"I won't be able to forget it, either, but we're going to have to stop talking about it, because we don't have any proof," Catalina said. "No one believes us. They think we still lack control or that we were under the influence of the energy in the cavern."

"What if he comes back?"

"The killer?" Catalina thought about that. "It would be a huge risk for him. He knows we can identify him."

"But he also knows there's no evidence that he committed murder."

"True," Catalina said. "Still, I don't think he'll want to take a chance like that if he can avoid it."

"I wonder what he and the guy with the glasses were looking for."

"Who knows?" Catalina said. "Dad told me that from time to

time strangers still show up asking questions about what happened in the caves all those years ago."

"Those two weren't asking questions. You saw them, Cat. They knew where they were going, and they had some kind of high-tech gadget that they were trying to tune. They were looking for something."

"I know," Catalina said. She hugged her knees and studied the fog. "I wonder if the killer found what he was searching for. Maybe that's why he disappeared."

Olivia perked up. "In that case he doesn't have any reason to come back."

"If he does, we'll tell our parents. That's all we can do. Meanwhile, we have to get our act together and at least look like we have full control. Otherwise we'll be stuck in this town for the rest of our lives. Dad says that on the outside they put people like us in institutions."

"Ms. Trevelyan told Mom that you and I will probably have some really bad nightmares for a while on account of we're at a sensitive state of development or something. She gave my mother a tisane to help me sleep."

"She gave my mom some, too."

Nyla Trevelyan was the local healer. If you broke a leg or developed heart problems or an infection, you made the trip down the mountain to a regular medical clinic. But if you were plagued with insomnia, parapsychological disorders or lack of control over your senses, you sought help from Nyla, because she was a member of the community. She understood that seeing visions and auras and other manifestations of the paranormal did not automatically mean you were crazy.

"Do you think we're going to have some kind of PTSD from this whole thing?" Olivia said.

"Who knows? We're from Fogg Lake. We're weird."

CHAPTER 2

Seattle, present day . . .

'm sorry to be the bearer of bad news," Catalina said. She used the gentle, consoling voice she reserved for announcements that she knew would either break the client's heart or send her into a rage. Or both. "I'm afraid our investigation turned up a lot of red flags. I'll be blunt. Angus Hopper is not the man he pretends to be."

That was putting it mildly, she thought. Hopper was a very bad piece of work. The background investigation she and Olivia had conducted had turned up strong evidence that he was a slick, smooth-talking con man who specialized in bilking vulnerable women out of their life savings. But that wasn't the worst part. Hopper had a history of violence.

"I know I should be grateful to you," Marsha Matson said. "You saved me from making what would no doubt have been the biggest mistake of my life. But I was hoping for a different outcome."

Matson was a thin, tense woman in her early forties. A successful real estate broker, she had made a considerable amount of money in the hot Seattle market. But her personal life was a string of disappointments. She had been married and divorced twice. In both cases she had been dumped for younger women. Now Catalina had been obliged to inform her that her latest Mr. Right was another Mr. Wrong.

"I understand," Catalina said. "My associate and I also hoped that the results would be more satisfactory. Here's what we know: Most of what Hopper told you about his past is a lie. He never served in the military, and he never received any medals. He did not graduate from Stanford. He never made a fortune with a tech start-up. But I think you suspected the truth. That's why you came to Lark and LeClair."

"There were just too many stories about his exploits in various war zones, and that garbage about the tech start-up sounded a little too good to be true." Marsha pushed herself up out of her chair and went to stand at the window. She stood quietly for a moment, watching the rain dampen the city. "I've been a businesswoman my entire adult life. I like to think I've got a fairly good bullshit detector, but it almost failed me this time."

"You were right to listen to your intuition," Catalina said. "Too many people fail to pay attention to what that inner voice is trying to tell them. They choose to believe what they want to believe, or they are afraid they'll look foolish or paranoid if they act on what their intuition is telling them."

It was that astonishing observation that had sparked Catalina and Olivia's decision to go into the private investigation business. They had been brought up to trust their intuition. Everyone in Fogg Lake accepted it as a normal and natural thing. Sure, occasionally it provided misleading or confusing information, and there were certainly times when people deliberately chose to ignore a subtle warning sign, but for the most part they at least acknowledged the risk.

It had come as a startling revelation to discover that people in the outside world routinely overrode their intuition, especially when it came to matters of money and matters of the heart.

Catalina and Olivia had founded Lark & LeClair six months earlier, in the wake of what they privately labeled Catalina's Total Fiasco. Catalina had had no option but to reinvent herself after the scandal that had cost her a job she loved and a relationship that, while admittedly not the kind to set the bed on fire, at least appeared to have a solid foundation.

For her part, Olivia could have happily continued with her career at a local art gallery, but she had pounced on the notion of joining Catalina as a partner in the new venture. Somewhat to the surprise of both, it turned out they had a knack for the investigation business.

Their business model was based on targeting a niche market—smart, savvy people who knew that it was a good idea to take a second look at a potential spouse who looked like Mr. Perfect, a charming investment counselor who promised you a steady return of 20 percent on your money or a long-lost relative who showed up just in time to get himself into your will.

Lark & LeClair had struggled at first, but business was finally starting to pick up, thanks to word of mouth from satisfied customers. The firm was careful not to advertise or promote the psychic angle. Catalina and Olivia feared it would draw people who wanted their palms read, their fortunes told and advice on which numbers to play in the state lottery. There was also a very real possibility that any claim of paranormal abilities would attract the attention of some flat-out crazies.

"After my last divorce I promised myself I would never marry again," Marsha continued. Her jaw tensed. "But sooner or later the loneliness gets to you."

"I understand," Catalina said. She waited because she knew there would be questions. The client always had questions.

Marsha sighed. "How did you do it?"

"How did we discover the truth about Hopper?"

"Yes. I did some research myself, online. I couldn't find anything but what he wanted me to find."

"I'm not surprised," Catalina said. "He did a good job of cleaning up his online profile. But my partner and I employ some extremely sophisticated search programs here at Lark and LeClair."

That was the truth, more or less. There was no need to explain that she and Olivia had begun the search by simply taking a very close look at Angus Hopper. It had been a straightforward, routine step for a couple of investigators who could see auras. She and Olivia had waited in a car outside the restaurant where Marsha and Hopper were scheduled to have dinner one evening. Olivia had examined Hopper's aura when he walked past the parked vehicle.

"That is one scary creep," she announced.

Catalina had studied the way Hopper focused his attention on Marsha and picked up a whisper of a vision.

"He's dangerous," she said. "He's hurt women before and he'll do it again."

After that it had been a matter of old-fashioned investigative work. Hopper had scrubbed a lot of his past off the Internet, but there wasn't much he could do about the memories of the people who had come in contact with him over the years. The women who had known him had nothing good to say about him. *Explosive temper. When I finally ended things, I thought he would kill me. He stalked me for weeks. I was so relieved when he finally left town.*

Catalina clasped her hands on top of her desk. "Hopper is smart. Thus far he has managed to keep from getting arrested. I think the women he's hurt were afraid to file charges. But sooner or later he'll go too far or get careless. He's a ticking time bomb."

Marsha pulled herself together, squared her shoulders and turned around. Her eyes were bleak but resolute.

"We were supposed to have dinner together tonight," she said.

"I'll let him know that I can't make it. Business. He won't think that's strange. Everyone knows real estate people work odd hours."

Something about Marsha's grim expression sent a chill of anxiety across Catalina's senses.

"Be careful," she said. "Keep your distance from him, Marsha. I told you, he's dangerous. The people we talked to said he has serious anger management issues."

Marsha had been about to move toward the door. She paused. "Do you think he'll try to hurt me?"

Catalina hesitated, sorting through possibilities. "My colleague and I believe that his first instinct is to ensure his own welfare. He is smart enough to want to avoid arrest. He's like a snake that would prefer to slither away out of sight rather than attack. But we think he is also somewhat unstable. Our advice is to slide out of the relationship without provoking him. Take a vacation. If his past behavior is any indication, he'll cut his losses once he realizes his con isn't working. He'll go hunting for another potential victim."

Marsha shook her head. "Some other poor fool who will fall for his lies, you mean."

Catalina got to her feet. "I want to be very clear about what happened here. You did not fall for Angus Hopper's lies. You heeded your intuition and you paid a substantial fee to this firm to investigate that con man. We confirmed your suspicions, but the only reason we were able to assist you is because you had the intelligence and common sense to question a man who seemed too good to be true. We hope you will accept the results of our inquiries."

Marsha looked surprised. "Of course. I'm not an idiot."

"I know. But some clients in your position refuse to deal with the facts that we present to them."

Marsha nodded somberly. "They wanted different answers."

"We always provide hard evidence, but you would be amazed by how many people ignore our advice."

For the first time Marsha's mouth curved in the barest hint of a smile. "Which is why you insist on getting your fee up front in the form of a retainer."

Catalina smiled, too. "Yep. We learned that lesson back at the start."

Marsha absorbed the small pep talk in silence for a few beats. Then some of the nervous tension seeped out of her.

"Thanks," she said. "I'll be careful, but what I'd really like is to see that bastard go to jail."

"We don't have the kind of evidence that will stand up in a court of law," Catalina said. "And none of the people we talked to are willing to testify. Eventually Hopper will cross the line and get caught, but until he does, he's a menace."

"He's also one hell of a con artist, I'll give him that. Thank you, again, Catalina. I'll be back if I run into any other dates who seem too good to be true."

Catalina hurried around her desk and crossed the room.

"Goodbye," she said. She opened the door. "And please remember what I said. You should thank your own intuition. You saved yourself because you were smart enough to sense that you were being conned."

"Right." Marsha gave her a wry smile. Tears glittered in her eyes. "Think that will keep me company at night?"

"I'm sorry," Catalina said again.

There was nothing else she could say. Sometimes she suggested that clients consult a counselor or a therapist but her intuition told her that Marsha would not take that advice well.

Marsha strode down the hall to the reception area. Daniel Naylor, ensconced behind the sleek receptionist desk, jumped to his feet and opened the outer door for her. She brushed past him and disappeared out into the hall.

When she was gone, Daniel closed the door and looked at Catalina.

"Is Ms. Matson depressed or just mad as hell?" he asked.

Daniel was in his early twenties and possessed the computer skills that Catalina and Olivia lacked. They had grown up in Fogg Lake, after all, where high-tech phones, laptops and other cutting-edge devices did not function well, if at all. Sure, they had picked up a working knowledge of computers in college, and they were becoming increasingly competent with the various programs required in the course of the investigation business, but there was no way they would ever become as nimble on the Internet as someone who had grown up wired to his tech, playing online games and navigating social media.

In addition to his skills, Daniel had a gift for putting tense, nervous clients at ease. He also had style. As if by magic, he made the casual street gear look that characterized Pacific Northwest fashion appear effortlessly cool.

"She's both depressed and pissed off," Catalina said.

Olivia emerged from her office. She had grown into a striking woman endowed with an artistic, bohemian vibe. Today she wore rust brown wide-legged trousers that flowed with every step. She had topped it off with a sleek long-sleeved silk blouse in deep yellow ocher. Her auburn hair was cut in an artful wedge that framed her hazel eyes and delicate features.

Next to Olivia and Daniel, Catalina always felt like a fashion failure. She had tried to find an appropriate style; really, she had worked hard at it. Olivia had taken her shopping innumerable times. But somehow nothing had ever felt right except her uniform of basic black. Today she was wearing black trousers, low-heeled black boots and a black crew-neck top. Her dark hair was caught back in a stern twist at the back of her head.

Olivia folded her arms and lounged in the doorway. "Marsha Matson is definitely pissed off."

"She's got every right to be angry," Daniel pointed out.

"Yes, but I worry that she'll confront Hopper face-to-face," Catalina said. "I tried to reinforce the idea that he could be dangerous if cornered but I don't think she was paying attention."

"You did all you could do," Daniel said.

"He's right," Olivia said. "All we can do is offer advice. It's not your fault if Marsha Matson doesn't follow through on your suggestion of how to handle Hopper."

"Right," Catalina said. "Now if only I could convince myself of that."

Olivia sighed. "If only. Well, let's just hope she calms down before she does anything rash, because I agree with you. Hopper is volatile."

"I'll give her a call later and see what sort of mood she's in," Catalina said.

Daniel glanced at his watch. "It's after five. Unless you need me for something else, I'll be on my way."

"That's it for today," Catalina said. "See you in the morning."

Olivia waited until the door closed behind Daniel before she turned to Catalina.

"Well, this is the big night," she said. "Emerson is cooking for me at his place. I've got to pick up the wine. Wish me luck."

"You know I wish you all the luck in the world, but are you sure you want to go through with your plan? Emerson's a nice guy. The two of you enjoy each other's company. Why take the risk of messing up a good thing by dropping the bombshell on him?"

"I can't wait any longer, Cat. Things are getting too serious between us. It wouldn't be fair to string him along. And to be honest, I need to know if our relationship is going to go somewhere good or if it's doomed."

"You think he's the one, don't you?"

"Maybe. I hope so. I know he's attracted to me. He's kind. Thoughtful. He cares about art and he's got a good relationship with his dog. A man's relationship with his dog says a lot about him. In addition, his aura is stable. Healthy."

"You know as well as I do that you can tell only so much about a man by viewing his aura," Catalina said. "Granted, Emerson Ferris is not a sociopath, and he's not mentally fragile, but that doesn't mean he'll be comfortable accepting the truth about you."

Olivia straightened her shoulders and got a determined look. "If he can't handle my psychic side, then I need to know now. Until I see how he deals with it, I'm trapped. I can't move forward with our relationship until I'm sure it's right for both of us."

"You know I understand," Catalina said. "But I'm so afraid he'll react badly. You were devastated when that bastard McTavers told you that you needed psychiatric help. I don't want to see you get hurt again."

Olivia's brows rose. "The same way you were hurt when you realized Ben Thaxter wanted to use you as a test subject for his crazy research project?"

Catalina held up both hands, palms out. "I admit I screwed up when I got involved with Thaxter, but I learned my lesson. Just because a man is curious about your psychic vibe doesn't mean he doesn't secretly think you're delusional."

"It's not like things worked out for you when you hooked up with someone who did understand and accept your talent," Olivia said. "Roger Gossard used you until he was afraid you'd become a liability to his business. When he concluded that you were a threat to his brand, he couldn't throw you under the bus fast enough."

"Okay, that relationship didn't end well, but there were extenuating circumstances. Once again, lesson learned."

Olivia's expression softened. "You got over Thaxter and Gossard and you will try again. Give me some credit. If Emerson tells me he thinks I should check into a psychiatric hospital, I will be hurt but I'll survive, just like you did."

"All right. I'll shut up now." Catalina crossed the room to hug her friend. "I really hope things go well tonight."

Olivia returned the hug. "I know you do. Don't worry, if it turns out to be a disaster, you'll be the first person I call. I'll stop by your apartment for some therapeutic wine and sympathy. But if you don't hear from me this evening, you'll know Emerson took the news well and that I'm spending the night at his place."

"Right." Catalina took a step back. "Just promise me you'll be careful, okay?"

"Careful?" Olivia's gaze sharpened. "Don't tell me you're concerned that Emerson might be dangerous."

"No, of course not. I just want you to protect yourself."

"I can't," Olivia said gently. "Not in the way you mean. But I can be strong. That's all that matters."

Catalina smiled. "Yes, that's all that matters."

CHAPTER 3

The need to contact Marsha Matson had become too intense to ignore.

Catalina stopped her small car in the circular driveway of Matson's home and sat quietly behind the wheel for a moment, absorbing the feel of the scene. There was nothing that jumped out at her, but she finally decided that things just felt off. Maybe it was the fact that the only light in the house emanated from somewhere deep inside. *Probably my imagination.* She had done too much crime scene work, she decided. It made a person jaded.

She left the car engine running and got out. Again she took a few beats to try to figure out what was bothering her. She could not identify the vibe, but whatever it was, it was not good.

There was only one way to find out if the client was all right.

Leaving the driver's-side door open, she went toward the imposing entrance. It was nearly eight in the evening, but it was April, so there was a little light left in the sky. The short, dark days of the Pacific Northwest winter had passed. The long days of summer were on the horizon.

Marsha Matson's home was located in an exclusive neighborhood in one of the little boutique communities clustered around the shoreline of Lake Washington. The residence was a testament to Matson's real estate success. It loomed two stories tall and sprawled across a large chunk of property.

Catalina was sure that there was a lot of electronic security.

The lights over the three-car garage revealed that all the doors were closed. There were no other vehicles in the driveway. If Marsha was home, she was alone. That was a good sign, Catalina thought, but she could not shake the uneasy sensation that had been riding her hard all evening. She had called Marsha three times over the course of the past few hours. On each occasion she had been dropped immediately into voice mail.

There could be any number of reasons why Marsha, a businesswoman who lived on her phone, might not be taking calls that night. One possible explanation was that the anger that had glittered in her eyes that afternoon had been transformed into an equally powerful depression.

Catalina went to the front door and paused to look up. Sure enough, a small camera was discreetly tucked under the eaves of the roof.

She hesitated before pushing the doorbell, still not certain that she was doing the right thing.

The vision whispered across her senses the instant her finger touched the doorbell.

Rage—murderous, howling rage—coalesced into a ghostly vision. She saw a man coming up the steps. He was the source of the wild fury.

Catalina gasped and instinctively jerked her finger off the bell. Now the darkness that gripped the interior of the house took on an ominous aspect that could not be ignored or explained away.

Common sense dictated that the smart move now was to call the police—assuming they would bother to respond. The last crime scene case she had worked for Roger Gossard had given her a reputation as a flake as far as law enforcement was concerned.

She hesitated, uncertain what to do next. Her intuition warned her that if Marsha was still alive it might be a bad idea to leave the scene. The intruder, assuming there was one, might feel compelled to carry out even more violent action in an attempt to silence his victim before the police arrived.

Catalina opened her purse and took out the dinner fork that she kept inside.

The door opened a scant few inches. Marsha appeared.

"Catalina." Marsha's voice was hoarse with panic.

The hall light was off but there was enough illumination emanating from the outside fixture to reveal her stark features. She stared at Catalina, desperate and terrified. It was clear now that she was not alone in the house. Angus Hopper was inside. That was the only thing that could explain the fear in Marsha's eyes.

A vision of Marsha lying dead on the floor, blood streaming from her slit throat, whispered across Catalina's senses. She suppressed the dreamlike image with an effort. Marsha wasn't dead—not yet, at any rate.

"Marsha," Catalina said, "what's wrong?"

"What are you doing here?"

"You didn't answer your phone," Catalina said. She clutched the fork very tightly. "I was worried about you."

"Go away," Marsha pleaded. "I don't want to see anyone tonight."

But her eyes sent a different message. Her gaze shifted briefly to her right. Catalina knew then that Hopper was standing just out of sight on the other side of the door. She had to assume that he was armed.

"All right," she said. "If you're sure you want to be alone?"

"Yes."

Catalina threw herself against the partially open door, slamming it inward with all her weight. Marsha stumbled back. There was a heavy thud when the door struck the man who had been concealed behind it.

Caught off guard, he was shoved hard against the wall. There was a muffled grunt. An object clattered on the tile floor.

Marsha yelped and rushed out the door.

"Run," Catalina shouted. "The car."

Marsha did not hesitate. She leaped down the steps. Catalina whirled around in an attempt to follow, but a big hand clamped over her arm and hauled her back. She did not try to free herself. She went with the momentum and rammed the fork upward in the general direction of her captor's eyes.

Startled, Hopper slackened his hold on her arm. Instinctively, he lurched back out of reach of the fork, but he did not release her.

"Bitch," he shouted.

Catalina stabbed again and again, wildly this time, going for whatever she could reach.

She knew she had connected with flesh when the fork met resistance. She kept jabbing. Hopper yowled in pain and rage, and suddenly she was free. She ran through the doorway. Marsha had the passenger-side door of the car open.

"Get in, get in," Catalina shouted.

Marsha bolted into the car and slammed the door shut. Catalina got behind the wheel, dropped the fork, closed the door and hit the lock button.

Hopper had taken a few seconds to pick up his knife, but he was moving fast. He reached the passenger side of the car an instant after the locks took effect. Blood flowed from the fork wounds on the side of his face. He wrenched the door handle. When he discovered that it wouldn't open, he pounded on the window with the hilt of his knife. Catalina heard glass crack.

She stepped hard on the accelerator. The little car leaped forward. In the grip of an unthinking rage, Hopper tried to cling to the vehicle. He managed to hang on for a couple of yards before he was thrown aside.

Catalina aimed the car down the driveway, heading toward the winding street. She gripped the wheel in both hands. She was shivering with the unnerving energy of raw adrenaline. She managed to make the call to 911 and promised to wait in a safe location until the police arrived.

Marsha stared straight ahead throughout the short, terse conversation with the emergency operator. When Catalina ended the call, Marsha finally emerged from her trancelike state.

"You were right about Hopper," she said. "I should have taken your advice. But I was so fucking angry. I called him and told him I knew everything about him and that I was going to file charges."

"What did he say?" Catalina asked.

"Nothing. He just hung up on me. The next thing I knew he was at my door with a dozen roses and a bottle of champagne. I couldn't believe it. As if I was going to fall for his lies again. He didn't take out the knife until he was inside."

"Are you all right?"

"No, but I will be, thanks to you." Marsha glanced down at the console between the two seats. "A fork? Really?"

"People think it's odd if you carry a knife or a gun in your handbag."

"But they don't take much notice of a fork."

"No," Catalina said. "They don't."

"Have you ever had to use it before tonight?"

"Once," Catalina said.

"What happened?"

Catalina focused on the narrow road. "I'm still here."

"I think I'll get myself a fork. Hell, make that a gun."

CHAPTER 4

"I'm afraid that Catalina Lark might be something of a problem," Victor Arganbright said. "And not just because she comes from Fogg Lake."

Slater Arganbright contemplated the feverish heat and energy of the casino lights on the Las Vegas Strip below the penthouse window. From where he stood in his uncle's office at the top of one of the tallest buildings in the city, he had a spectacular view. It was two thirty in the morning, but in Las Vegas the night was always on fire. What intrigued him now, as usual, was the darkness of the desert that lay just beyond the city.

He had been awake when Victor had summoned him with a cryptic phone call. That was not an unusual condition for him these days. He had not slept well since the last case. Things had improved a little—the nightmares came less frequently now—but it was still the norm for him to snap into wakefulness on a rush of energy every morning around two. Sometimes he was able to go back to sleep. Sometimes he was doomed to stay awake until dawn.

Still, there were signs of progress. They no longer had to keep him locked up in the attic. Baby steps.

He turned around to confront his uncle.

"Tell me about Catalina Lark," he said.

Victor grimaced. "It's complicated."

Victor was in his early midfifties and in excellent physical shape, which he attributed to a regimen of daily laps in his indoor pool, a mostly vegetarian diet—he did eat fish on occasion—and red wine at dinner. He had the strong, bold profile and fierce amber eyes that ran in the male line of the Arganbright family.

Today Victor's features were set in the grim expression that was his default mode these days. Five years ago, when he had assumed the helm of the Foundation in what some of the staff referred to as a hostile takeover, he had been energized by the daunting task of transforming the secretive organization into a modern, smoothly functioning operation. He'd had some success, but in the past few months he had become obsessed with what he was convinced was a mortal threat, not only to the Foundation but to the country.

The problem for Victor was that with the exception of his husband, Lucas, no one else believed the danger actually existed. The truth was that rumors questioning Victor's stability were starting to circulate among the Foundation staff. Some wondered if he had fallen down the rabbit hole of a conspiracy theory. That theory had a name—Vortex.

Aware of the rumors about him, Victor no longer talked openly about his concerns. But Slater and Lucas and others in the family were well aware that he had not stopped obsessing over the legend. There was a driven quality about him. His amber eyes were shadowed with the resolve of a man who has a clear vision of the task in front of him; a man who fears time is running out.

The only outward indication of his obsession lay in the paintings that currently covered the walls of his paneled office. The pictures were everywhere, hanging one on top of the other. Several more were stacked on the floor. A few were valuable works of art by the old masters. Others had been created by modern artists. There were also a number of sketches done by Victor himself.

All of the paintings in the room were focused on the same theme: the Oracle of Delphi.

Most of the pictures depicted the Oracle in the classic pose, draped in a hooded robe and seated on a three-legged stool that straddled a crevice deep inside a cave. In that position she inhaled the mysterious vapors that wafted up from the fissure in the rocky floor of the cavern.

Under the influence of the unknown gases, the Oracle hallucinated and saw visions. She delivered prophecies and predictions, usually in the form of cryptic phrases that had to be interpreted by those who paid handsomely to obtain the otherworldly information.

The oracle business had been a very profitable enterprise for the ancient city-state of Delphi, Slater thought, but he was pretty sure that wasn't why Victor was obsessed with the ancient legend. Victor already had money—a lot of it. He had made a fortune with his hedge fund before retiring to take control of the Foundation.

His first major change was to move the organization from its old headquarters in Los Angeles to Las Vegas. He had made no secret of his reason for the decision. In a town that specialized in creating the illusion of endless night, a world in which Elvis impersonators, magicians, ageless entertainers, shady characters and those afflicted with gambling fever all coexisted, it was easy for an enterprise dedicated to paranormal research to vanish into the shadows.

"Walk me through this," Slater said. "Why is Catalina Lark going to be a problem?"

Victor heaved a melancholy sigh. "There was an unfortunate incident in Seattle several months ago while you were recovering."

"You mean while I was locked in the attic."

Victor glowered but evidently decided to move on.

"A man named George Ingram died," he said. "The body was found in a vault in his private gallery. The death was attributed to natural causes, but Ingram was a . . . collector, so I decided to take a look at the scene."

When Victor used the term *collector* it went without saying that the individual he was talking about was not a standard-issue connoisseur of art. It meant the person was obsessed with objects, artifacts and antiques that had a connection to the paranormal.

"You wanted to know if Ingram was murdered because someone was after an artifact in his collection," Slater said. He did not make it a question.

"I knew something of Ms. Lark's talent and I was aware that she had a Fogg Lake connection. I asked her to consult on the case." Victor grunted. "Paid her very well for her time, I might add. It's not as if I stiffed her when it came to the bill for her services."

Victor sounded defensive now. A sure sign that he had really screwed up.

"What kind of assistance did you request, and what went wrong?" Slater asked.

Victor had a computer for a brain. He could leapfrog over a dozen scraps of data and reach the logical conclusion. But sometimes you had to take things step-by-step. He tended to skip right past pesky little details that indicated he might have miscalculated.

"It was just a routine analysis job," Victor muttered. "Nothing to it. All she had to do was take a close look at the scene of Ingram's death."

Take a close look was one of Victor's favorite sayings.

"What's her talent?" Slater asked.

"She . . . senses things."

"A lot of people from Fogg Lake sense things," Slater said. "Be more specific."

Victor switched his brooding gaze to one of the paintings of the Oracle of Delphi. He contemplated it as though it contained some secret that he needed to know, as if people's lives depended on acquiring that knowledge.

"Miss Lark sees visions," he said quietly.

"Hallucinations?"

"No, the real thing," Victor snapped. "There's a difference between hallucinating and seeing visions, and you damn well know it."

"Speaking from experience, I can tell you that there are times when it can be tough to tell the difference."

Within the paranormal community, the ability to control hallucinations was the working definition of sanity. It was what made it possible to pass for normal.

"Miss Lark's visions are a manifestation of her strong intuition," Victor said. "She can read someone's aura and pick up on the vibe of what the individual is likely to do next."

Slater glanced at the nearest Oracle painting and shook his head. "You're not going to tell me that she can see the future, are you? That kind of nonsense is for the Freak crowd."

Over the years, a number of those who had been affected by the vapors released on the night of the Fogg Lake Incident had found themselves unable to cope with their new senses. Those who failed to gain control of the psychic side of their natures lost the ability to use logic and reason and old-fashioned common sense. All too often they fell into cults or obsessed over conspiracy theories. Some ended up in the locked wards of psychiatric hospitals.

The Freaks had appeared online a couple of years ago. The group had popped up on the Foundation's alert file almost immediately, because several people with links to Fogg Lake had found their way into the secretive group.

Until recently Victor had not been particularly concerned, because the Freaks had appeared to be just another relatively harmless bunch of conspiracy theorists.

Recently, however, the Freaks had begun to work their way up Victor's long to-do list. There was some indication that one individual in particular was trying to gain control over what had, until now, been a loosely linked crowd of whack-jobs.

Victor shook his head. "Catalina Lark isn't one of the crazies. She has full control of her talent. The reason she will be a valuable asset is that not only can she pick up on an individual's future intentions, she can read the energy prints that a perp or a victim leaves behind at the scene of a crime."

Slater got a ping. Curiosity sparked across his senses. "She can analyze crime scene heat?"

"The same way you can pick up the energy infused into artifacts," Victor said. "To be clear, I'm as certain as I can be that this is not a Freak case. There's something else going down in Seattle."

"What, exactly?"

"Another collector died three days ago. Jeremy Royston. His body was found in his vault. The death was attributed to natural causes. Heart attack."

"Anything missing from the collection?"

Victor snorted. "By now I'm sure the place has been cleaned out. Somehow the raider crews always seem to get to the scene before the Foundation people arrive."

"But you think that Royston was murdered for a particular artifact?"

"I think there is a possibility that is the case, yes. I want you to investigate and confirm my theory."

"Why?"

Victor was silent for a moment. Then he heaved another sigh.

"Because I think that someone or some group is trying to find the old Vortex lab," he said.

"People have been looking for that facility for decades. There's no record that it ever existed."

"There's no official record that any of the lost labs existed," Victor said. "But we know that they did."

A case focused on a possible Vortex link was most likely a waste of time, Slater thought. But any job was better than returning to his office in the Foundation museum. Victor wasn't the only one who had become the subject of rumors and speculation in the halls of the archives, museum and research labs.

"I'll go to Seattle for you and take a look at the scene," he said. "And I will ask Ms. Lark for her assistance. You said you paid her bill. What did you do that makes you think she might not be willing to help the Foundation again?"

"Nothing," Victor muttered. "What happened was not my fault."

This is not going to be good, Slater thought.

"What exactly did happen?" he asked.

"There was some unfortunate publicity in the media. But that was after I left town."

"Define *unfortunate*," Slater said.

Victor cleared his throat. "A reporter somehow got hold of the fact that a psychic had been called to the scene of Ingram's murder. What followed was a social media frenzy. It didn't last long, but there were accusations hurled around. The press declared Ms. Lark a fraud."

"And?"

Victor sighed. "The owner of a Seattle-based consulting firm that does sophisticated crime scene analysis was not helpful when he told a reporter that if Ms. Lark was not an outright fraud she was most likely delusional and should seek professional help. Ms. Lark lost her position as a career counselor. It was after that incident that she and her friend Olivia LeClair decided to open their own investigation business."

"I see."

Victor brightened. "I believe their firm is holding its own and may even succeed. But a start-up business always needs cash. It occurs to me that they might be very pleased to consult for the Foundation."

"Or not." Slater studied Victor for a moment. "Why do I get the feeling that you aren't telling me every detail of the fallout from the Ingram case?"

Victor drummed his fingers on the top of his desk. "In addition to losing her job, I think Ms. Lark's personal life may have been somewhat affected by the media storm."

"In what way?"

Victor heaved yet another sigh. "Ms. Lark was apparently involved in a personal relationship with Roger Gossard at the time."

"Who is Gossard?"

"The owner of that crime scene consulting company that I just told you about."

"Gossard is the person who told a reporter that if Catalina Lark wasn't a fraud she was delusional and should seek help?"

"Evidently." Victor sat forward with a purposeful air. "To be absolutely clear, what happened between Lark and Gossard after I left town was not my fault, either. Relationships fall apart all the time."

"Can't argue with that."

Victor slanted him a wary glance. Neither of them mentioned Roanna Powell. There was no need. Relationships did, indeed, fall apart—especially if one of the parties involved had to be locked up for a month due to instability of the paranormal senses.

"Moving right along," Slater said. "I will contact Ms. Lark and request her help, but considering the fact that you left her in a situation that can only be described as the sum of all FUBAR, I don't think we can expect her to welcome our business, even if we do pay our bills."

"Well, she might turn us down," Victor admitted. "But it's worth asking her to consult. She's good, Slater. I've never met anyone who could read a crime scene as clearly as she can. And we need all the help we can get on this. We're not just chasing another Vortex lab rumor this time. Two collectors are dead and I am convinced that they were murdered by whoever is behind this project. We need to move fast."

"Why send me?" Slater said. "Why not one of the other cleaners?"

"Because I know that while you are not convinced of my theories concerning Vortex, you'll do a thorough job. I don't trust the regular team to take this problem seriously. Besides, no one is better than you when it comes to tracing objects with a paranormal provenance. Also, for what it's worth, I think you've got the best shot at convincing Ms. Lark to help us."

"Why?"

"Because her talent is similar to yours. You hear voices. She sees visions."

"Made for each other, huh?"

Victor glared. "I'm just saying that the two of you have something in common."

"Is that right? Has she ever been locked up because she's delusional?"

"No, and neither have you," Victor shot back.

Slater smiled a cold, humorless smile. "Not officially. But the only reason I didn't wind up in Halcyon Manor six months ago was because you and Lucas kept me locked in the attic until the hallucinations finally resolved."

Victor snorted. "Don't exaggerate. This penthouse does not even have an attic."

"Details."

"You were injured. Your parents were beside themselves with worry. You needed a quiet place to recover. Lucas and I provided it. That's all there was to it. Now, try to forget what happened six months ago. It's over. Morgan is dead. You're alive and stable. That's all that matters. You need to focus here. We've got a possible Vortex problem. We have to deal with it."

Slater thought about that. He would never be able to forget the disaster that had happened six months earlier. There was still one burning question that had to be answered. But he could not continue to drift through the dusty storerooms of the Foundation archives pretending he was back at work.

"What else can you tell me about Lark and this case?" Slater asked.

"Lucas put together a file for you," Victor said. He broke off at the sound of a knock on the door. "Come in, Lucas."

The door opened. Lucas Pine strolled into the room. He looked at Victor, brows slightly elevated.

"Did I hear my name just now?" he asked.

Charming, with a warm smile, a gracious manner and an innate sense of style, Lucas was the exact opposite of Victor in many ways, but the two had been together for nearly twenty years. They had recently formalized the relationship with an over-the-top Vegas wedding hosted at one of the big, glamorous casinos on the Strip. Slater's mother held the opinion that the enduring relationship was a classic example of the old theory that opposites attract.

There was no denying that Lucas and Victor complemented each other in a way that made them a formidable team.

"Uncle Victor just finished explaining to me that he managed to piss off the investigator I might need to assist me in the Seattle case," Slater said.

"Right," Lucas said. "That would be Catalina Lark. Victor threw her whole life into the toilet six months ago."

"What happened was not my fault," Victor grumbled. "And for the record, she seems to be doing fine now."

Lucas ignored him. "You're going to have your work cut out for you, Slater, but Ms. Lark does have an exceptional talent. It would be very good to have her consult. Try to keep all contact with her on a face-to-face basis if possible, though. Your phone is heavily encrypted, but we think you should stay off of it as much as possible."

"Understood." Slater glanced out the window. It was past three now. Maybe he could still catch a couple of hours of sleep before he left for Seattle.

"I've got you booked on a six fifteen flight to Seattle," Lucas continued. "You've got just enough time to pack a bag and head to the airport. The flight time is about two hours and forty minutes. Here's the file. You can review it on the plane."

So much for a few hours of sleep.

"I'm flying commercial?" Slater said. "I don't get to use the Foundation jet?"

"Don't be ridiculous." Victor snorted. "Talk about a red flag to whoever might be watching. Besides, do you know how much it costs to put that plane in the air?"

"Petty cash for you," Slater said.

"Victor is right," Lucas said. "No sense announcing the fact that the Foundation has taken an interest in the Royston murder."

"If people are watching, they're going to figure that out right quick once I start asking questions," Slater said.

"Every minute of time we can buy up front gives us just that much more of an edge," Victor said. "Go figure out what the hell is going down in Seattle."

"On my way," Slater said.

He went into the hall and closed the door. The thick carpet hushed his footsteps as he made his way through the penthouse.

Out of nowhere, a little rush of exhilaration and anticipation flashed across his senses. It had been a while since he had felt the familiar stirring sensation. The last time had been just before the Morgan case six months ago.

He wondered if the whisper of excitement was an omen and then reminded himself that he didn't believe in omens and portents. He tightened his grip on the file. He would focus on the unknown Catalina Lark instead.

He walked swiftly through the elegant, high-ceilinged rooms, heading toward the grand foyer, where the butler was waiting.

When he turned one particular corner, he was very careful not to look at the closed door of the room at the end of the hall. He saw enough of the attic in his nightmares.

———

Victor waited until the door closed behind Slater before he pushed himself out of his chair and crossed the room to the wall of windows overlooking the Strip.

"He still thinks that we locked him up in an attic, Lucas," he said.

"He doesn't really believe that." Lucas moved to stand beside Victor. "Slater knows we did what we had to do to protect him."

"Why does he keep insisting he was locked away in some damned attic?"

"Because we did lock him up. He was hallucinating wildly. His mind obviously translated that room at the end of the hall into an attic. He probably picked up the imagery from some old horror movie that he saw years ago. It's okay. He's stable now. He has been for months."

"When I think of what that bastard did to him . . ."

"The radiation he was exposed to in that rogue lab six months ago may have permanently affected his senses, but it didn't change the man. Slater is still Slater. You gave him exactly what he's been needing—a job."

"I hope we're doing the right thing."

Lucas reached for Victor's hand. "It's not like we had a choice. We need someone we can trust on this case. Someone who knows what's at stake. Someone who won't immediately dismiss the possibility that Vortex may be involved."

"For the past five years I've tried to tell myself that with Rancourt gone, it was finished."

"Secrets have a bad habit of climbing up out of the grave."

"You know I don't like metaphors."

"In this case, I don't think it's a metaphor," Lucas said. "It may be the truth."

"Rancourt is dead. We know that for a fact."

Lucas tightened his grip on Victor's hand. "Yes."

"We destroyed all the files and the artifacts that we found in his lab, but what if we missed something?"

There was nothing reassuring he could say, Lucas thought.

"We're doing all we can do," he said. "We're staying vigilant."

CHAPTER 5

Catalina awoke on the last tendrils of the old nightmare, the one in which she and Olivia tried to flee deep into the Fogg Lake caves to escape the stranger who had just murdered a man. But no matter how hard they struggled, they could not find the right current of energy. Each time they attempted to enter a tunnel, they found themselves at the edge of the lake.

"We have to go into the caves again," she tells Olivia. "It's the only way to escape."

"We can't go inside," Olivia explains in the unnaturally calm tone of dreams. "If we do, we will go mad and throw ourselves into the deepest part of the lake. We will drown."

But the dreamer tries another path. Once again she finds herself at the edge of the bottomless lake. She realizes that she is holding a fork and suddenly understands that they can use it to find their way through the caves.

She turns to tell Olivia that everything will be okay now.
Olivia is not there.

Catalina sat up abruptly, her pulse skittering, and swung her legs over the side of the bed. She knew that most people would probably turn on the lights and walk around for a few minutes in an attempt to suppress the dream images. But if you were raised in Fogg Lake, you learned to analyze your dreams.

It didn't take any great insight to understand why the old dream had come back tonight. The anxiety of the past had been roused from the depths by the drama at Marsha Matson's house.

There was no need to be alarmed. The fact that Olivia had not texted or phoned was a good thing. It indicated that the big date with Emerson Ferris had gone well. Olivia was no doubt sound asleep at that very moment, wrapped in the arms of her lover. She would probably be glowing when she walked into the office a few hours from now.

Catalina went to the window. A fiery sunrise illuminated the sky over the Cascades. It had been a long night. Hopper had vanished by the time the police arrived on the scene, but he had left plenty of evidence inside the house. The bottle of champagne had his fingerprints all over it. There were traces of his blood on the front porch. Best of all, the security camera had caught almost everything.

In addition to the statements that she and Marsha had given, she had been able to provide the cops with a great deal of Hopper's personal information, including aliases that he had used over the years. The authorities were certain it would not be long before he was taken into custody.

After the police had finished, Marsha had declared that she could not spend another night alone in the big house. Catalina had driven her to a downtown hotel that had plenty of reassuring security and waited until she had checked into a room.

Catalina had returned to her apartment building, where there was also a respectable security presence, including a twenty-four-hour concierge on the front desk, a lot of surveillance technology and a private guard who patrolled the garage and the perimeter of the building at night. She and Olivia had good security inside their own apartments, too. When you were in the investigation business, you got a little obsessed.

There had been other cases that had ended badly. She and Olivia usually dealt with those by having drinks together and talking. But Olivia had not been available this time. She had spent the night with the man of her dreams.

Maybe Emerson Ferris was the right person for Olivia. Catalina tried to analyze her doubts about Ferris. There was nothing obviously wrong with him. She and Olivia had both researched him thoroughly before Olivia went out on a second date. By every objective measure he was a good man, just as Olivia had said that afternoon. He was honest. Stable. Successful. Kind to animals. And he shared Olivia's artistic interests.

Maybe I've gotten too cynical, Catalina thought. Maybe there was hope after all for a couple of Fogg Lake girls who were trying to pass for normal in the outside world.

The fire in the sky was fading now, transforming into a cloud-streaked dawn. Catalina turned away from the scene. The restlessness that had kept her awake for much of the night was getting more intense, but she could not identify a legitimate cause. She wasn't on the verge of a full-scale anxiety attack, she decided, but she could not shake a persistent sense of dread.

She went to the closet and found her workout clothes. She would join the other early risers in the fitness center on the top floor of the apartment tower. Maybe exercise would help her calm down.

An hour later she showered, made a pot of coffee and sat down to her customary breakfast: unsweetened Greek yogurt, peanut butter on a slice of rye toast, and blueberries. The meal was as predictable as her wardrobe. Maybe she needed to get a life. On the other hand, she had nearly been murdered the previous night, so maybe her life wasn't so boring after all. It was a matter of perspective.

By the time she finished she was so unnerved she dared not finish the coffee. She was afraid the additional caffeine might push her over the edge.

She could no longer resist the urge to contact Olivia.

She tried a text first. When there was no response, she made the call—and was promptly dumped into voice mail. Just as she had been the previous evening when she had tried to get in touch with Marsha Matson.

Where had that thought come from? There was no connection between the Matson case and Olivia's big date with Ferris. Her imagination was starting to slip into overdrive again, just as it had last night.

Last night someone had very nearly been murdered.

"Stop it," she said aloud to the empty kitchen.

There was a fine line between intuition and a vivid imagination, but the line existed. It had to be respected. Obviously the problem this morning was that her nerves and her frazzled senses were still recovering from the encounter with Angus Hopper. She had to cling to common sense and logic, both of which held that there was no reason to worry about Olivia.

She pulled out her laptop and worked on some notes from a case that had closed earlier in the week. When she finished she checked the time. It was just after eight. The offices of Lark & LeClair opened at nine. The walk to work took about fifteen minutes. There was no reason she could not go in a little early. She wondered if Olivia and Mr. Right were enjoying a leisurely morning in bed or maybe having a champagne breakfast to celebrate their relationship.

It was also possible that Olivia had come home this morning to shower and dress for the office. But if that was the case, why hadn't she answered her phone? Oh, wait, maybe she had forgotten to switch it back on.

Catalina pulled on the black trench coat that Olivia had given her, slung the strap of her large handbag over her shoulder and went toward the door. Halfway there she changed course and went into the kitchen. She needed a replacement for the fork that the police had taken as evidence.

She rummaged around in the cutlery drawer and found a large fork, one that had been designed for use along with a serious knife for carving big hunks of meat. She had never cooked a hunk of meat that required such oversized implements, but she had developed a great appreciation for sturdy, well-made forks.

She wedged the fork into her bag and let herself out of the apartment. She took the stairs to the floor below and knocked on Olivia's door. There was no response. Olivia had probably packed a small bag in preparation for an overnight with Ferris. She was no doubt planning to head straight to the office from his place.

Using the key Olivia had given her, Catalina entered the apartment. She punched in the security code to turn off the alarm and walked slowly through the one-bedroom space. The two of them were as close as sisters, but when it came to their choice of interior decor, they were exact opposites. Her own place was done in a Zen-like palette of off-white and pale gray punctuated with discreet hits of glossy black. Olivia's was in the hot colors of a flaming sunset—gold, burnt orange and bright red.

The closet door stood open. Some of the clothes Olivia had evidently considered for the special date were scattered across the bed. They had not made the cut. The new scarlet slip dress was gone, however, and so were several items from the bathroom, including her toothbrush.

That settled it. Olivia had been anticipating a successful date and packed accordingly.

"You had better show up at the office on time, pal," she said softly. "Or I'll come looking for you."

Catalina closed and locked the apartment and went down the hall to the elevator. When she stepped out into the lobby, Robert leaped to his feet behind his polished desk. He had once had dreams of an acting career. That ambition had not gone well, but he had reinvented himself as the quintessential concierge.

"Ms. Lark," he said. "I was just about to call you to warn you."

Catalina stared at him, panic-stricken. "Why? What's wrong?"

Grim-faced, Robert gestured toward a small cluster of people gathered on the sidewalk outside the building.

"The TV people showed up a few minutes ago," he said. "I was able to prevent them from coming into the lobby, of course, and I gave them absolutely no information about you. However, the person in charge is that reporter from the local TV station. Brenda something."

"Brenda Bryce." Catalina suppressed a groan. "You know it's going to be a bad day when she shows up at your front door. I wonder how she found out so soon about what happened at the Matson house last night. She's got good sources, I'll give her that."

"There was another incident?" Robert asked. His tone was one of deep concern but the expression in his eyes betrayed his excitement and curiosity.

"Unfortunately, yes. I didn't see anything about it in the morning news so I was hoping . . . Never mind. Will you help me get past her? I don't think that she and the cameraman can move too fast, not with all that gear. Once I'm in the clear I'll be okay."

Robert turned and strode toward the door. "Follow me."

He pushed open the heavy glass doors and led the way out onto the sidewalk. He held up his cell phone.

"Your attention, please," he said, raising his voice to be heard above the traffic in the street. "I cannot prevent you from standing out here, but I warn you that if you attempt to bar Ms. Lark's progress in any way or if you lay so much as a finger on her, I will call nine-one-one immediately and notify the police of an assault in progress."

The cameraman kept his distance, but Catalina knew he was filming her. Brenda Bryce edged around Robert, stepped directly in front of Catalina and aimed the microphone.

Brenda was not quite as beautiful and glamorous in person as she appeared on TV, where she had the benefit of artfully arranged lights. But with her sharp feline features, long blond hair and cosmetically enhanced bosom, she was still a woman who turned heads on the street. She had, in fact, caused several people who were on their way to work to stop.

Nothing drew a crowd like a TV camera crew loitering outside a door.

"Catalina Lark, I understand that you were involved in a violent confrontation last night. Do you attribute your presence at another crime scene to your so-called psychic talents?"

Catalina had learned the hard way that there was no good response to a question from Brenda Bryce.

"No comment," Catalina said.

She dodged around Brenda and walked very swiftly through the small group of curious people.

"Is she the fake psychic?" a woman asked Brenda.

"Who says she's a fake?" the cameraman shot back.

"Just one or two questions, Ms. Lark," Brenda said.

Catalina gripped the strap of her handbag and kept moving. She had on low-heeled booties. Brenda was in four-inch heels. It was no contest. Catalina increased her lead with each step.

Behind her, Robert started shooing people away from the lobby doors.

A few of the curiosity seekers trailed after her for a time, asking her for psychic readings, but eventually they abandoned the chase.

By the time Catalina reached the lobby of the office building that housed Lark & LeClair, she was a little winded, tense with anger and vibrating with anxiety.

Daniel was already behind his desk. He took one look at her when she came through the door and got to his feet.

"Are you all right?" he asked.

"I'm fine. Has there been any word from Olivia?"

"No." Daniel frowned. "Should there be some word from her?"

Catalina glanced at the clock. "In another five minutes she'll be late. She's never late."

Daniel raised his brows. "The hot date, remember? She's probably having a late breakfast with Mr. Perfect."

"Probably," Catalina said.

Daniel exhaled slowly. "You think something's wrong, don't you?"

"Olivia knows I would be worried about her by now," Catalina said. "She should have checked in. She's not answering her phone. I'm going to call Ferris."

"I'm not sure that's a good idea," Daniel said.

"I can apologize later."

Emerson Ferris answered on the fourth ring. He sounded groggy; maybe hungover. Maybe angry. Whatever the case, it was clear from his first words that he was not in a good mood—certainly not in the mood one would expect from a man who had spent the night with a lover.

"No, Olivia isn't here," he growled. "Who the hell is this?"

"Catalina Lark, her friend and business partner. We've met a few times, remember?"

"Oh, yeah, I remember you. Well, you can tell your friend and business partner that I got the message. But, shit, she could have texted me to say it's over. She didn't have to ghost me. I spent half the day on that meal and she didn't even bother to let me know that she wasn't going to make it. I thought she cared. I was so wrong about her."

Catalina stopped breathing. She clutched the phone so tightly it was a wonder the device didn't shatter.

"Are you saying Olivia didn't show up at all last night?" she whispered.

"Yeah, that's exactly what I'm saying." Emerson paused. "Why? Do you know something I don't know?"

"No," Catalina said. "I don't, and that's got me scared half to death."

"What the hell?" Sudden alarm erased the growl in Emerson's voice. "Where's Olivia?"

"I have no idea," Catalina said. "Why do you think I called you? I'm going to hang up now and make some other phone calls."

"Holy shit, do you mean you're going to start calling the hospitals? Do you really think something happened to her?"

"I just told you, I don't know," Catalina said. "But something is very wrong. I've got to go now. Give me your word that you'll call me if you hear from her."

"Yeah, sure." Emerson's voice sharpened. "I'll get in touch right away. What about her car? Is it gone?"

"Her car is still in the apartment garage. She said she was going to use a ride-hailing app to go to your place."

"Maybe the car service can tell you when they picked her up and where they took her."

"Trust me, I'm going to start there."

"Let me know what you find out, okay? Call me immediately. Now you've got me worried, too."

"I'll be in touch," Catalina said.

She hung up the phone and looked at Daniel. "Olivia never showed up at Emerson Ferris's condo."

Daniel reached for his own phone.

"I'll call the hospitals," he said. "You deal with the ride-hailing company."

Twenty minutes later they both put down their phones. Catalina had to fight to suppress the raw panic that was eating her up inside.

"The car service guy says Olivia canceled the pickup," she managed, trying to maintain a semblance of calm. "I called all of her other friends. No one saw her last night."

"The hospitals have no record of admitting anyone by that name," Daniel reported. "What in the world is going on? It's not like Olivia to just up and vanish."

"No, it's not," Catalina said. She grabbed her coat and handbag and headed for the door. "You stay here and start going through the morning news reports. You're looking for anything that happened in the Seattle downtown area last night. Car accidents. Fires. Shootings. Robberies. Kidnappings. *Anything.*"

"Got it." Daniel started to swivel his chair toward the computer. He paused. "You do know what they say about the boyfriend or the husband. When a woman goes missing—"

"The cops look at the boyfriend or the husband first. Everyone knows that. I'm going to check out that angle. Ferris sounded genuinely surprised and concerned when I talked to him on the phone a few minutes ago, but I intend to confront him in person. It's easier to get a read on someone that way."

"Hold on. I don't think you should meet him alone. I'll come with you."

"Thanks, but we'll worry about that later. First I want to retrace Olivia's steps last night. I checked her apartment this morning. It was obvious that she went back there and changed her clothes after she left the office yesterday. I know she requested a pickup from the ride-hailing service and then canceled a short time later. I need to find someone who might have seen her during that time period."

"What about the police? Are you going to file a missing persons report?"

"Yes, but at this point I have no grounds for suspecting foul play. I want to see what I can find out on my own first."

Daniel gave her a knowing look. "You think the cops will blow you off because of the Ingram case, don't you?"

"Yep. There wasn't an ounce of evidence to indicate that Ingram had been murdered, at least not the kind of hard evidence the police can use. All I could tell them was that I thought he had been killed, possibly with poison or some drug that stopped his heart. They found nothing to back up my theory."

"It's their job to find the hard evidence," Daniel said. "They had no right to label you a fake psychic."

"They didn't actually say that I was a fake until Roger Gossard told them and that reporter Brenda Bryce that I was probably delusional."

"Gossard was trying to cover his own ass."

"At the expense of my ass," Catalina said. "Get going on that computer search. Call me if you find anything."

"I'm on it, Boss."

Catalina went out into the hall and closed the door. She formed a strategy while she waited for the elevator. The first step was to go back to the apartment tower and try to retrace Olivia's steps. Someone must have seen something. This was a city, after all. There were people on the streets and security cameras everywhere these days.

_____

The only good news that morning was that the TV crew and the curiosity seekers were no longer hanging around in front of the apartment building. She went upstairs and made herself walk through Olivia's apartment again, this time with her senses heightened. There was no trace of panic or fear in the atmosphere, nothing that indicated violence.

She took the elevator downstairs to the lobby and asked Robert to contact Andrea, the woman who had been at the concierge desk the previous evening. He made the call and handed the phone to Catalina.

"I spoke to Olivia when she left," Andrea said. "I could tell she was really looking forward to the evening. She went outside to wait for her ride. Usually the cars pull up right out in front in the loading zone. But the driver must have sent a message telling her he was waiting on the side of the building. I saw her glance at her phone, and then she walked around the corner. I lost sight of her after that."

"Thanks," Catalina said.

She went outside and followed the route Olivia had evidently taken. It led to a quiet side street. Marge was in her office, the alcove of a service door. She sat on her bedroll. She wore the heavy down-filled coat Olivia and Catalina had given her several months earlier. There was a six-pack of sodas on the ground next to her. A battered shopping cart containing all her worldly possessions completed the furnishings.

No one knew Marge's last name. No one knew her age, either, although Catalina and Olivia had concluded that she was probably in her forties. Life on the street aged a woman fast. She was not big on conversation, nor did she ask for money. Instead, she regarded most passersby with a suspicious glare. The majority of those who noticed her in the alcove kept their distance. The assumption was that she had some serious mental health issues. Catalina and Olivia were pretty sure they knew why Marge gazed at people the way she did. Marge perceived human auras.

Catalina approached her with some caution. You never knew what to expect.

"Hello, Marge," Catalina said.

"Wondered when you'd show up. Took you long enough."

Marge spoke in a rough voice that, at some point in the past, had been wrecked by cigarettes or, quite possibly, too much screaming. In a rare conversational moment, she had confided to Catalina that she had spent some time locked up in a secret research lab. She said she had screamed night and day until they finally let her go.

"I'm trying to find Olivia," Catalina said.

"Gone," Marge said. "I saw 'em take her away."

Catalina fought back the panic. She warned herself that you couldn't always take Marge too literally.

"Who took Olivia?" she asked.

"The clones from Riverview."

This was getting worse by the second. But questioning Marge was a tricky business.

"Did Olivia know the Riverview clones?" Catalina asked, searching for a path through Marge's worldview, which was organized according to an elaborate conspiracy theory involving evil human scientists who worked for the rulers of the planet Riverview. The Riverview folks planned to conquer Earth, but they were still in the exploration and discovery stage. Hence the occasional alien abduction.

"Olivia didn't know who was in the car," Marge said. "Soon as she realized there were clones inside, she tried to get out, but they wouldn't let her."

"What kind of car?"

"The wrong car," Marge said. "That's how they grabbed me, too. Tricked me into getting into the wrong car and then they took me away."

Catalina tried again. "What color was the car that Olivia got into?"

"Black."

"Can you describe it?"

"Big one. Sort of like a cross between a truck and a regular car."

An SUV, Catalina decided. Unfortunately, that described a huge percentage of the vehicles on the road in the Pacific Northwest, including the one that she and Olivia had purchased together for their occasional trips to Fogg Lake. The mountain roads were not well maintained in the vicinity of the lake. Access to the town often required a rugged vehicle, not the nondescript little compacts they used in the city for errands and for occasional stakeouts.

Marge popped the top on a can of soda and waited.

"Can you describe the people who took Olivia?" Catalina said.

Marge frowned. "Bad energy."

"What color was their hair?"

"Couldn't tell. The windows of the car were dark. Just caught a glimpse of some of the energy around the driver and the guy in the back seat."

"Did you notice the license plates?"

Catalina asked the question with no real hope of a helpful answer.

"No plates," Marge said. "I looked."

That came as startling news.

"You checked for license plates?" Catalina asked.

"I may be crazy but I'm not stupid. Knew you'd come around looking for Olivia."

"Why didn't you tell a cop what you saw?"

"Cops think I'm just a crazy old lady. If I told 'em what I saw they'd take me to some clinic where they would shoot me full of drugs and make me go numb again."

"The cops think I'm a crazy lady, too," Catalina said.

And maybe she would be in Marge's place now, she thought, if her parents hadn't raised her in Fogg Lake and instilled in her the importance of gaining control of her second sight so that she could pass for normal.

"Nah, the cops don't think you're crazy," Marge said. She winked.

"They just think you're a fake psychic. Pretty good disguise, by the way. Wish I'd thought of it a few years back. If I'd played my cards right, I coulda made some real money."

"Why didn't you tell me what happened to Olivia before now?" Catalina asked. "I've lost so much time."

Marge chugged more soda and lowered the can. "I don't know where you live."

"What do you mean? I live in the apartment building right behind you. Surely you knew that?"

"Can't go around the corner. That's Riverview territory. Had to wait for you to come find me. Knew you would. What took you so long?"

Catalina reminded herself that Marge lived in a strange landscape that only she could see. There was no point berating the poor woman. She was doing her best to survive.

"Do you have any idea where the clones in the big black car took Olivia?" Catalina asked.

"Expect they took her to hell. That's where they took me. I'll bet they've got her locked up in hell right now. You're gonna look for her, aren't you?"

"Yes," Catalina said.

"That's good. But you're gonna need help. You can't walk into hell unless you've got someone to watch your back."

Catalina went very still.

"Who will help me, Marge?" she asked.

Marge concentrated hard for a moment and then gave a short, brusque nod.

"Someone who knows about the clones. They're a tough crowd. You're gonna need someone who can deal with that bunch."

The disheartening news was that Marge was right. It would be infuriating to have to make the call to Victor Arganbright to ask for help, but given what she had just learned, she didn't have much choice.

She needed professional assistance from someone who would take her fears seriously, someone who wouldn't make her waste time filling out forms.

Catalina rose to her feet. "You may be right, Marge. But *shit*."

Marge started to raise the soda can but she paused and squinted up at Catalina.

"Watch out for the needle," she said.

"What needle?"

"The clones slapped something over Olivia's face and then they stuck a needle into her shoulder when she tried to get out of the car. Just like they did to me when they took me away."

A hypodermic syringe, Catalina thought, the same type of weapon that had been used to murder a stranger fifteen years earlier in the Fogg Lake caves. It had to be a coincidence. Drugs were obviously an easy way to subdue a captive. There couldn't possibly be a connection to the murder in the caves.

"Marge," she whispered, bracing herself for the worst possible answer to her next question, "I know you can see auras. Do you think those people in the black car murdered Olivia?"

"I could see her energy through the car window when they drove off. She was still alive, but . . ."

"What, Marge?"

"It looked like she was going to sleep," Marge said. "She'll wake up in hell. Just like I did."

CHAPTER 6

Catalina was halfway back to the office, walking fast, when her phone vibrated. She yanked it out of the pocket of her coat and glanced at the screen. Daniel.

"Please tell me you've got a lead on Olivia," she said.

"Nothing yet, but you need to get back here now."

"Almost there. Why? What happened?"

"There's someone here to see you. Says it's urgent. Says it's about Olivia."

"Put him on the phone," Catalina said.

"Hang on," Daniel said.

The voice that came on the line was masculine, eerily calm, cool and controlled. It was, she concluded, the kind of voice that could lead you out of a burning building. It was also a voice that, under the right circumstances, could scare the living daylights out of you.

"My name is Slater Arganbright," he said.

"Oh, shit," Catalina whispered.

"I realize you've got some history with my uncle. We can talk about that later. Right now we've got other priorities. I understand your business partner, Olivia LeClair, is missing."

Okay, so she had been on the verge of calling Victor Arganbright. It was one thing to put in a call for help. It was something else entirely to discover that someone from the Foundation was already on the scene. That information left two gut-wrenching possibilities: either Victor Arganbright had known that Olivia was in danger and had failed to warn her in advance, or his so-called Foundation was behind the kidnapping.

"Did Victor Arganbright's thugs take Olivia?" she said. It was all she could do not to scream into the phone. "Because I swear, if you harm her, I will find a way to destroy your Foundation, even if it takes me the rest of my life."

"No, we didn't take your friend," Slater said. "And for the record, my uncle doesn't employ thugs. Just people like me."

It wasn't the denial that brought her to a stunned halt in the middle of the sidewalk. She had been prepared for that. It was highly unlikely that anyone in his right mind would admit to a serious crime like kidnapping, especially not while he was speaking on the phone. For all Slater Arganbright knew, she was recording his words.

It was the incredibly unemotional way he spoke that stopped her cold. His voice sounded far too flat, unnaturally so. There should have been some heat in the denial; a hint of outrage, at the very least. After all, she had just pulled out a verbal jackknife by virtually accusing him, or at least his uncle, of a major federal crime.

"How did you know Olivia was kidnapped?" she said. She still sounded fierce and accusatory. She did not give a damn. She was dealing with an Arganbright.

Whose help she might need.

Damn, damn, damn. Shit.

That was the third time she had used the word *shit* in the past

few minutes. Her language was deteriorating rapidly. That was probably not a good sign. *Control, Catalina. You must exercise control.*

"When I walked into your office a few minutes ago your receptionist said you were out looking for your friend," Slater explained in
his eerily uninflected voice. "I was told no one appears to have seen
or heard from Ms. LeClair since late yesterday. Considering that I
came to Seattle to ask you and Olivia for some professional assistance, it's unlikely that her disappearance today is a coincidence."

Still no emotion in the words. Just flat statements of facts. Or flat-
out lies. There was no way to be sure. It was as if she was talking to
a robot.

Two could play that game.

"What do you want, Arganbright?" she asked, trying to channel
her inner Philip Marlowe. She was a private investigator, after all. She
even had a trench coat, and she was wearing it today. It was a very
stylish trench. Olivia had given it to her when they embarked on
their new business venture.

"We can talk about why I'm here in Seattle when we meet," Slater
said. "We shouldn't be having this conversation on the phone."

With an effort of will, Catalina forged through the small trance
she had plunged into when she heard the Arganbright name. She
lurched forward, once again walking as swiftly as possible, almost
trotting.

"I'm on my way back to my office," she said. "Stay right where
you are, Arganbright. Don't make a move or I swear I'll call the cops
and tell them you're responsible for the disappearance of my friend.
I'm sure the Foundation has some good lawyers who will be able to
keep you out of jail, but I'll make damn certain that the Arganbright
name is all over the media before Victor can make me shut up. And
what's more, I'll mention that little private lab he's operating there in
Las Vegas."

"It would be better if I come to you," Slater said. "Is there a busy office building or a hotel near your present location where you can wait until I get there?"

So much for her puny threat. Evidently it hadn't even ruffled his hair as it went past. The truth was, she wasn't in a position to be anything more than a minor inconvenience for Victor or his Las Vegas operation, and they both knew it. Informing the media that the Foundation Arganbright currently controlled was engaged in paranormal research wouldn't do any real damage. Who cared if some eccentric gazillionaire had set up his own lab to run some crazy-ass experiments? Vegas had a history of eccentric characters. Think Howard Hughes.

"No," she said, abandoning Philip Marlowe and settling for coldly polite, "there is no suitable location where I can hide out and wait for you. I'm only about three blocks away from my office. I will be there in a few minutes. Do. Not. Leave."

There was a long pause at the other end of the connection. Maybe Robot Man was trying to figure out how to respond to her refusal to follow his orders. Evidently he was not programmed to handle rejection.

"All right," Slater said finally. "But stay on the phone. Keep to the busiest streets. Make sure there are people around you at all times. Above all, don't get into any cars. No taxis. No ride services."

Catalina caught her breath. "My witness says that's how they grabbed Olivia. How did you guess?"

"You've got a witness?"

There may have been a slight edge on Slater's words now.

"Yes," she said. She was not about to offer him any more information. Not yet, at any rate. "Now tell me how you knew that the kidnappers faked a ride service pickup."

"I didn't know about that angle," Slater said. "I just went with the logical and most obvious assumption. Kidnapping usually requires a vehicle. Historically, unmarked vans have been popular for that purpose. But these days it's obvious that a vehicle that looks like a car from a ride-hailing operation would be a smart option. No one takes any notice of a black car pulling over to the curb to pick up a passenger."

"Oh, right." She felt like an idiot. Of course there would have been a vehicle of some kind involved.

"Do me a favor," Slater continued. "Make sure you use all your senses on the way back here."

The edge on his voice got sharper. Her level of wariness and the anxiety that accompanied it shot up another notch. At this rate it wouldn't be long before she was in a state of full-blown panic.

Who was this man, and what was he doing in her already complicated life?

"I suppose your uncle told you about my talent?" she said.

"He mentioned it, yes."

"He told you I was one of the Freaks from Fogg Lake?"

"I'm not from Fogg Lake but I'm in the same category as you. A genuine, but not yet certified, freak."

Robots did not crack jokes.

"What's that supposed to mean?" she asked, deeply suspicious now.

"Let's just say that my family made sure I didn't wind up with an official diagnosis."

"I see."

"Obviously your family took good care of you, too," Slater said. "And that's enough getting-to-know-you conversation for now. You need to focus. Crank up all of your senses."

"Please stop talking like that. You're making me nervous."

"Talking like what?"

"Never mind."

She braced herself for the jolt that she always got when she went all the way into her other vision. First came the rush of heightened awareness. For a couple of seconds she was being spun around inside a disorienting kaleidoscope. The world got sharper but people took on a ghostly aspect. Their auras whispered, sparked, flashed and glowed. Their footsteps left seething prints on the sidewalk.

And then she got control.

With control came the prickling chills of dread. When she walked down a busy city street with her senses running at full blast the world was transformed into a jungle. The potential for danger was everywhere. Each and every person she passed was a threat until proven otherwise.

"Are you running hot?" Slater asked.

"Yes," she said, her voice very tight now as she struggled to process the tsunami of information her psychic vision was transmitting. She had to steel herself to make the three-block trek to her office. It was not going to be a walk in the park.

"Promise me you'll stay on the phone," Slater said.

"I'll stay on the phone," she said, "but don't expect an extended conversation. I've got to concentrate."

"To maintain control. Trust me, I understand."

For the first time there was more than just an edge on his voice. There was a faintly human quality now. She got the impression that he just might know exactly how much effort it took to remain anchored to reality when you found yourself trying to interpret the world through a storm of visions.

Luckily the sidewalk was not very crowded. The morning surge of workers on their way to the office was over and the noon lunch frenzy was still a few hours away. Nevertheless, walking through downtown Seattle with her talent engaged was always an intense, exhausting experience. The fact that it was daytime made no difference. Her other vision transformed every individual who came within a range of twenty to thirty feet into a luminous figure that had to be scanned, assessed and categorized according to her intuition's definition of threat level.

Each illuminated figure pulsed with hot energy that created constantly shifting, complex patterns. Every man, woman and child was a three-ring circus with various performances taking place simultaneously. For those with the vision to see it, the truth was that humans really could walk and chew gum at the same time. It was an unnerving talent.

Each individual was capable of thinking about a problem at work while anxiously trying to ignore the new chest pains. A person could carry on a conversation on the phone that elicited a range of conflicting emotions, all of which seethed in his or her aura. Some people she passed were hovering on the verge of an anxiety attack. Some were brooding. Some were angry.

And for Catalina, the sense of a potential threat did not end once a person had moved out of range, because she was forced to wade through the hot energy of the footprints that had been left behind. Sure, in most cases the prints cooled rapidly and faded into the countless footsteps that had already been laid down on the sidewalk. But the speed with which most prints sank to the undetectable level was no help when you were trying to dodge the still-fresh energy tracks of a man who wanted to hit someone or a person who was mired in deep depression.

A few of those she passed left prints so hot and so tainted with unwholesome energy that they would burn for hours before they cooled to the point where they were no longer disturbing.

She found herself playing a game of hopscotch on the sidewalk, hastily sidestepping a hot print, skipping over one that seethed with some very unstable energy, darting around a trail of footsteps that boiled with rage.

She was all too aware that those who noticed her weaving a convoluted path down the sidewalk concluded that she was just another crazy street person, albeit one who was better dressed than the average bag lady. They avoided eye contact and adjusted their own courses to give her plenty of room.

Deep down, in spite of all the training her parents had provided and all the tricks she had learned to employ in order to pass for normal, sometimes she did wonder if maybe she really was one of the crazies.

She jumped or flinched or otherwise reacted to every odd spike in every aura around her and to each hot print on the sidewalk. She was constantly in fight-or-flight mode. How could that possibly be normal?

Two more blocks. The woman in the dark blue jacket radiated the thin, irregular energy of chronic stress. Catalina's senses registered her as *No immediate threat.*

The man passing on the left had shafts of anger spiking in his aura. *Potential threat.* Catalina quickened her pace to move out of range. The angry man did not notice her. His rage was directed at someone or something else, but that didn't make him any less dangerous. People with anger management issues often lashed out at anyone who got in their way.

The young man coming toward her was glued to his phone. Whatever he was viewing was creating spikes of intense excitement that Catalina's senses interpreted as unhealthy obsession or addiction. She decided he was probably playing a game. *No threat.*

Cell Phone Guy was clearly unaware of the woman on the bicycle approaching him from behind. She, in turn, was focusing her attention on a car, not on Cell Phone Guy.

A vision of the bicyclist crashing into Cell Phone Guy and sending both of them into the street where they would be struck by a car ghosted across Catalina's senses. *Threat.* Her intuition was alerting her, telling her to move out of the way so that she didn't get tangled up in the imminent collision.

She overrode the warning, grabbed Cell Phone Guy by the arm and hauled him out of the path of the bicyclist. In the process he dropped the phone on the sidewalk.

"What the hell?" Cell Phone Guy yelped in startled surprise and a flash of panic.

"Sorry," Catalina said. "I'm really sorry. I thought—"

"What's going on?" Slater's voice crackled in her ear.

She ignored him because Cell Phone Guy had just scooped up his phone and was glaring at her. His aura was flaring with anger now.

Potential threat.

"Are you crazy, lady?" he snarled.

The bicyclist whipped past, heedless of the near collision.

"Catalina, talk to me," Slater ordered.

"Not now," she said. She lowered the phone to deal with Cell Phone Guy. "I'm so sorry. I thought that bicyclist was going to run into you. Is your phone okay?"

Cell Phone Guy's anger began to fade but he was clearly annoyed. He glared and then he examined his phone. Relief spiked for an instant in his aura before it was demolished by another wave of angry alarm. He started checking his pockets. She sighed.

"I didn't take your wallet," she said.

When he discovered his wallet was where it was supposed to be he gave her one last disgusted glare and walked swiftly away.

"Everything okay?" Slater asked.

"Yes," she said. "Some guy on a phone was about to get hit by a woman on a bicycle. At least I think he was about to get hit. It looked like both of them were going to wind up in the street and maybe get struck by a car. I pulled the man out of the way. He dropped his phone in the process. Let's just say he was not particularly grateful."

"No good deed—"

"Goes unpunished. I know."

"How far away are you?"

"About two blocks."

"Walk fast. You're making me nervous."

"How do you think I feel?"

Out of the corner of her eye she caught sight of a man in running gear coming up fast on her left. The runner had been directly behind her until now, which explained why he had not registered on her senses.

Immediate threat.

As the runner drew up alongside her, she could see that he looked to be in his early thirties, tall and in excellent physical condition. He was loping along at an easy, steady pace, not even breathing hard.

It wasn't only his proximity and the swift way he had closed the distance between them that set off all of Catalina's psychic klaxons. It was the almost invisible bands of pale energy that whispered in the runner's aura.

Blank.

It wasn't true that blanks had some bandwidth missing from their energy fields. That was a myth that had developed because most of those who could perceive auras couldn't detect the deceptively pale radiance that was the calling card of the average sociopath.

Catalina had never had any trouble detecting the freakish vibe of a true human monster. She had encountered blanks often enough to recognize one immediately if he or she got within range. But she never got past the chill of dread that a brush with a blank sent across her senses. Crossing paths with one was a lot like chancing upon a snake while out on a stroll. The snake, at least, had a valid excuse for being a ruthless predator.

"Oh, shit," Catalina muttered.

Maybe she should just abandon the effort to control her language today.

Propelled by instinct and intuition, Catalina pivoted away at a right angle from the man in running gear, swiftly putting as much distance as possible between the two of them. She knew the sudden move would make her appear even more alarming to those around her. She tried to cover the action by glancing quickly at her phone as though she had just received new directions for a destination.

"Damn it," Slater said. "What's going on?"

Wow. He was cursing now. Catalina decided that indicated some degree of emotion. But she was too occupied with keeping track of the blank to respond.

The runner flew past without seeming to notice her. He never broke stride. One of the interesting things about blanks was that they were so utterly convinced of their own strength and cleverness that it rarely occurred to them anyone could see them for the frightening beings they were. But, as Catalina's parents had frequently pointed out, everyone had blind spots. For blanks, the weakness was invariably overconfidence in their own supposed superiority.

The runner's aura faded rapidly and vanished altogether as he moved out of range. By the time he reached the corner he looked like any other fitness-minded man trying to get in a morning workout.

No longer a threat.

Catalina discovered she could breathe again. She pulled her frazzled senses back in line and prepared to resume the grueling hike through the human jungle. But she was still focused on the close brush with a blank. She did not notice the powerful aura of the man directly in front of her until it was too late.

She walked straight into the arms of the stranger and came up hard against his very solid chest—and an aura unlike any she had ever encountered. For a couple of beats she was once again tumbling around inside the kaleidoscope.

"Oh, shit," she yelped.

Even when she was in her normal senses she disliked touching or being touched by anyone except the people she knew and trusted. The sensation of colliding with a complete stranger was a thousand times more disturbing when all her senses were engaged and on high alert.

It wasn't the heat of the unknown aura that shocked her. It was the jarring sense of intense intimacy. Aura incompatibility was one of the many reasons why her romantic relationships always ended in disaster. Even a simple kiss was a balancing act. When it came to actually engaging in sex she had learned the hard way that she had to keep a tight rein on her senses. Letting go in bed had one of two dramatic effects on her partners. Men either concluded that she was an exciting dominatrix or else they ran for the hills. Regardless of which outcome prevailed, the end result had led her into a series of spectacularly boring relationships that sputtered along for a while and then collapsed.

But the darkly radiant energy field that had just slammed into her own was profoundly not boring. For a few seconds she was literally dazzled. She was unaware of anything or anyone else around her. All her senses were flaring and all of them were focused on the man in whose arms she stood.

"Sorry," he said. "Didn't mean to startle you."

She knew that voice. A moment ago she had been listening to it on her phone. Her already disoriented senses did another unstable spin, trying to find a new balance.

"Slater Arganbright?" she said.

"Yes. Apologies for the clumsy introduction."

He still had his hands on her, and her senses were still spiking and flashing.

"Oh, shit," she muttered.

Frantically she lowered her senses and tried to untangle herself. He released her very quickly, as if he had been the one who had been burned by the collision of their auras.

"Are you all right?" he asked.

Annoyed, she straightened her shoulders and regained her composure.

"You don't have to act like I'm going to fall apart," she said. "I'm not fragile or delicate. You took me by surprise, that's all. I was . . . focused on someone else."

"What's going on? You sound breathless."

"I was walking quickly because you insisted that I get back to the office right away, remember? Just got too close to a blank, that's all. Or, rather, he got too close to me. I didn't see him coming until he was next to me."

"Trust me, I know how it feels." He glanced briefly over his shoulder. "The runner with the gray jacket?"

"Yes." Catalina peered past Slater's shoulder. The runner was no longer in sight. "You noticed him?"

"I caught a glimpse of his aura. He was strong."

That was interesting. A lot of people who could detect auras were able to tell that something was off about a blank's energy field but very few could actually see the cold heat of a blank's aura.

"You could see the bad light in his field?" she asked.

"Yes." Slater looked at her with a thoughtful expression. "He got close to you, didn't he?"

"Yes, but I don't think he even noticed me. He's long gone now, thank goodness. How did you find me out here on the street?"

"No big mystery to it," Slater said. "I have a photo of you. Your receptionist described the coat you're wearing and gave me your most likely route back to the office."

"I see."

"Also, it's not like there are a lot of women walking down the street who are trying to avoid the hot footprints."

She groaned. "In other words, I looked like I was drunk or crazy?"

"Not to me. I knew exactly what you were doing."

She wasn't sure how to deal with the information her senses were providing about Slater Arganbright. The heat in his aura was breathtaking. Even though she was no longer using her second sight, she would never forget the way his energy field had felt when it collided with hers. Summer lightning.

She had never before experienced anything like the sensation.

Now that she had calmed down and put some distance between them, she had a chance to study the man in more detail. He wasn't big and bulked up. He was leopard-sleek, and leopard-powerful. The sharp planes and angles of his face had a severe, ascetic cast. His dark hair was cut short in a no-nonsense style. Even though the sun illuminated the street in the warm glow of springtime, Slater seemed to be enveloped in shadows. There was a grim, haunted quality in his amber eyes.

It was obvious he had not bothered to shave that morning. He didn't look as if he had spent much time putting together his sartorial look, either. He wore a pair of rumpled-looking, multipocketed cargo trousers, a black T-shirt, an extremely distressed leather jacket and low boots that appeared as well-worn as the jacket. He had the strap of a sturdy-looking backpack slung over one shoulder. He might be built like a big cat but he dressed like a cross between a tech ace and a biker.

To her chagrin she'd had to exert a little raw willpower to shake off the mesmerizing impact of his eyes. But maybe she should cut herself some slack. After all, she had been through a lot in the past twenty-four hours.

"Tell me what you want from me in exchange for helping me find Olivia," she said. "Because that's what this is about, right?"

"My uncle obviously left a bad impression."

"No shit."

"We can talk about that later."

"As far as I'm concerned, it's too late to discuss your uncle's actions. The damage has been done. I'm on the other side. I prefer not to be reminded of all the details."

"Right," Slater said. "In that case let's stick to the problem at hand."

"My friend Olivia is missing. That is the problem at hand. You seem to know something about the situation. I want answers and I want them now."

"I don't have many. All I can tell you is that I'm pretty sure I'm chasing the people who grabbed her. You said on the phone you found a witness, someone who saw Olivia kidnapped?"

"Yes."

"I want to talk to her," Slater said.

"I just did. All Marge knows is that yesterday evening someone tricked Olivia into getting into a black car, an SUV of some kind. No license plates. There were two people in the car. She thinks she saw one of them use a syringe to inject some drug into Olivia. That's it. That's all Marge could tell me."

"She thinks she saw one of them inject Ms. LeClair with a drug? That's interesting."

"The problem with Marge as a witness is that she interprets everything through her own personal conspiracy theory. In her world the bad people are all from a planet named Riverview and they use drugs to subdue their victims."

Slater looked interested. "Any idea how she picked up the specifics of her theory?"

"Sure, Olivia and I did a little research. Turns out Riverview is the name of the psychiatric hospital where Marge was incarcerated for a couple of years. The doctors used a lot of drugs on her in an attempt to rid her of her fantasies."

"What kind of fantasies?"

Catalina pulled up her steeliest smile. "Marge is considered crazy because she sees auras."

"Does she have a connection to Fogg Lake?"

"I don't think so."

"Statistically speaking, there is a small percentage of the population with a naturally occurring sixth sense. Over the years a lot of people have claimed to see auras or tried to invent gadgets to read energy fields. The experts at the Foundation believe that some psychic ability is probably a latent talent in many people, but no one knows what is required to kick-start it."

"You mean it takes something like what happened to the residents of Fogg Lake on the night of the explosion in the caves."

"Evidently. Whatever the case, if you don't grow up in a community that takes psychic ability as normal, it's difficult to learn how to control your talent and even harder to figure out how to pass for normal. Sounds like your friend Marge never got the hang of it."

"Sadly, no."

"Let's go talk to her."

CHAPTER 7

Tony Harkins yanked open the door of the black SUV and vaulted into the passenger seat. He slammed the door, wiped the sweat off his face and pulled a bottle of water out of the console.

"Almost had her," he said. He gulped some of the water and lowered the bottle. "But for some reason she suddenly turned and shot off in another direction."

Deke eased the vehicle away from the curb and out into traffic. "We knew it was a long shot trying to grab her on a busy street. Think she picked up on you?"

Tony reflected briefly on the abrupt way Catalina Lark had veered off to the right when he had come up beside her.

"Nah. Pretty sure she saw someone she knew and changed course to meet him."

"Did you see the guy?"

"I got a quick look at him just before I turned the corner. Probably a boyfriend."

"We need to get her but we can't risk another near miss. She's got some talent, like the other one. Sooner or later she'll figure out what's going on."

"Relax, we'll pick up Lark tonight or tomorrow. How hard can it be to grab a single woman in Seattle?"

"No more spur-of-the-moment shit," Deke said. "We need a real plan, because we have to get it right next time. There's a lot of money at stake here."

"You don't have to tell me that." Tony drank some more water. "Score of a lifetime."

"Think Lark will recognize you if she sees you again?"

"I doubt it. But so what if she does? I'm just a guy who happened to be out for a run. If she sees me again she'll assume that I live somewhere in the neighborhood. No big deal."

"Huh."

"What?"

"Maybe the easiest way to handle this is a straight-up introduction," Deke said. "You intercept her, tell her you're new in town and that you saw her on the street today when you went for a run. Ask her for the name of a place that does a good happy hour in the area. You invite her to have a drink with you. You put the drug in her glass."

Tony gave that some thought. He smiled.

"The old game," he said.

"It always worked in the past. No reason it wouldn't work again."

"It worked because we were careful to pick the right targets," Tony said. "Don't forget, Lark is not a normal. We don't have any idea how strong she is."

"The drug worked just fine on LeClair. No reason it won't work on Lark. You just need to get close enough to give her a dose. That will take care of her senses, whatever they are, for a few hours."

"Or maybe a few days," Tony said. "Olivia LeClair was still out of it when we took her to the pickup location. I think we used too much. If she doesn't wake up, the client is going to be pissed."

"So we'll cut back a little on the dose we give Lark," Deke said.

He brought the SUV to a halt at a stoplight. He smiled in anticipation of the action.

Tony met his brother's eyes in the mirror, eyes that were the exact same shade of blue. There was no bond like the bond that existed between identical siblings.

CHAPTER 8

Marge was still huddled in her alcove, seated atop the bedroll. There was another empty soda can on the ground beside her.

When she saw Catalina and Slater coming toward her, she stiffened.

"It's all right, Marge," Catalina said. She went forward quickly. "This is Slater Arganbright. He's going to help me look for Olivia."

Marge fixed Slater with an assessing gaze. "Huh."

Slater ignored the less-than-encouraging greeting. He crouched in front of Marge so that he was face-to-face with her.

"I would appreciate your help, ma'am," Slater said. "I'm after the people who kidnapped Olivia but I don't have much to go on. I could really use a good description of the men who drove off with Ms. LeClair."

Catalina was relieved that he was speaking to Marge in a calm, professional manner, as if she were a normal person.

Marge studied him for a long moment. "Never seen anyone like you. That's some weird energy you've got goin' on."

"So I've been told," Slater said.

Marge accepted that and let it go.

"Not much I can tell you," she said. "Couple of clones from Riverview grabbed Olivia and shot her full of some crap. She went to sleep real quick. They took her away. They've got this secret research lab where they do experiments on people."

Catalina stifled a sigh. Marge was evidently about to launch into her conspiracy theory.

Slater was unfazed.

"Tell me more about the clones," Slater said. "Were they male or female?"

Marge perked up a little at the question. Probably because Slater seemed to be taking her seriously, Catalina thought.

"Male," Marge said. "One in the back seat. One in front. Didn't see the clone in back until Olivia tried to get out of the car. He reached out to haul her back inside. That's when I got a quick look at him. Got a glimpse of the driver at the same time. It was the one in back who used the needle on her. Poor Olivia is going to wake up in hell."

"Not if we find her first," Slater said. "You're sure the two men in the car were clones?"

"Didn't get a good look at their faces, but I saw their auras. No two auras are one hundred percent identical, but those two were so close most folks would have a tough time telling them apart."

"Twins," Slater said quietly.

Catalina glanced at him, startled. She turned back to Marge. "Are you saying the two men who grabbed Olivia were identical twins?"

"If they were human you could call 'em twins," Marge said. "But those two weren't human. They're from Riverview. That makes 'em clones."

Time to give Slater some credit, Catalina thought. Two minutes into the interview with Marge and he had already extracted a description that might prove extremely valuable.

"What else did you see in the energy fields of the two people in the car?" Slater asked.

Marge eyed him. "You see energy fields, too?"

"Yes," Slater said. "Not the way you do, but yes, I can sense them."

Marge nodded with a sage expression. "Right. You're one of the cleaners from the Foundation, aren't you?"

Catalina could have sworn her jaw dropped. "You know about the Foundation?"

"Met someone at that secret lab the Riverview bastards operate," Marge said. "Another captive. He talked about it. I remember he told me that if the people from the Foundation found out we'd been kidnapped they'd send the cleaners to rescue us. No one ever showed up to get us out of that place, though, so I figured he was just another crazy. But a while back Olivia told me Catalina was working for a client from Las Vegas. She said he ran a Foundation that understood people like me."

"There's a lot about people like you and me and Catalina that the Foundation still doesn't understand," Slater said. "But we're working on it." He took a card out of his pocket and handed it to Marge. "If you get kidnapped again and taken to Riverview or anywhere else that you don't want to be, you make sure you tell whoever works there that they have to call that number. The cleaners will come and get you."

Marge looked dubious. "What if the clones won't make the phone call?"

Slater smiled coldly. "You tell them that as soon as Catalina and Olivia figure out that you're missing, they'll make the phone call.

And if that happens, the folks at Riverview will find themselves dealing with a lawsuit as well as the cleaners. Trust me, someone will make that call."

"Okay," Marge said. She studied the card, her lips moving silently. Then she nodded once, satisfied. "Got a pretty good memory for numbers. But just in case, I'll keep this card handy."

She tucked it under her knit hat.

"Anything else I should know about the clones who took Olivia?" Slater asked.

"That big car they were driving looked real new," Marge said. She shrugged. "And the one who used the needle on Olivia knew what he was doing. Expect he'd done it before. That tell you anything?"

"It tells me I'm dealing with professionals," Slater said.

"Exactly," Marge said. "Talent like that doesn't come cheap. Takes money to set up an operation slick enough to make a woman vanish without a trace."

"Money and resources," Slater said. "You're right, Marge, this has all the hallmarks of a sophisticated operation."

Catalina looked at Slater and then at Marge. Somewhere along the line they both appeared to have forgotten about her. The whole thing felt a little unreal but there was no getting around the reality of what had just happened. A stranger with a very weird aura had immediately been able to establish communication with a homeless woman whose psychic senses had been scrambled by drugs.

Marge eyed Slater. "Has your energy always been like it is now?"

"You know how it is, Marge—you can't see your own aura," Slater said. "But people have told me that mine was always a little different. Six months ago it got a lot different because something happened to me."

Marge squinted knowingly. "The clones used drugs on you?"

"Radiation."

"Yeah? What kind?"

"I have no idea."

Marge nodded. "Changed you, though."

"Evidently," Slater said.

"What are you now?"

"Still trying to figure it out," Slater said.

CHAPTER 9

"Talk to me, Arganbright," Catalina said. "I want to know everything you know."

Slater considered how and where to begin. It wasn't easy to concentrate on her question, because he was still adjusting to the effect she was having on his senses. When they had slammed into each other on the street a short time ago it was as if he had been plunged straight into the heart of a different version of the "Sleeping Beauty" fairy tale. In this story he was the sleeper, and he had been awakened not by a kiss but by the electrifying energy of Catalina's fierce aura.

Or maybe this wasn't some psychic edition of "Sleeping Beauty." Maybe this story had more in common with *Frankenstein*. That would make him the monster. Marge's question whispered through him. *What are you now?*

They were less than a block away from the offices of Lark & LeClair, walking quickly. After leaving Marge, Catalina had said very little. He knew she was trying to figure out what the hell to do about him.

He had been warned that she was going to be a problem. What he hadn't realized until the moment she walked into his arms was that she would prove to be an exciting problem.

He had known that she was smart. Victor had also made it clear that she was a strong talent and that she was in full control.

He studied her now, trying not to be obvious about it. She was no longer using her psychic senses, so her aura was not as fiery as it had been when they had slammed into each other. But the fact that her energy field was calm did not diminish the effect she had on him.

He was just as intensely aware of her vibe now as he had been earlier when they had collided on the street. The difference was that without the distraction of her intoxicating aura he was aware of other, more subtle things—the rich, lustrous brown of her tightly bound hair; the cool challenge in her green eyes; the aloof image projected by the black trench coat and low black boots.

He was intrigued, curious, fascinated, *thrilled* to be this close to her.

"I'm sorry I got here too late to save Olivia LeClair," he said.

Catalina shot him a somber, searching look. "Do you know who took Olivia and why?"

"I don't have any solid answers for you. Just a theory."

"That's more than I've got. Talk fast, Arganbright."

"Three days ago a collector named Royston was murdered. The circumstances of his death are similar to those of the Ingram murder."

"Ingram was the victim in the case your uncle asked me to investigate."

"Right. Both of the victims were known to be eccentric and secretive. Both were obsessed with acquiring objects with a paranormal provenance. Victor is convinced the deaths are related. He believes someone is looking for a particular artifact."

"What artifact?" Catalina asked.

"We don't know, but Ingram and Royston were both known to be obsessed with objects linked to what may have been the old Fogg Lake lab."

"What makes you think Olivia's kidnapping is linked to the murders?"

"I don't like coincidences, and it would be a hell of a coincidence if your friend, who has a very specific connection to Fogg Lake, just happened to get kidnapped three days after Royston's murder."

Catalina caught her breath. "You think that whoever killed Royston found what he was searching for and then went after Olivia."

"It's more than that. If I'm right, it's all connected to the murder you and Olivia witnessed fifteen years ago."

Startled, she looked at him and then quickly glanced away. "You know about that?"

"Rumors of murder have a way of leaking out. The story of a couple of Fogg Lake kids who thought they witnessed a killing made it into the Foundation files. It was noted because one of the Foundation researchers disappeared right around the time of the murder. His name was John Morrissey. His body was never found."

"Was there a Foundation investigation?"

"The Foundation was under different . . . management at the time."

"Oh, yeah, right." Catalina made a face. "Rancourt was still in charge in those days. Your uncle didn't take over until, what? Five years ago?"

"Victor was appointed director of the Foundation five years ago. He is well aware that his predecessor left a legacy of distrust."

"No shit."

"Out of curiosity, is 'no shit' your default mode?"

"It seems to be today," Catalina said. "Believe it or not, until this morning my language was a little more refined."

"I'll take your word for it. As I was saying, at the time of the Fogg Lake murder, Stenson Rancourt was in charge of the Foundation. He more or less inherited the job from his father."

"Everyone in Fogg Lake knows that the Rancourts were no better than a mob family. They used the Foundation to make millions. Billions, probably."

"Things are different now," Slater said.

"Sure."

"Moving right along, due to Stenson Rancourt's lack of interest in Morrissey's disappearance, the investigation was minimal. It went nowhere."

"And yet," Catalina said, "Olivia and I still wound up in a Foundation file."

"I'm afraid so." Slater hesitated, telling himself that he should probably shut up now. But Catalina deserved some answers. "That did not happen under Rancourt's regime. You and Olivia landed in the files because Victor has begun an effort to identify everyone who might have some connection to the old Bluestone Project. The people of Fogg Lake and their descendants are of particular interest to him."

"I've got news for your uncle—we don't want his attention."

"Try to put your animosity aside for thirty seconds and consider the facts on the ground. Your friend has been kidnapped and there is every reason to believe her disappearance is connected to something that happened in Fogg Lake fifteen years ago. Do you really think regular law enforcement has a chance in hell of finding her before it's too late?"

Catalina clutched the strap of her handbag with the determination of a patient about to undergo a tooth extraction without the benefit of an anesthetic.

"No," she said.

They had reached the entrance of the office building that housed

Lark & LeClair. He opened the door for Catalina and followed her into the small lobby and then into the elevator.

"Enough with the history lesson," she said. "Where do we start looking for Olivia?"

"We're going to pay a visit to the owner of a local gallery who specializes in antiques with a paranormal provenance. No one knows more about the rumors circulating in the underground market of paranormal artifacts than Gwendolyn Swan. She's got a shop here in town."

The elevator doors opened. Catalina moved briskly out into the hall. He fell into step beside her.

"I've never heard of an antiques shop that specializes in those kind of artifacts."

"Gwendolyn Swan tries to keep a very low profile, for obvious reasons. Any hint of the paranormal attracts some extremely odd people."

"Trust me, I know exactly how she feels," Catalina said. "I became the human equivalent of a tacky tourist attraction myself six months ago, thanks to your uncle."

Slater followed her out of the elevator and kept his mouth shut. He did not have the time or the energy to continue defending Victor and the new management of the Foundation.

They reached the door of the Lark & LeClair office. Slater opened it and stood aside to let Catalina stride past him into the room.

She came to an abrupt halt and stared at the man standing by the window.

"Oh, *shit*," she said. "This really is not my day."

CHAPTER 10

D aniel leaped to his feet behind the reception desk. He was at once anxious and apologetic. "I'm sorry, Ms. Lark. Dr. Gossard said it was really important that he talk to you."

Slater got a silent ping as the name popped up in his memory. Dr. Roger Gossard was the head of the security consulting firm Victor had mentioned . . . *What happened between Lark and Gossard after I left town was not my fault, either. Relationships fall apart all the time.*

Roger Gossard looked like he had been sent from central casting to play the part of a lean and hungry CEO who was going places and taking his cutting-edge forensics investigation business with him.

Catalina regarded him with a mix of antipathy and impatience.

"What are you doing here, Roger?" she asked.

Gossard smiled, showing a lot of very white, very straight teeth, but tension and wariness shivered in the atmosphere around him. He flicked an uneasy glance at Slater and then smiled at Catalina.

"Good morning, Cat," he said.

Catalina started to take off her trench coat. "I've told you before, do not call me Cat."

Daniel was still on his feet behind his desk. He looked as if he was afraid he might have to throw himself between Catalina and Gossard in order to prevent bloodshed.

"A police detective called while you were out," Daniel said. "He indicated that you were involved in an attempted murder sometime last night. He said to tell you that they picked up Angus Hopper an hour ago. What happened? Are you all right?"

Catalina switched her attention to Daniel. "To be clear, I was not involved in an attempted murder. I was almost murdered. There's a distinct difference."

Daniel grimaced. "Sorry, that didn't come out right."

"You said they picked up Hopper?" Catalina hung her coat on a coatrack. "That's the first good news I've had this morning."

Daniel glanced at his notes. "Evidently Hopper showed up in an emergency room with what appeared to be puncture wounds from a, um, fork."

Roger chuckled. "Figures."

Daniel kept going. "It's been a tough morning, Boss. First Olivia goes missing. Then Arganbright shows up claiming he has to see you immediately, a matter of life and death. The police call to tell me that you were attacked at Matson's house. Then, just to put the cherry on top of my latte, Dr. Gossard walks in demanding to talk to you."

"I'm sorry," Catalina said. "I didn't get a chance to tell you about Hopper because Olivia's disappearance is a lot more important. Priorities, Daniel."

"Right." Daniel collapsed into his chair, dazed. "Priorities."

Roger's brows kicked up. "What's this about Olivia?"

"Never mind," Catalina snapped. "It's none of your business."

Slater cleared his throat. "I'm feeling a little out of the loop here, too. What's this about an attempted murder and a fork injury?"

Daniel looked at Catalina. She waved one hand.

"Go ahead," she said. "Tell him."

Daniel straightened in his chair. "Last night one of our clients came close to getting her throat slit by an ex-boyfriend. According to the police, Catalina arrived on the scene just in time to interrupt the proceedings. Evidently there was a struggle. Catalina somehow managed to do some damage to the perp with a fork. Fortunately both women escaped."

Slater looked at Catalina. "A fork?"

Roger snorted, clearly suppressing laughter.

Daniel eyed Catalina with a grim expression. "You may want to think about upgrading to a gun, Boss."

Catalina ignored him. She glanced at Slater and jerked a thumb at Gossard.

"This is Roger Gossard," she said. "Excuse me, *Dr.* Roger Gossard. I forget what the PhD is in."

"Forensic psychology," Roger said smoothly.

"Whatever," Catalina said. "Roger, here, runs a consulting business. Does some contract work with various law enforcement agencies and is available as an expert witness for any law firm that can afford him. Roger, this is Slater Arganbright."

Roger walked quickly across the small space and held out his well-manicured hand.

"A pleasure, Slater," he said.

Slater shook the offered hand once and broke contact. "*Dr.* Gossard." He put a little emphasis on the title.

Roger chuckled and waved that aside. "Roger, please. Any friend of Cat's and all that."

"Don't call me Cat," Catalina said.

Roger chuckled as if the protest was an old joke they had often shared. He fixed Slater with a deeply curious expression. "Are you one of Catalina's clients?"

It struck Slater that the explanation was as good as any he could have come up with on the spot. It had the advantage of being the truth. Sort of.

"Yes," he said.

Catalina gave him a startled look but she did not correct him. She returned her attention to Roger.

"I'm still waiting for an explanation, Roger. Why are you here?"

"Got to admit I'm curious about what happened at your client's home last night," Roger said.

"You can't expect me to discuss that with you," she said. "Client confidentiality. I'm sure you understand."

"Of course," Roger said, annoyed but evidently resigned. "I came here to discuss some business. Shall we go into your office? I just need a few minutes of your time."

"No," Catalina said. "I'm in a hurry. Say whatever it is you have to say so that I can get back to work."

"Fine." Roger's mouth and eyes tightened at the corners, but he kept his voice as smooth and polished as his attire. "I dropped by this morning because I want you to look at a scene for me."

"You have got to be joking," Catalina said. "You want me to consult for you? After what you did to me?"

"I admit I didn't handle things well," Roger allowed. "I apologize. But I'm sure you can appreciate my situation. It's critical that my consulting work be viewed as cutting-edge technologically and rigorously scientific. I couldn't afford to have my name or my firm's name linked with that of a woman who claims to be psychic."

"I never claimed to be psychic. You told Brenda Bryce, Girl Reporter, that I was a flake who claimed to have paranormal talents. You got me fired from my career counseling job. I ended up dealing with a stalker because of those stories in the press."

Roger finally displayed some emotion—outrage.

"I had nothing to do with you losing your job, and you can't blame that crazy stalker on me," he said. "It's not my fault that your former boss was afraid you might attract the wrong sort of clients at that counseling agency. I heard he wound up with a line of people demanding an appointment with the psychic who could talk to the dead. He had to dump you. You were ruining his business."

"Really? You're going to blame what happened on *me*? In case you didn't notice, I was the innocent victim in that fiasco."

Roger regained control with a visible effort. "Look, I said I'm sorry. But you've moved on." He swept out a hand to indicate the office. "Looks to me like you're doing great."

"That is not the point," Catalina said between her teeth.

Roger shot another uncertain glance at Slater and then turned back to Catalina. "This is not the time or the place to discuss the past. I am prepared to pay you your usual consulting fee—"

"No."

"Charge whatever the hell you want," Roger said. "I'm just asking for some of your time. This is a straightforward murder-for-insurance-money case. I want you to confirm my own theory of the crime."

"You mean you want me to provide you with a theory of the crime so that you can look brilliant. Forget it, Roger. Even if I was in the mood to give you some help, I don't have time right now. I've got other problems."

Roger still appeared annoyed, but he was managing to come up with a little concern as well.

"Is this about Olivia?" he asked. "Are you sure she's missing?"

"Positive."

"How long has she been gone?"

"She hasn't been seen since yesterday evening."

"That's not even twenty-four hours. Odds are she's fine. Probably took off with a new boyfriend. Look, can you just let me have five minutes to lay out my case for you?"

"Nope." Catalina folded her arms and gave Roger a smile that looked as if it had been carved out of the heart of a glacier. "I'm sure you can understand that I have to put my own business interests ahead of yours."

Roger's lips thinned. "You're making this personal, Cat. That's a mistake. If you're serious about your business, then consider the fact that I am in a position to bring a lot of additional work here to Lark and LeClair. We'll keep our association confidential, of course."

"So that Lark and LeClair won't get any credit for solving your cases and so that your firm won't be embarrassed by having the media find out that you sometimes ask a psychic investigation agency to consult for you."

"We're talking a lot of money, Cat. Many of my clients are lawyers. When it comes to defending one of their wealthy clients, cash is no object."

"That does it." Catalina unfolded her arms and yanked open the door. "Leave. Now. Or I'll call the police and have you thrown out. There must be some legal grounds I could use."

"Loitering," Daniel said. "Trespassing."

He reached for the phone.

Roger looked as if he was going to make a stand, but he must have realized it was pointless.

"You're making a mistake, Cat," he said. He went toward the door. "I'll be in touch when you've had a chance to cool down."

Catalina did not deign to respond to that. She simply closed the door very firmly behind him and turned to Daniel.

"Anything else about the arrest of Angus Hopper that you can tell me?" she said.

Daniel glanced at his notes. "The detective who called said they'll want another statement from you. Evidently there are a few questions regarding your weapon of choice—"

"That is not amusing."

"Just kidding," Daniel said quickly. "The detective told me he thinks they've got more than enough to keep Hopper off the streets. Your turn. Did you get any leads on Olivia?"

"One very tiny lead," Catalina said. "According to Marge, the two men who grabbed Olivia may be twins."

Daniel frowned. "Weird. When do we call the police?"

Slater decided it was finally time to insert himself into the conversation.

"I don't think there's any point bringing in the cops," he said. "Not at this stage. For one thing, we haven't got much to go on. I'm sure that Marge was telling the truth, at least the truth as she sees it, but I doubt if the police will take it seriously. They're more likely to focus initially on the man Olivia was supposed to meet last night."

"Emerson Ferris," Daniel said.

"I'm convinced now that Ferris had nothing to do with grabbing Olivia," Catalina said. "The problem with concentrating on him is that we'll lose valuable time looking for the kidnappers."

"It does seem unlikely that this Emerson Ferris is behind the kidnapping, but we can't overlook the possibility that he's involved," Slater said. "We need someone to keep an eye on him while you and I chase other leads."

"That would be me," Daniel said. "Stakeouts are my specialty. I'm on my way."

He punched a key to send the phones to voice mail, pulled a small black backpack from a drawer, grabbed his jacket and went out the door.

Catalina looked at Slater.

"Before we go off to see that gallery owner, I want some more answers," she said. She swung around and went briskly down the hall. "My office, Mr. Arganbright."

It was not a request.

CHAPTER 11

Catalina dropped into the chair behind her desk and watched Slater set his backpack on the floor. He cast a longing glance at the pot of coffee sitting on the burner.

"Mind if I have a cup?" he asked. "I didn't get much sleep last night."

"Help yourself," she said. "It's not exactly fresh. Daniel made it first thing this morning. Pour a cup for me, please, while you're at it. I could do with a stiff jolt of caffeine myself."

Slater nodded. He picked up the pot and poured two mugs. He put one of the mugs on her desk.

She wrapped both hands around the large mug, taking comfort from the warmth. "Tell me why you think Olivia and I are involved in the murders of those two collectors. And then explain how this relates to what we saw fifteen years ago."

"I don't have all the answers," Slater said. He sank down into the client chair, took a healthy swallow of the coffee and slowly lowered the mug. His eyes got very intent. "But I agree that you need some background. I came here today to ask you to assist me in what was supposed to be an unrelated inquiry. Obviously the situation has changed."

"Obviously."

"What do you know about the Bluestone Project and the lost labs?" Slater asked.

"Not much. The project and the labs associated with it are more or less an urban legend in the paranormal community. *Conspiracy theory* might be a more accurate term. Supposedly, back in the late nineteen fifties, the government established a highly classified program to explore the possibilities of various forms of psychic energy."

"Bluestone was not a legend or a conspiracy theory. It was very real. It was designed to be a paranormal version of the Manhattan Project."

"The research and development program that produced the first nuclear weapons during World War Two?"

"Right," Slater said. "During the Cold War that followed World War Two, certain government agencies were concerned because it appeared that what was then the Soviet Union was engaging in serious paranormal research."

Catalina wrinkled her nose. "Imagine that. Someone in the government actually took the woo-woo thing seriously."

Slater gave her a bleak smile. "Who knew?"

"Go on."

"Like the Manhattan Project, the various labs associated with Bluestone were established in rural locations. We believe that most, if not all, of the Bluestone labs were located in the West and the Southwest. The theory was that if the enemy discovered one lab and sabotaged it, the entire project would not be destroyed."

"You think that Fogg Lake was one of those sites."

"We assume so, yes."

"Because of what happened that night decades ago," Catalina said.

"Whatever went wrong that night apparently made the government agency responsible for overseeing Bluestone extremely nervous. Ultimately the decision was made to shut down the entire project. Orders were given to destroy the labs. Every record and file, every scrap of paper associated with the project was supposed to be burned. There were no digital records in those days, so it was assumed that it would be a relatively simple matter to erase every trace of Bluestone. But this was a government project, so . . ."

"So of course some paperwork survived."

"And some of the artifacts associated with Bluestone survived. Hence the collectors' market."

Catalina studied him for a long moment. "Are you a collector?"

"Yes."

"You said collectors tend to be eccentric and weird."

Slater nodded and drank some coffee. He lowered the mug. "I try to disguise my little obsession by working in the Foundation's museum. I'm in the security department. I'm in charge of tracking down potentially dangerous artifacts with a paranormal provenance and transporting them to Foundation headquarters in Las Vegas."

"I can see how a job like that might give you a convenient cover for collecting just about anything."

"Works for me," Slater said.

"Have you recovered a lot of artifacts?"

"We have a number of objects stored in the museum vaults," Slater said. "But only a few are considered dangerous."

"Have you ever found an actual lab?"

"No."

"Then how can you be certain they even existed?"

Slater's mouth curved in a wry smile. "To repeat, Bluestone was a government operation. It was highly classified, but it required funding, a lot of it. Money, even dark money, always leaves a trail."

"You found that trail?"

"Not me. The Foundation has experts who specialize in tracking financial operations. But although they've come up with hints and clues, there is still a lot we don't know about the project. It's hard to make a big research operation like Bluestone vanish, but I've got to hand it to whoever was in charge of closing down the project. He or she did a hell of a job. All we've got at this point are rumors, legends and some scattered artifacts."

"You think that Morrissey and the man who killed him were searching for the Fogg Lake lab the night that Olivia and I witnessed the murder."

"Yes."

Catalina picked up a sleek black pen and tapped it gently against her coffee mug. "Let's go back to my original question. What makes Ingram's and Royston's deaths so important to the Foundation?"

"We're paying particular attention because there are some new rumors circulating in the underworld market. There are indications that someone is trying to find one particular lab. Of all the facilities, it was the one that was treated as the most highly classified. The code name was Vortex. It was a real black box operation."

"Why was it special?"

"It was focused on developing technology designed to weaponize paranormal energy. There are some hints in the archives that suggest the Vortex lab may have been successful or, at the very least, came up with a few working prototypes."

"Do you think the Fogg Lake lab was the Vortex operation?"

"We don't know. It may not be the Vortex lab, but I think whoever is searching for Vortex has taken an interest in the Fogg Lake facility."

"Assuming it even exists."

"You and Olivia and I, along with everyone else who can trace their ancestors back to Fogg Lake or the Bluestone Project, are evidence that it existed," Slater said.

Catalina eyed him closely. "What's your connection to Fogg Lake? I grew up there. I don't remember an Arganbright family."

"None of my people are from Fogg Lake but the residents of your hometown aren't the only ones with a connection to the Bluestone Project. A wide range of paranormal research was carried out in all of the labs. The Arganbrights carry the results of one of those experiments in our DNA."

A shiver of intuition crackled through her. "Well, well, well. I'm going to take a flying leap here. You think the Arganbrights were affected by experiments done in that mysterious Vortex lab, don't you?"

Slater hesitated and then shrugged. "There is some family lore indicating that my grandfather may have worked in the Vortex lab. We've never been able to prove it because he didn't survive the closure of the labs. My father suspects Granddad was killed by someone who thought he knew too much. What we do know is that there's a strong psychic vibe in the bloodline and that it showed up first in my father's generation. Everything after that is pure conjecture."

"Do you think the explosion on that night was caused by some sort of paranormal weapon? A bomb, maybe?"

"Maybe." Slater got to his feet and put his empty mug on the counter. "Ready to go talk to Gwendolyn Swan?"

"Yes." Catalina rose and walked around the end of the desk. "Where is her shop located?"

"Pioneer Square."

"That's not far from here," Catalina said. "It will be faster if we walk."

She went to the window and looked down at the street. A van marked with the familiar logo of a local TV station was just pulling up in front of the building. The passenger-side door opened. Brenda Bryce got out. A man with a video camera emerged from the van. They headed toward the lobby doors.

Catalina turned away from the window. "We'll use the loading dock entrance in the alley."

Slater glanced down at the TV crew. "You do have a problem with the local media, don't you?"

"Yep, thanks to good old Uncle Victor and Roger Gossard."

"Don't worry." Slater picked up his pack. "I'll handle security on the street so you don't have to waste a lot of energy running hot. On the way you can tell me what you did with a fork last night."

CHAPTER 12

The escape through the alley went off without a hitch. It was a relief not to have to walk down the street with all senses firing. With Slater handling security, as he called it, Catalina discovered she could allow herself to relax somewhat for the first time that day. No more stepping over hot prints on the sidewalk. No more flinching every time a person with a disturbing aura drew near. No more confrontations with Brenda Bryce and her crew.

True, she found herself checking the faces of those around her, searching for two people who looked enough alike to be twins, but aside from that she felt she could let down her guard, at least for a while. *As long as Slater is keeping watch.*

Okay, it was weird to have a bodyguard from the Foundation at her side, but her life had taken a weird twist.

Under other circumstances the vibe of an energy field as fierce as Slater's would have made her deeply uneasy. She had never been so close to such a powerful aura. But now that she had recovered from the shattering jolt that had arced through her when they had collided, she was surprised to discover she had already adjusted to his unusual aura.

Adjusted might not be the right word. The truth was, she found it exciting to walk down the street with Slater Arganbright. Thrilling, even.

That was probably not a good sign.

The fact that he was from the Foundation was a serious complication. The reality, however, was that she had no choice but to accept help from the secretive organization. Victor Arganbright had the kind of resources she might need to try to save Olivia.

She decided her reaction to Slater's nearness could be attributed to the fact that her own energy field was badly frazzled from recent events. A person couldn't perceive their own aura, so she didn't know how hers looked to Slater or to anyone else who could detect human energy fields. But she had a bad feeling that her aura was probably sparking and flashing like a busted neon sign.

Sooner or later the crash will hit. You couldn't go flat-out, as she had been doing most of the time since the scene at Marsha Matson's house, without paying a price. Energy was energy, and she had burned a lot of it lately. The fact that she hadn't gotten more than a couple of hours of fitful sleep during the night only made things worse.

"I get that you read the scene at your client's house last night," Slater said when she finished her story. "You picked up on the fact that Hopper had a weapon and that he was behind the door. You rescued your client and yourself. Nice work, by the way."

"Thank you. We try to be a full-service agency for our clients."

He smiled a little. "I've got one question."

"The fork."

"Why did you happen to have one in your handbag?"

"I owe your uncle for that," she said.

"You don't sound overly grateful."

"After I read the Ingram crime scene for him six months ago, your uncle thanked me and left town that same day. I played the good citizen and contacted the police. I told them there was reason to believe that Ingram had been murdered. They investigated the death. No evidence was found. Case closed. But word got out that a woman claiming to be psychic had called in a tip about a possible murder. Brenda Bryce ran with the story. That's when things got complicated for me. Some very odd people started showing up at the career counseling firm where I worked."

"I heard something about that."

"I became a media sensation here in Seattle for about twenty-four hours. But that was long enough. Most of those who tried to get an appointment with me wanted lucky numbers for the lottery, or they wanted me to tell their fortunes. The ones that really gave me the creeps were the folks who asked me to contact spirits on the Other Side."

Slater shook his head. "Some people still believe it's possible to talk to ghosts."

"I tried to explain that being psychic is not the same thing as being a medium and that anyone who claimed to be able to contact a ghost was either a fraud or seriously deluded. I pointed out that if I could predict which numbers would win the lottery I would have played them myself long ago and retired to a beach in Hawaii. And then there were the so-called paranormal researchers who wanted to study me, as if I were a lab rat."

"In other words, thanks to Uncle Victor, you ran headfirst into the buzz saw that most of us with any drop of talent try to avoid."

"Unfortunately, one of the nutjobs who read about me in the papers concluded that I was a demon straight from hell. His name was Earl Plunkett. He called himself a demon slayer. He stalked me for a while, and then he came after me one evening as I was leaving a restaurant with Olivia."

"Ah, I think I'm getting a psychic vibe about the fork," Slater said.

"Olivia and I were having drinks and dinner and talking about our plans for an investigation agency. Plunkett was outside the restaurant in an alley. I caught a glimpse of his aura. So did Olivia. We had planned to walk back to our apartment building, but we decided to call a ride instead. We waited inside the restaurant until the car arrived. At the last minute I realized it might be a good idea to have some sort of weapon. I grabbed a fork off the table."

"What happened?"

"We hurried across the sidewalk to jump into the car. Earl the Demon Slayer ran out of the alley. He had a knife in one hand. I managed to block him with the car door. That jolted him long enough for me to jab the fork at his eyes. He panicked and ran. The cops picked him up less than twenty minutes later."

"Is he in jail?" Slater asked.

"Of course not. He's out on bail. But so far he has stayed away from me."

"Damn. Victor did not do you any favors, did he?"

"He paid his bill, but that's about all I can say on his behalf. Considering that you're family, I'm sure you have a much kinder view of him."

"I dunno about that. He and his husband, Lucas, kept me locked up in the attic for a month."

That brought her to a halt on the sidewalk. "What?"

"Long story," Slater said. "Let's save it for later. But thanks for clarifying your feelings toward Victor. I think I've got a fairly good understanding of why my uncle thought you might not be thrilled with the idea of assisting me."

He resumed walking. She had to hustle to catch up.

"And I've got a very realistic understanding of why I need you to help me find Olivia," she said.

"Allies as long as we're facing the same enemy, is that it?"

"Looks like it," Catalina said.

Slater stopped at the entrance to a dark, narrow passageway between two equally dark buildings. "Swan's shop is halfway down this alley."

Catalina eyed the uninviting thoroughfare. "Picturesque. I'll give it that much."

"Antiques shops like quaint locations."

"There's quaint and then there's eccentric."

"Anyone who deals in paranormal artifacts is, by definition, eccentric," Slater said.

"You're a collector."

"Yes."

"Is that your way of telling me that you are eccentric?"

"I don't know if I am or not," Slater said. "*Eccentric* is one of those labels that other people slap on an individual. I doubt if true eccentrics view themselves as eccentric."

"Good point. Do you consider Gwendolyn Swan eccentric?"

"She's quite normal for a dealer who specializes in paranormal artifacts."

"That doesn't exactly answer my question."

"Sorry," Slater said. "It's the best I can do."

"How did you become acquainted with her?"

"A couple of years ago Lucas discovered that she was acquiring artifacts with a paranormal vibe for certain clients. Victor sent me here to contact her and see if she was the real deal."

"I take it she was."

Slater smiled ruefully. "Let's just say that the first time I walked into her shop I dropped several thousand dollars on a nice little Roman ring set with a stone engraved with an image of Medusa. The damned thing was only worth a few hundred bucks at most. It didn't even have a Bluestone lab provenance. It was a couple of thousand years older. But I couldn't resist the vibe of the stone."

"In other words, Gwendolyn Swan saw you coming?"

"Ms. Swan not only has a talent for picking up paranormal arti-facts, she's a natural-born saleswoman. Trust me, you'll be lucky if you get out of her shop today without buying something."

"I grew up in a town full of artifacts with a paranormal prove-nance. Heck, my neighbors are living artifacts. I'm one. So is Olivia. I have no interest in collecting stuff that has a psychic vibe, believe me. All right, I get why you are interested in Gwendolyn Swan, but what makes her useful to your uncle?"

"A river of hot gossip flows through the underground market in paranormal antiquities," Slater said. "Much of the work of the Foun-dation depends on that kind of gossip. Gwendolyn Swan is an excel-lent resource because she is among the first to hear all of the important rumors."

"Does she charge a fee for the information she provides?"

"Sure," Slater said. "No such thing as a free lunch in the paranor-mal underworld."

CHAPTER 13

Gwendolyn Swan was in the basement, struggling to drag the body into the vault, when she heard someone bang on the front door of the shop. She ignored the muffled noise, hoping the customer would notice the Closed sign in the window and go away.

She tightened her grip on the dead man's ankle and leaned into her task. She managed to haul most of the torso inside the vault. Only the head and both arms were still outside.

The pounding on the front door continued, more insistent this time. Collectors. They tended to be obsessive.

She was breathing hard and her forehead was damp with perspiration by the time she finally got the rest of the body over the threshold. She slammed the heavy door shut and set the lock.

The pounding was still going on upstairs. With a sigh she paused in front of an old looking glass that glittered with dark energy and checked her hair. She looked like she had just finished a workout.

She took a moment to remove the hair clip, shake out her shoulder-length, honey-brown hair and reclip it into a neat twist. She took off the full-length leather apron she had put on to deal with the body and dusted off her jeans. The crystal in the locket around her neck glittered briefly in the old Victorian mirror.

She paused at the foot of the steps to survey the basement. Everything appeared to be in order.

The pounding upstairs continued.

"I'm on my way," she called.

She hurried up the steps, opened the door at the top and went through the back room and out across the sales floor.

Damn collectors.

She plastered a cheerful, welcoming smile across her face and opened the front door of the shop.

She dropped the smile immediately when she saw who stood on the step.

"Slater Arganbright," she said. "Well, well, well. I heard you had gone into seclusion and were probably painting watercolors at Halcyon Manor."

"You know you can't always believe everything you hear, Gwendolyn," Slater said. "This is my consultant, Catalina Lark. Catalina, meet Gwendolyn Swan."

"How do you do?" Catalina said.

"Your name rings a bell," Gwendolyn said. "Would you happen to be Catalina Lark the fake psychic, who told the cops that she was sure someone had been murdered?"

Catalina winced. "I am never going to live that down."

Gwendolyn mustered some reluctant empathy. "I realize things must have been rough for a while after the media got ahold of that story."

"Very rough," Catalina said. "But, hey, Victor paid his bill."

Gwendolyn gave her a grim smile. "Sorry to say there is always a risk of becoming collateral damage when you get involved with the Foundation."

"Believe it or not, I had already figured that out," Catalina said. She eyed Slater. "Halcyon Manor?"

"I'll explain later," Slater said. "Sorry to bother you, Gwendolyn, but I'm working a case for my uncle. I'd like to ask you a few questions."

Gwendolyn gave him her brightest smile. "You know me, anything for the Foundation. Come on in."

She stepped back to allow her visitors through the front door, took a quick peek outside to make sure there was no one lurking nearby, and closed and relocked the door.

She went back across the room to put the barrier of the sales counter between herself and the man from the Foundation.

So much for the rumors about Slater Arganbright. He was not only very much alive, he was evidently stable enough to navigate a city street. Of course, that particular test set a very low bar. There were a lot of crazies on the streets of any big city, including Seattle.

That said, there was definitely something different about Slater, she concluded. She could see auras, but she didn't have a strong talent for reading them. Her psychic strengths lay in another area. To her senses the energy fields around people appeared as little more than a pale glow. The brightness varied somewhat depending on the health and vitality of the person. As far as she could tell, Slater was relatively strong, but it looked like some damage had been done.

"You know I'm always delighted to help you find an interesting piece for your private collection, Slater," she said, "but you make me nervous when you're working a case for your uncle."

"I get that a lot," Slater said.

Catalina surveyed the gloom-filled sales floor. She looked disappointed.

"Do these things all have a paranormal provenance?" she asked.

Surprised by the question, Gwendolyn looked at her.

"What makes you ask?" she said.

"I don't know. I guess I just expected more energy or something."

Gwendolyn smiled. "You guessed right. Everything up here is a reproduction. The real artifacts are downstairs in the basement."

"I see," Catalina said.

Gwendolyn turned back to Slater. "All right, we've got the pleasantries out of the way. What can I do for you?"

"I need whatever information you may have heard regarding a very hot artifact from one of the lost labs that surfaced recently and may have found its way into Royston's vault."

"You know as well as I do that lab rumors circulate all the time in my business."

"Let me be a little more precise," Slater said. "I'm looking for an artifact hot enough to have attracted the attention of someone who was willing to commit murder to get it."

Gwendolyn went very still. "I heard Royston died of natural causes."

"Uncle Victor has his doubts."

"Before we go there, you should know that I have recently raised my fees."

"I'll make sure Uncle Victor is aware of that," Slater said.

At least she could count on turning a profit today, Gwendolyn thought. Catalina Lark was right—Victor Arganbright always paid his tab.

She moved out from behind the desk. "We'll talk downstairs."

She led the way through the cluttered back room and opened the stairwell door. At the top of the stairs she flipped a light switch to illuminate the steps. She descended first.

When she reached the bottom, she turned to watch Catalina and Slater come down the stairs.

"Welcome to the real sales floor," she said.

CHAPTER 14

Shivery frissons of awareness danced across Catalina's senses as she went down the stairs into the dimly lit basement. The atmosphere in the room below Gwendolyn Swan's shop reminded her of the interior of the Fogg Lake caves. The tendrils of energy emanating from the individual artifacts combined into a breathtaking wave of paranormal heat. It was disorienting.

She looked around, amazed. "This place is really hot."

"Gather enough objects with a strong vibe in one room and even people with normal senses can pick up some of the energy," Gwendolyn said.

Intrigued, Catalina walked to the nearest case and studied the miniature scene inside. The setting was a glamorous masked ball. The room was draped in crimson velvet. A miniature chandelier was suspended from the ceiling. In one corner a trio of musicians held dainty instruments. Figures dressed in elegant costumes and masks crowded the floor.

Initially it was the exquisite workmanship of the ballroom tableau that fascinated Catalina. But when she got close to the case, her senses started to flash and flicker in reaction to the scene. The sensations were both ominous and compelling.

"What in the world?" she whispered.

The impulse to touch the glass case was irresistible. She reached out one hand.

"Careful," Slater said. "Some of these objects are unpredictable."

But it was too late. Catalina's fingers had already made contact with the glass. The strains of an eerie waltz emanated from the corner where the musicians played their tiny instruments. The figures on the dance floor began to move.

Gwendolyn chuckled. "The Masked Ball is similar to an old-fashioned music box, except that instead of having to wind it up, you just touch the glass. It conducts the energy of a person's aura and activates the mechanism. Interestingly, most of my clients can't get it going, even those with a lot of heat in their auras. It only responds to certain wavelengths. That's why I haven't been able to sell it. Congratulations, Catalina. Looks like you have the magic touch. I can give you an excellent price on it."

"No, thanks," Catalina said.

The miniature ballroom scene was fascinating, but as she watched the dancers whirl faster and faster around the floor, she was aware of a growing sensation of dread. It was as if the figures in their elegant costumes were somehow compelled to keep up with the strains of the eerie waltz.

She tried to take her fingers off the glass and step back. She discovered that she could not move. She watched in gathering horror as the crimson drapes parted, revealing a miniature figure dressed in a long black cloak and a bloodred mask. He gripped a small gold cane in one gloved hand.

"Catalina?" Slater said sharply. "Are you all right?"

The master of the ball began to raise the gold cane. The music sent more unpleasant shivers across Catalina's senses.

"Oh, shit," she whispered. "Stop, damn it."

A rush of fear-driven energy gave her the willpower she needed to overcome the pull of the miniature ballroom. With a small yelp she yanked her fingers off the glass and scrambled to take a couple of steps back.

For the second time that day she collided with Slater. Her senses were hot and, she belatedly discovered, so were his. There was an electric moment of contact, and then Slater gripped her arms and set her firmly to one side.

"What the hell?" he asked. He spoke very softly, as though curious and intrigued but not alarmed.

He released her and went toward the glass case. Catalina pulled herself together and saw that the miniature scene had gone still. None of the figures moved. The unpleasant music had ceased. The figure in the black cloak had disappeared behind the velvet drapes.

"Well, that was certainly interesting," Gwendolyn said. She joined Slater at the display case. Together they examined the tableau. "I've never had a client who could do anything more than activate a few of the dancers."

"Where did you get this piece?" Slater asked.

Gwendolyn sighed. "The usual source—the estate of a dead collector. As I told you, I haven't been able to sell it. Those who lack whatever the vibe is that activates it aren't interested in it. Those who can activate a few of the figures have the same reaction Catalina did just now. No one wants it in their collection."

Catalina shuddered. "I think I know why. There's something very disturbing about that miniature scene."

"Evidently," Gwendolyn said.

"What happens when the figure in the black cloak raises the gold cane?" Catalina asked.

"I have no idea," Gwendolyn said.

"I'm no expert on paranormal antiques," Catalina said, "but for what it's worth, I think that thing may be dangerous."

Gwendolyn gave her a thoughtful look. "I'll keep that in mind."

"That miniature didn't come from any of the lost labs," Catalina said. "It looks old."

"Nineteenth century, to be precise," Gwendolyn said. "There's nothing new about the paranormal, Catalina. People have been messing around with it since humans discovered fire." She turned back to Slater. "What, exactly, are you looking for?"

"I think something from the Fogg Lake lab ended up in Royston's vault," Slater said. "Someone murdered him for the artifact. Three days later, Catalina's friend Olivia LeClair was kidnapped. We're looking for her."

"You think the killer found whatever he was looking for in Royston's gallery and then concluded that he needed Olivia LeClair?" Gwendolyn asked.

"Yes."

Gwendolyn snapped a quick, searching look at Catalina. "I'm sorry to hear about your friend. Have you contacted the police?"

"No," Catalina said. "At this point we don't have much to go on. I didn't want to waste any time filling out the paperwork. To be honest, I don't think they would take Olivia's disappearance seriously. And even if they did, this seems to be connected to something that happened in Fogg Lake years ago. I hate to admit it, but I have a feeling someone from the Foundation has a better chance of finding her."

Gwendolyn gave that some thought. "Has there been a ransom demand?"

"No," Catalina said.

"And we're not expecting one," Slater added. "We think this is about locating one of the lost labs, probably the facility believed to have been established in the Fogg Lake caves."

Gwendolyn frowned. "Are you saying that for some reason the kidnappers think Olivia LeClair can help them?"

"That's the only theory we've got at the moment," Catalina said.

Slater looked at Gwendolyn. "What was in Royston's vault that might have convinced his killer he needed Olivia LeClair?"

Gwendolyn shook her head. "I don't know. All I can tell you is that a month ago there were rumors that a cache of goods with a Fogg Lake provenance had come on the market. But none of the items passed through my shop. It was a private auction. Invitation only. There was no description of the goods. I heard Royston got a few valuable items. So, yes, he probably had some Fogg Lake artifacts in his vault, but I can't tell you what they were."

"By now the raiders will have cleaned out Royston's vault," Slater said. "You know how fast they move."

"Somehow they are always the first to know when a collector dies," Gwendolyn said.

"Have any of the usual suspects shown up at your back door offering you objects that may have come from his gallery?" Slater asked.

Gwendolyn raised her chin. "I do not deal in stolen goods. My reputation is spotless and you damn well know it, Slater Arganbright."

"I'm not accusing you of illegal sales," Slater said, impatient now. "In fact, I don't really give a damn if some of the items in this basement have a murky provenance. I just need to know if you've heard of anything from Royston's collection."

Gwendolyn's mouth tightened. Then she sighed.

"All right," she said. "A couple of lowlife raiders came around offering some objects they claimed were from Royston's gallery. Nothing special, though—a few desk accessories, an old-fashioned calculator and a coffeepot. It was all the right vintage, and there was the residual heat that items pick up when they are in a room full of hot energy for a long period of time. I took the calculator. It's still here if you want to see it."

"Yes," Slater said. "I'd like to take a look."

Gwendolyn crossed the room to a table that was covered with antique office equipment. She gestured toward an old calculating machine.

"Help yourself," she said. "Late nineteen fifties, I believe. Definitely warm, but not hot enough to be interesting to a serious collector."

Slater examined the big, clunky-looking machine with a thoughtful expression. "I agree."

He moved on to another item in the display, an antique typewriter. He touched it lightly with his fingertips and then lost interest. He moved on to another object.

Catalina noticed a large clockwork figure dressed in a vintage nurse's costume: a crisp white dress, white shoes, white stockings and a white starched cap. The doll was about four feet tall. It gripped a syringe in one mechanical hand.

Curious, Catalina started to cross the crowded space to get a better look. She stopped abruptly when she realized she had just stepped into a pool of all-too-familiar energy.

Death.

A ghostly vision started to take shape. It was too vague to make out any details, but she thought she saw a man fold up and collapse on the floor.

"Something wrong, Catalina?" Gwendolyn asked.

"No, I'm fine." Catalina rubbed the back of her neck. "It's just really, really hot in here."

"Yes, it is," Gwendolyn said. "But it's not the heat that gets to those of us with a strong psychic vibe, it's the death factor."

Catalina whirled around. "What?"

"Sorry, didn't mean to startle you," Gwendolyn said. "It's just that a lot of the most powerful paranormal artifacts from the past come from crypts and tombs. I do a lot of business in grave goods.

Death has a vibe. Even people who are not particularly sensitive get uneasy down here in my basement."

"I see," Catalina said. "That explains it. I've experienced something similar at museums but nothing as strong as this. How do you handle it day in and day out?"

"One gets accustomed to it," Gwendolyn said. "I hardly notice the energy in here anymore. Are you finished, Slater?"

He turned away from the display table. "For now. I appreciate the help, Gwendolyn. You'll let me know if you hear of anything else that might be connected to Olivia's disappearance."

"Yes," Gwendolyn said. She hesitated. "I can contact some of the other dealers, if you like. Most of them won't want to talk to someone from the Foundation, but they might answer some questions from me."

"Thanks," Slater said. He appeared surprised by the offer. "I would appreciate it. You've got my number. If you get any leads, anything at all, contact me immediately, night or day. We're dealing with a kidnapping. That means we're on the clock."

"I understand," Gwendolyn said. She looked at Catalina. "I know you must be very worried. I hope your friend is okay."

"Thanks," Catalina said.

Gwendolyn turned back to Slater. "I'll start contacting my associates immediately."

She led the way up the staircase. When she reached the landing she turned off the lights. Catalina paused to look down into the darkened basement. The display cases were no longer illuminated, but there was enough energy from the collection of artifacts to make the underground chamber glow with a faint radiance. She could feel the currents seething in the atmosphere.

Death had a vibe, but there was a difference between old and new. The frissons of dark energy that had tugged at her senses felt very fresh.

CHAPTER 15

"Pretty sure Gwendolyn Swan was lying," Catalina said. "I'm almost positive that someone died in her basement recently."

Slater had just selected another french fry from the massive pile on his plate. He paused and gave her a searching glance.

"Someone or something?" he asked. "Seattle is a nice city, but I'm sure it's got rats like every other big city, especially in the older sections."

"Someone. Trust me, I can tell the difference between a dead animal and a dead human."

They were sitting in a popular downtown restaurant, drinking strong coffee and eating a lot of protein and carbs in the form of extra-large orders of fish and chips. Catalina had chosen the venue because it was convenient, because it featured booths that allowed for private conversations and because she did not want to spend time or energy trying to decide where to eat.

She and Slater were not eating the healthiest meal on the planet, but they had both expended a lot of energy in the past few hours. Between the burn and the lack of sleep, they needed fuel that would hit their bloodstreams in a rush.

"Okay, I'm not doubting you," Slater said. "Just going for a little clarification. There was a lot of hot energy in that basement, and as Swan said, many of those artifacts were probably grave goods or other items that are associated with death and violence in some way."

"Yes, and I know that sort of energy can often mask the kind of heat I sense, but what I picked up in that basement was fresh. Probably within the past twenty-four hours."

"Huh." Slater munched the french fry and picked up another one. "Violent death?"

"Got news for you, Arganbright—for me, every death feels like an act of violence."

"Point taken." Slater forked up a bite of the fried fish while he reflected on that. "So, professionally speaking, how do you figure out the difference between a murder and a death from natural causes?"

"It's not always simple or straightforward. Things can get murky. What I look for is the energy of a killer. When that is present, I know I'm looking at a murder scene."

"All right, don't keep me in suspense. Did you pick up that kind of energy in Swan's basement?"

"No." Catalina drank some coffee and put the cup down very carefully. "That's why I hesitated to mention it. I've been telling myself all that radiation confused my senses. But the more I think about it, the more I'm convinced that someone did die in that room, and not long ago. A few hours at most."

"But you didn't find any trace of the killer?"

"I don't think so. But the atmosphere in that basement is really heavy. Who wants to collect things that come out of crypts and graves, anyway?"

"Me. For the Foundation's museum. What's more, we often

compete with museums and collectors around the world for grave goods. Where do you think that old stuff sitting in museum galleries comes from? A lot of those items survived precisely because they were sealed in a tomb or a crypt."

"Okay, I get the historical value. I just don't like to think about that sort of provenance too much, that's all."

Slater ate a few more french fries while he contemplated her words.

"Would you be able to tell if Gwendolyn Swan murdered someone in her basement?" he asked.

"Maybe. Maybe not. The currents in that place are really strong."

"Some of those objects are extremely dangerous."

Catalina shuddered. "Like that miniature ballroom scene?"

"It felt ominous, didn't it?"

"Yes."

"Let me run a scenario for you," Slater said. "What if a couple of freelance raiders broke into the basement and one of them grabbed a particularly dangerous artifact and got zapped? Maybe the accomplice hauled the body away. No would-be burglar would want to leave that kind of evidence behind for the police to find."

"That works," Catalina said. "Sort of. Why would Swan leave dangerous artifacts lying around where they might accidentally kill a client?"

"She wouldn't do that intentionally. Pretty sure she keeps the potentially lethal pieces in her vault. But if she wasn't aware of the hazard, she probably wouldn't lock it up."

"She didn't mention that there had been a break-in recently."

"She might not even suspect it, not if the raiders didn't actually steal anything." Slater got a thoughtful expression. "It's also possible that she had some reason not to mention a recent burglary, especially one that resulted in a dead guy."

"In my opinion, Gwendolyn Swan was lying, or at least not telling us the whole truth."

Slater's mouth curved in a faint smile. "No one in the hot artifacts business ever tells the whole truth, especially not to someone from the Foundation."

Catalina sniffed. "Can't say I blame them. How far do you trust Gwendolyn Swan?"

"Define *trust*," Slater said.

"Excuse me? I sense deep cynicism and a jaded view of human nature."

"When I know what someone wants, I trust them to pursue that objective. As long as I keep the individual's goal in mind I know exactly where, when and how far I can trust that person. Swan is fascinated with hot artifacts and she likes to make money selling them and the rumors that are attached to them. That's really all I know about her aside from the fact that she has a degree in archaeology and spent some time on digs in South America."

"You know that my goal is to find Olivia," Catalina said.

Slater put down his fork and reached for his coffee. "I share your objective. I also want to find Olivia LeClair. That makes us allies."

"You want to find her because you think she can help you solve your case."

Slater's eyes got very cold. "And because she's an innocent victim who just happened to witness a murder when she was a teen. It really pisses me off when the bad guys use civilians."

The intensity in his voice startled her.

"'Civilians'?" she said.

Slater swallowed the last of his coffee, put the cup down and moved his empty plate aside. He leaned forward and folded his arms on the table.

"I know you don't have much use for my uncles or the Foundation, but like it or not, it's the only operation that has the resources required to deal with the bad guys regular law enforcement can't handle."

"Criminals who possess a strong psychic vibe." Catalina sighed. "I get that. But I don't like the idea of a rogue organization operating in the shadows. Like my father says, there's no accountability. No oversight. Who polices the Foundation? That's what I want to know. Your uncles might have cleaned things up a little when they got rid of the Rancourts, but they still operate the Foundation in a secretive way. It's a relief to know that, currently, at least, they seem to be mostly on the same side as regular law enforcement—"

"Mostly?"

Catalina smiled a steely smile. "I'm trying to give the Foundation the benefit of the doubt."

"Gee. Thanks."

"Here's where the real doubts come in. What's to keep the Foundation from going back to the way things worked when the Rancourts ran it?"

Slater regarded her for a long moment. "Does everyone from Fogg Lake hold that view of the Foundation?"

"Not everyone," she admitted. "There are a handful who think those of us in the paranormal community need some organization or agency we can turn to when it's clear that regular law enforcement can't handle the situation."

"The kidnapping of a woman who sees auras, for example? Or the murder of a couple of collectors who specialized in artifacts with a paranormal vibe?"

"Yes," Catalina said. "Situations like that. But for the record, as far as I'm concerned, the idea of a rogue organization operating in the shadows with its own police force is . . . deeply disturbing, to say the least."

"Well, damn," Slater said. "You really don't know, do you?"

"Know what?"

"Here's a quick history lesson, Catalina. The government did not shut down every single agency that was involved with paranormal research and development when it closed down the Bluestone Project. Some farsighted individuals realized that the problem of policing bad guys who possess paranormal talents was not going to vanish just because the labs had vanished. One small agency was kept open. But it's seriously underfunded and unable to provide genuine oversight. Which is why the Rancourt family was able to gain control of the Foundation and remain in control for so long."

"Are you telling me that the Foundation is supposed to report to some no-name government agency?"

"Oh, it has a name. Just not a very well-known name. The Foundation is a private research-and-development lab under contract to the Agency for the Investigation of Atypical Phenomena."

"Never heard of it."

Slater smiled. "That is, of course, the whole point. The government learned its lesson years ago. The vast majority of voters are convinced that serious paranormal research is a waste of money and resources. No one running for office at any level wants to be accused of funding that kind of work. Therefore the Agency is careful to keep a very low profile."

"So, what you're telling me is that the Foundation is a front for this Agency for the Investigation of Atypical Phenomena?"

"It's not the first time a clandestine agency has used a corporate front. All sorts of government entities, including the CIA, fund an enormous amount of investigation and research through private contractors, academic institutions and corporations."

"Yes, I know," Catalina said. "But this is the first I've heard about this weird little agency."

"I just wanted you to be aware that the Foundation is not some rogue vigilante operation."

"If you don't mind, I'm going to reserve judgment on that. Tell me about Halcyon Manor."

Slater's jaw tightened. "You haven't heard of that, either?"

"Not until Gwendolyn Swan mentioned it."

"Halcyon Manor is a private psychiatric hospital that specializes in treating people with disorders of the paranormal senses. It's located outside of Las Vegas."

Catalina had been about to finish her coffee. Shocked, she set her cup down with exquisite care.

"Are you serious?" she asked.

"Trust me, it's not the kind of thing I make jokes about, at least not these days. It's run by the Foundation. In addition to handling serious parapsych disorders, it has a special wing that houses the criminally insane talents who can't be safely dealt with in the regular prison system."

Catalina shook her head. "I suppose I should be beyond stunned after all that's happened today, but oddly enough, I'm not. The hits just keep on coming. Between you and me, I think it's safe to say that your uncles and the Foundation have a serious problem when it comes to public relations with Fogg Lake and other people in the paranormal community."

"Oh, yeah. The Rancourts left us with some baggage."

The glass doors at the front of the restaurant opened to admit two people, one of whom was all too familiar.

"Oh, shit," Catalina said.

"Are we back to that?" Slater asked.

"Yep." Catalina fixed her attention firmly on what was left of her coffee.

Slater turned his head just enough to see who or what had caught her attention. "Roger Gossard."

"Uh-huh."

"Who is that with him?"

"I have no idea."

Roger's companion was a stunningly attractive woman who appeared to be almost a decade younger than him. Her long blond hair fell in waves to her shoulders. She wore a tight pencil skirt, a white top and a sleek little jacket that accented her curves to perfection. Her heels were very high. She had one dainty arm tucked into Roger's elbow.

"An amazing coincidence?" Slater asked, one brow slightly elevated.

"Not really," Catalina said. "More like bad judgment on my part. This is one of Roger's favorite restaurants. I wasn't thinking when I suggested we eat in this place. Oh, well. It will be fine. We're all civilized adults."

"Good to know, because the last thing we need is a public scene. We've got enough trouble as it is."

Catalina glared at him. "Trust me, there won't be a scene."

"What makes you so sure?"

"Because Roger won't want that any more than I do. I'm a threat to his brand."

"Right. The brand thing."

"One of these days I may get around to sending your uncle a thank-you note for all that he did to ruin my professional and personal relationship with Roger. I'm sure eventually I would have figured out that things were not going to work for us, but Victor Arganbright made certain the relationship collapsed on an accelerated timetable."

"Was it a good relationship?"

"It was a relationship, okay? It lasted nearly two whole months. That, for your information, was a record for me. A personal best."

"I'll mention your gratitude to Victor next time I see him," Slater said.

"Don't bother. It's not what you'd call deeply sincere. Let's get back to you. I believe we were discussing Halcyon Manor. Swan implied that you spent some time there. Is that true?"

Slater seemed to brace himself, as if preparing to deliver a blow— or take one.

"No," he said. "I did not end up in Halcyon Manor."

"Whew. That's a relief."

"The only reason I wasn't locked up there," Slater continued, jaw clenched, "is because Uncle Victor and Uncle Lucas kept me hidden away in a locked room in their penthouse while I . . . recovered."

"Recovered from what?"

"Like I told Marge, I got hit with a dose of radiation at the end of my last case. Before you ask, no, I don't know what kind of radiation. The source was a machine that generated energy through some unknown crystals. Initially my psychic senses were completely iced. For a time I thought I had lost them altogether."

Ruthlessly, Catalina tried to suppress a rush of sympathy. There was no need to feel sorry for Slater Arganbright. But the thought of what he must have gone through when he woke up to discover that his paranormal senses had been blinded made her shudder.

"That must have been a horrible feeling," she said. "But obviously you recovered."

"Maybe. The truth is, I don't know what the hell is happening to me. I don't know what I'm becoming. I haven't admitted this to Victor and Lucas, but given the fact that you and I are going to be in very close contact for the foreseeable future, you have a right to know."

"What is this truth?"

"I don't sleep very well these days because I wake up in the middle of the night wondering if I'm becoming one of the psychic monsters that the Foundation hunts."

CHAPTER 16

O kay," Catalina said. "I did not see that coming. It certainly will add some spice to our relationship."

Slater's eyes tightened at the corners. "You aren't taking this seriously, are you?"

"I'm pretty good at figuring out what people are about to do next, remember? Not perfect, mind you, but my ability is way above average."

"So?"

"So I don't see any signs of instability in your energy field. You're in full control. And given the nature of my talent, I'll get some warning if you suddenly do become a psychic vampire or a crazed human monster."

"If I'm so stable, why do I feel like I'm . . . changing?"

She shrugged. "Probably because you're still healing."

Slater hesitated. "That's what my uncles tell me."

She smiled very sweetly. "There you go, then. If you can't trust the word of the director of the Foundation and his husband, who can you trust?"

"I'm trying to give you a heads-up about a potentially serious complication."

She stopped smiling and leaned forward slightly. "Here's the thing, Slater. I don't have time to take your personal problems seriously. All I care about is finding Olivia. As long as you are helpful in that regard, I don't give a damn who or what you might turn out to be. Are we clear on that?"

Some of the shadows in his eyes seemed to dissipate.

"Clear," he said.

She heightened her senses a little and suddenly she understood.

"You told me about that radiation hit you took and your concerns because you were hoping I could tell you what it is that is changing in your aura, didn't you?" she said.

He sat back, resigned. "It occurred to me that with your talent you might be able to give me some idea of what's going on."

"Hey, I'm a *fake* psychic, remember?"

There was no humor in Slater's eyes. He was, she realized, very, very serious.

She was not sure why she wanted to reassure him. Maybe she just wanted to assure herself that he was not turning into one of the monsters. As he had said, she was stuck with him for now. She tried to find a way into what had become an extremely delicate conversation.

She leaned across the table again and lowered her voice to barely above a whisper.

"What do *you* think is happening to your parasenses?" she asked.

"I told you, I don't know."

"You may not know the final result, but you must have some feel for what is going on in your energy field. Maybe you're just more powerful than you used to be. Could be that's the only thing that's different—the degree of heat in your aura."

"I don't think it's as simple as that. What I'm going through now reminds me too much of what it was like when my psychic senses first began to develop. I was twelve or thirteen. Remember how it felt?"

She winced. "Don't remind me. There were times when I would be walking home from school in Fogg Lake and stroll straight into a full-blown hallucination."

"Try to imagine that experience on steroids. That's what happened to me after I was hit by that radiation. Except that the hallucinations were a thousand times worse than they were when I was a kid. I thought I really was going mad. My uncles won't admit it, but I know they wondered the same thing. Fortunately for me they decided to give me some time to recover. But I was a walking disaster. That's why they had to lock me up for about a month."

Catalina had been about to drink some more coffee. She shivered and put the cup down instead.

"Being locked up for any length of time would have driven me mad," she said. "I don't do well in confined spaces. How did you get through it?"

"At night they laced my food with sedatives in an effort to calm the nightmares, but the drugs never worked for more than a couple hours at a time. They didn't want to keep me totally sedated, because they were afraid that might make it impossible for me to get control of my senses."

"They were probably right. Sounds like you spent a month in hell."

"The attic."

"What?"

"Not exactly hell." Slater's mouth kicked up in a humorless smile. "In my hallucinatory state I imagined that I was locked up in an attic. Isn't that what they did with crazy relatives in the old days?"

"I've heard that."

Slater studied her for a moment longer. She got the feeling he was making a decision.

He reached into the pocket of his jacket and took out a small leather case. He opened the case without a word. She glanced at the medical device inside.

"An auto-injector?" she said. She met his eyes. "Are you allergic to something?"

"Maybe the effects of some unknown radiation." He closed the case and handed it to her. "Take it. Use it if you think it's necessary."

"I assume we're talking about using it on you?"

"It's a powerful sedative. It will take me down very fast, at least for a while. With your talent, you'll probably get some warning if I'm about to turn rogue. If you do decide to use it, do it fast. The needle will go through fabric, so aim for whatever part of me is within reach. After you inject the sedative, call Uncle Victor. He'll know what to do. You still have his number, right?"

"Yes, I know how to reach him. You're serious, aren't you?"

"Yes."

There was no point arguing, she thought. If Slater was uneasy about the stability of his psychic senses, she probably ought to be worried, too.

She took the leather case and slipped it into the pocket of her trench coat. In a crisis she was more likely to be wearing the coat than carrying her handbag.

"All right," she said. "That's that. Now can we talk about our real priorities?"

"You don't appear to be shocked by my big reveal," Slater said.

"Maybe later." Catalina signaled the waiter. "Right now I've got other things at the top of what has become a very full agenda. We need to get to the scene of Royston's murder."

The waiter arrived with the bill. Slater took out his wallet.

"Business expense," he said.

"Definitely," Catalina said. "As far as I'm concerned, the Foundation can pay for everything involved in this mess."

"Easy for you to say. You're not the one who will have to justify every single receipt to the accounting department."

"It's not my fault your uncles are cheap."

The waiter returned with the credit card. Slater signed the slips, pocketed a copy for himself and got to his feet.

Catalina slid out of the booth and prepared to walk the gauntlet of booths to the front door. It was the only way out of the restaurant. The route would take them straight past the table where Roger sat with his companion.

She led the way, setting a brisk pace while silently counting off booths.

Four to go.

Three.

Two.

In a few more seconds she would be past Roger's booth. She would pretend not to see him. She was very sure he would return the favor. At the most they might exchange the barest of small nods. Civilized adults.

"You're leaving me in the dust back here," Slater said.

She suppressed a sigh and forced herself to slow down to a normal pace.

He caught up with her.

One booth left.

She kept her gaze fixed on the front door but out of the corner of her eye she saw Roger glance up. For a second he was looking straight at her. There was no way they could ignore each other now.

"Catalina," he said. "I didn't know you were here."

There was no help for it. The civilized, adult response demanded a brief pause.

"Slater and I just finished lunch," she said. "Got a busy afternoon ahead."

"This is Alicia," Roger said. "Alicia, this is Catalina."

Catalina gave Alicia her new-client smile, polite and professional. "Nice to meet you," she said.

Alicia blinked, as if she wasn't sure of what she was supposed to say next.

"Hi," she said. Then she switched her attention to Slater and immediately found her footing. "Hello. I'm Alicia."

Slater nodded politely but he did not offer his name.

"Got to run," Catalina said. "See you later."

"Right," Roger said, clearly relieved that she was not going to linger.

The brand thing.

Catalina started toward the door again, Slater beside her.

Without warning there occurred that brief lull in conversation that happens periodically in a crowded space. It was only a small wave of silence destined to disappear in a matter of seconds. But one lone voice continued talking.

"Is that her?" Alicia asked. "The psycho you told me about? The one you said was crazy?"

Catalina froze. Slater halted beside her.

"We're all civilized adults here," he said very quietly.

"Maybe not," Catalina said.

She turned on her heel and walked the three steps back to the booth where Roger and Alicia sat. The restaurant had gone still. Forks paused in midair. The waiters were locked in a time warp. It was as if a spell had been cast across the room.

Catalina stopped at the table. Alicia's eyes widened. She looked as if she was on the verge of panic. Roger's jaw clenched and his eyes narrowed. Catalina knew that he was frantically trying to come up with a way to handle whatever came next.

She smiled.

"Boo," she said.

She might as well have dropped a live grenade on the table.

Alicia squeaked and scooted to the far corner of the booth.

Roger flinched. In the next instant he recovered. Anger leaped in his eyes.

"Damn it, Cat," he said, "that was not funny."

She swung around again and nearly collided with Slater for the third time that day.

"Are we done here?" he asked.

"Yes," she said. She flashed him her most dazzling smile. "We're done."

Behind them the spell was shattered by a lot of frenetic motion and sound. Cups clattered in saucers. People resumed conversations. Waiters swung into action.

Outside on the street, Catalina walked in silence for a moment or two.

"I behaved like a civilized adult back there, didn't I?" she said after a while.

"Depends on your definition of the term," Slater said. "But revenge is still revenge, and you know what they say about embarking on that journey."

She sighed. "That business about first digging two graves? I don't think it will come to that, but I can tell you one thing."

"What?"

"Payback doesn't feel nearly as good as it should."

"Karma bites."

CHAPTER 17

Gwendolyn Swan picked up the receiver of the landline phone and called a familiar number.

Trey Danson took the call on the first ring.

"What's wrong?" he asked.

His voice went well with the image that he took pains to project—that of a brilliant attorney and financial advisor; a man who could be trusted to be discreet; a man who would keep your secrets and make your legal problems go away quietly. His main business was handling estates and trusts for wealthy individuals. That meant he kept a lot of secrets.

"Guess who just walked into my shop looking reasonably sane and wanting to know if I'd heard any rumors about artifacts from the collection of a certain dead collector," Gwendolyn said.

"Shit. The fucking Foundation is already on this?"

"Afraid so. And Victor didn't send one of the regular cleaners, either. Slater Arganbright is in town and asking questions about

Royston. What's more, Arganbright was not alone. Catalina Lark was with him."

"Slow down. Are you saying that the Foundation sent *Slater Arganbright*?"

"It's not like I'm going to make a mistake about the identity of an Arganbright, now, is it?"

"The rumors said that if he survived he would be spending the rest of his days in a locked room at Halcyon."

"Well, he survived and he's in Seattle."

"What about his talent?"

"It's not exactly the sort of question you can ask a person." Gwendolyn touched the crystal locket at her throat. "It was obvious that he's still sensitive to the vibe of paranormal objects, but there's something different about him."

"What?"

"I don't know. All I can tell you is that when it comes to artifacts, he's as strong as ever. Lark is strong, too. When I took the two of them downstairs, they both reacted to the atmosphere."

"That doesn't mean anything," Trey said. "Most people with even minimal talent can sense that kind of energy if they find themselves in a confined space where there are a lot of hot artifacts."

"Yes, but Lark was able to activate the dancers in the miniature ballroom. She got the master out from behind the curtains, too."

"All right, so she's strong. That's not exactly a surprise. I already knew she does some crime scene work. The one we have to worry about here is Arganbright."

"You mean he's the one *you* have to worry about. I sell information and artifacts. That's all. You paid me to let you know if anyone came around asking about Royston's collection. I've done that. Now I'm out of this. You're on your own."

She ended the call before he could say anything else and put down the phone. The problem with Danson was that he had enough talent to make him both clever and dangerous. He paid well for rumors and information, but no amount of money was worth the risk of getting dragged any deeper into his current project. She did not want to tangle with the Foundation.

She picked up the phone again and made another call. The voice that answered on the first ring was male and gravel-rough.

"Pest control."

"I found another rat in the trap today," she said. "I'd like it removed as soon as possible."

"It will be taken care of tonight."

"Thank you."

Gwendolyn ended the call and picked up a duster. The artifacts business was a dirty business. It sometimes seemed as if she spent half of each day cleaning up.

CHAPTER 18

Catalina shoved her hands deep into the pockets of her trench coat and watched Slater press a small electronic device against the high-tech lock on the back door of the big house. She heard a faint humming sound and then a muffled click.

Slater dropped the gadget into one of the many pockets of his cargo trousers and opened the door. He aimed the beam of a flashlight down a shadowed hallway.

Catalina got a flicker of curiosity.

"You've done this before, haven't you?" she asked.

"Don't worry, we're not in danger of getting arrested for burglary. Royston left his collection to the Foundation. I'm here as a representative of the Foundation's museum."

"Okay, if you say so."

"According to the report, Royston's gallery and vault are downstairs in the basement."

"Like Swan's salesroom? Oh, joy. Another basement full of heavy energy."

"Collectors like basements because they offer an extra level of security. The surrounding ground absorbs a lot of the paranormal radiation, which means freelancers and raiders are less likely to detect a cache of hot objects."

"Is that why the lost labs were set up in places like the Fogg Lake caves?"

"Probably." Slater led the way down a wide corridor. "The caves there would have been a naturally secure location. The Foundation experts think that in other cases vast underground tunnel complexes had to be constructed to house the labs."

Catalina followed him along the hallway, aware of whispers of energy lifting the fine hairs on the back of her neck.

Slater stopped in front of a metal door and used the lock-picking device to open it. Stairs stretched down into the darkness. Currents of energy wafted upward.

Slater found a bank of switches on the wall. The lights came up, revealing a large belowground display room. Many of the shelves and glass cabinets were empty. There was a lot of residual heat radiating from the walls, floor and ceiling, but not much from the handful of artifacts scattered around the chamber.

Catalina followed Slater downstairs. When she reached the bottom of the steps, she paused to look around.

"You were right, this gallery has been cleaned out," she said. "There's some serious energy from whatever used to be in here, though."

"Royston was eccentric, and so was his collection," Slater said. "But as I told Gwendolyn Swan, the good stuff, most of which would have been stored in the vault, is long gone. The raider crews always seem to be the first to hear about the death of a major collector. It's uncanny. But in this case I think someone else was here even before the raiders."

"The killer?"

"Or killers," Slater said. He gestured toward a heavy steel door at the far end of the room. "There's the vault. The body was found inside. No signs of foul play. It looked like a straight-up heart attack."

"But you don't believe that."

"No."

Catalina moved a little deeper into the room and cautiously opened her senses. Sure enough, the whispers of fresh death shivered in the atmosphere.

"I hate crime scene work," she said.

She did not realize she had spoken aloud until Slater responded.

"Uncle Victor told me that in the past you've done it only when asked and only because you felt you had a responsibility to do it," he said.

"It's hard to say no, not when you know there's a murderer on the loose and you might be able to pick up some information that will help law enforcement catch him."

Slater watched her as she paused near a glass-and-steel case. "You know, there are some talents who actually get a thrill out of the work."

"Well, hey, good news for Victor, right? In the future he can dig up someone who gets a kick out of murder scenes to read crime heat for him."

"The problem with consultants who derive a thrill from this sort of work is not only that they are creepy but that you can't be sure they're not embellishing their results."

She had been about to move on to another row of shelving but she turned her head to look at him over her shoulder.

"What do you mean by 'embellish'?" she asked.

"They lie."

"Ah. Frauds."

"Not always," Slater said. "They might have a little talent, maybe even enough to pick up a hint of violence or death, but that's all they can detect, so they use their imaginations to enhance their reports. They inevitably end up giving law enforcement a lot of false leads or leads that are so vague they are meaningless. 'The body is buried near water.' 'The killer is obsessed with mirrors.'"

"So when the body is found or the killer is apprehended it's impossible to say that the psychic was wrong, because there usually is some water in the vicinity and almost every house or building has a couple of mirrors."

"Right. The really good crime scene people are like you—they hate the work but they do it because they feel they have a responsibility to help law enforcement. And when they can't offer anything helpful, they're up-front about it."

"I saw the way you responded to some of the artifacts in Swan's gallery. What's that like for you?"

"Depends on the provenance of the object," Slater said. "Some whisper to my senses. Others shout. I tend to resonate most strongly with the dark stuff."

"Same with me."

"You see visions. I hear voices. In another time and place people would have either revered us as seers and prophets or hunted us down with pitchforks and knives."

"These days they just label us as delusional and try to medicate us or confine us to a locked ward in a psychiatric hospital." Catalina sighed. "Which is why my parents drilled into me the importance of acting normal."

"I got the same lectures," Slater said. "Something in common, right?"

"Uh-huh."

Catalina stopped at the open door of the vault and looked inside. The space was not large, about the size of a walk-in closet. It was lined with glass. Most of the shelves, which were constructed of glass and steel, were empty. There were only a few artifacts left, including a vintage black telephone with an old-fashioned rotary dial, a plastic case full of small index cards, a desk lamp and some odds and ends that looked like they had been taken from an old lab.

"I wonder what the index cards were for?" she said.

Slater moved past her into the vault and raised the clear plastic lid of the case. He flicked through some of the cards.

"It's a file of addresses and phone numbers," he said. "In the era of the Bluestone Project all data was stored on paper. Uncle Lucas is going to love this."

"Why would he want it? If that file is from the Bluestone Project, most of the people involved are either very old or dead by now."

"Lucas is in charge of building a database of the descendants of anyone who might have been connected to Bluestone."

Catalina made a face. "Does it strike you that your uncles might be a tad obsessive?"

"It's often my first thought in the morning and usually my last at night. At the moment they are obsessed with the possibility that the Vortex lab was real and so were the weapons it created."

"Do you really believe psychic energy can be weaponized?" Catalina asked.

"Over the years the Foundation has come across a few devices that appear to have been designed as weapons, but no one has been able to operate them, let alone actually fire them."

"Why?"

"The theory is that in order to be activated, a paranormal gun would probably have to be tuned to the user's personal vibe. That's a technical hurdle that hasn't ever been solved, at least as far as we know. Still, the rumors of a lab that succeeded in creating some prototype weapons have never stopped circulating."

Catalina sniffed. "Neither have the rumors about the dead extra-terrestrials in the freezers at Area Fifty-One. Everyone knows those sorts of stories are strictly conspiracy theory junk."

Slater picked up the vintage telephone. "Sort of like the stories about the residents of a certain small mountain community having extrasensory perception because a few generations back their ancestors were subjected to some unknown gases released in a mysterious explosion?"

Catalina sighed. "That doesn't qualify as a conspiracy theory."

"Why not?"

"Because it's true."

She watched him lift the telephone receiver and put it to his ear. Experimentally he used a finger to turn the rotary dial in a full circle.

"Is it hot?" she asked.

"No more so than other office equipment that has been housed in a paranormal environment," he said. "But I love these old phones. As handheld communications devices they absorbed some really interesting energy. I've never come across one quite like this, though."

"Why? What's different about it?"

Slater examined the base of the instrument. "No label, brand or serial number. Also, it feels a little too heavy for a vintage phone. It's probably from the Fogg Lake caves, because artifacts from that facility were the main focus of Royston's collection. That makes me curious."

"I wonder why the raiders didn't take it."

"It doesn't have the kind of heat that appeals to raiders—or to the Foundation curators, for that matter," Slater said. He hesitated. "But evidently Royston considered it important enough to store in his vault."

Catalina stepped through the doorway of the big vault. "Wow. There is a lot of hot energy in here, isn't there? *Oh, shit.*"

She jumped back, jolted by the currents of violent heat that she had just stepped into. Her pulse kicked up. Frissons of ice and fire arced across the back of her neck. A ghostly vision began to coalesce.

She retreated a few more steps, putting a little space between herself and the pool of energy.

"What did you pick up?" Slater asked.

She took a couple of deep, steadying breaths. "You were right. Someone died in here, and he was not alone. The killer was here, too."

Slater watched her very intently. "No blood was found at the scene. There was no evidence of blunt force trauma. Cause of death was heart attack."

"Let me take a look."

Catalina wrapped her arms very tightly under her breasts and made herself move back into the seething currents. Cautiously she heightened her talent.

Once again the vision began to take shape, fading in and out, never quite coming into sharp focus. She tried to describe what she was seeing, vaguely aware that her voice took on an eerie, otherworldly note. She could not help it. She was, after all, trying to communicate from somewhere deep inside a nightmare.

"The victim is standing here where I'm standing now," she said in her dream voice. "He is not alone. There was another person. The victim is startled by something . . . A sharp pain. He is not frightened, not at first. Then he realizes that something terrible is happening to him. He can't breathe. His heart is beating too fast, pounding. He knows that he is dying. Fear. Rage. Panic."

The terrible energy left by the victim's mounting horror was a palpable force sending waves of violent dread through her, threatening to shatter her own senses. She fought for control, struggling to overcome the urge to run for her life; to hide.

Strong hands closed around her shoulders, hauling her out of the pool of death energy.

"It's all right, Catalina." Slater's voice shattered the vision. He wrapped his arms tightly around her, enveloping her with his aura. "I've got you. It's over. Done. You're safe."

She shut down her other senses and found herself once again in the world that most people defined as real. Her normal senses took charge. That was when she realized Slater was still holding her. She could not resist the temptation to burrow deeper into the warmth and energy of his embrace. *Just a few seconds,* she promised herself. *Just long enough for me to catch my breath.*

It had been a very long time since anyone had comforted her after a vision.

She was pretty sure the last time had been when her mother had come into her bedroom to calm her after she had begun to experience the nightmares that had heralded the onset of her talent. The era of parental sympathy and concern had not lasted long. Once the true nature of her new senses had become apparent, her mother and father had immediately begun to emphasize the necessity of gaining control over her strange new ability. *You've got to learn to handle the visions or you'll never be able to live a normal life in the outside world.*

She knew they had meant well and that their insistence on control was for her own good. Nevertheless, neither of them could see the things that she saw. They could not comprehend how disturbing the dreamlike visions were. They imagined them to be waking dreams but the truth was that they were so much worse because, in a sense, the visions were all too real.

"Most people who see me like this want to get as far away from me as possible," she said, her voice muffled by Slater's leather jacket.

"What did you say?" Slater asked.

Mortified, she raised her head and took a step back. His hands fell away from her shoulders.

"Sorry," she said, avoiding his eyes. "I don't usually get that disoriented. I think the heavy atmosphere in here made the vision a lot more powerful than it would have been otherwise."

"That's not surprising." Slater gave it a beat before he continued. "Do you think it affected the accuracy of the vision?"

She managed a wry smile. "You know, that's one of the things I'm starting to admire about you, Mr. Arganbright. You're very good at going straight to the bottom line. No, the energy in here didn't affect the accuracy of the vision. It just made it stronger. Someone was murdered in here. Given that it was Royston's body that was found, I think it's safe to conclude he was the victim. I also picked up the hot prints of one other person."

"Any chance there might have been two other people?"

His focus on the crime made it easier for her to pull herself together. He wasn't freaking out. He wasn't looking at her as if he was wondering if she should be locked up in an asylum. He was treating her as a qualified, professional investigator. That realization warmed her almost as much as the feel of his arms around her had a moment ago.

"You're thinking about Marge's clones, aren't you?" she said. "I'm almost certain that there was only the one other person here inside the vault," she said. "But there wouldn't have been room for two killers."

"Good point. It would have taken only one to do the job."

Catalina opened her senses again and moved around the vault. "The killer was . . . excited."

"By the kill?"

She hesitated, trying to analyze the energy. "No, that was an act of cold-blooded violence. I think he was excited because he found whatever it was he was looking for."

"And three days later Olivia gets kidnapped."

Catalina looked at him. "I think you're right. Olivia was taken because of something the killer found here inside Royston's vault. That means there is some connection to what happened in those caves fifteen years ago. But how could Royston have been involved?"

"Looks like he had the bad luck to acquire the wrong artifact," Slater said. "So much for his safe room."

"What safe room?"

Slater indicated the latch on the heavy steel door. "Collectors usually design their vaults to function as safe rooms in the event of a home invasion by freelancers or thieves. But that concept doesn't work well if you invite the killer right into the vault. Evidently that's what happened here."

"That would seem to indicate that Royston knew his killer."

"Not necessarily. The murderer may have forced him to open the vault."

"How?"

"Something as simple as a gun to the head would probably do the trick."

Catalina thought about that. "I don't think so. Royston wasn't afraid, not at first. He was . . . elated."

"In my experience there are only a couple of things that get an obsessive collector like Royston excited—adding a new artifact to the collection or showing off a particularly valuable acquisition to a rival."

"Maybe the killer posed as a collector or the representative of a potential buyer."

"That might have worked," Slater said. "But he would have had to be a very good actor to convince Royston. Collectors tend to be secretive and suspicious. We need to get to Fogg Lake."

"What? That's a three-and-a-half-hour drive. Four hours if the weather turns bad. We don't have time to go to Fogg Lake. The kidnappers won't be hanging out there."

"We've got to find out what that original crime scene can tell us."

You can't go back into the caves. You will go crazy. You'll throw yourself into the lake and drown.

Catalina pushed the old nightmare to the back of her mind and struggled to come up with a logical reason for avoiding the caves.

"If we go to Fogg Lake today we'll be stuck there overnight," she said. "You can't get in or out of town after dark because of the fog."

"We have to start at the beginning," Slater insisted.

"There's no way a couple of murderous sociopaths like those two clones could hide in Fogg Lake. That is still one very small town. Everyone knows everyone else. Strangers stand out."

"I don't expect to find them there," Slater said, impatient now. "But with luck we'll get some sense of whoever is running those clones."

"But—"

"We don't have time to argue, Catalina. I'm sorry, but you're going to have to trust me."

"Trust you? Just because you're from the Foundation? We should be looking for those two men who grabbed Olivia."

"I'm not going to ignore those damned twins. I'll have Victor send someone to Seattle today to run down any leads that originate here in this gallery. The Foundation cleaners are good."

"Yes, but they work for your uncle."

"Believe it or not, I know what I'm doing here," Slater said.

She had to give him that much, she thought. He was the expert when it came to chasing old artifacts, and it looked like they were after one. She had to trust him. Olivia's life might depend on it.

"All right, I agree that you're the expert," she said. "If you're convinced there are answers to be found in Fogg Lake, then I guess we'd better get on the road. It's a long drive. We have to arrive there before it gets dark, otherwise we'll end up sleeping in the car overnight while we wait for the fog to lift."

Slater did not look thrilled by the reluctance of her capitulation, but he gave her a brusque nod.

"Thanks," he said. "The sooner we get there, the sooner we can conduct the investigation. We'll stop by your apartment so you can grab whatever gear you think you'll need. I don't suppose your hometown ever got around to allowing a hotel or a B and B to open?"

"Of course not. Fogg Lake has a long and proud tradition of discouraging tourism."

"Yeah, I heard that."

"Relax, we can stay in my parents' house. They have a home here in Seattle and a condo in Scottsdale but they still spend some part of each summer at the lake. I think they held on to the Fogg Lake house in case I, uh—"

"In case you what?"

"In case I, you know, have kids and need to raise them in a safe environment."

"Right." Slater nodded. "Kids. Speaking of parents, where are yours now?"

"They're away on a world cruise."

"What about Olivia's mother and father?"

"Olivia's father died when she was just a baby. Her mother was killed in what the authorities called a hiking accident about a year and a half ago."

"Sounds like you and Olivia aren't so sure about that."

"Olivia thinks she was murdered but we've never been able to find any proof. When you die in the mountains, nature has a way of concealing the evidence."

"True."

"We can't even establish a possible motive. If she was killed, it was probably a random act of violence. Maybe she surprised someone who was running a drug lab. We just don't know." Catalina cleared her throat. "We'd better get moving. Long drive."

"Yes," Slater said. He still had the old phone in one hand. "Grab that tray of index cards for me, will you?"

"All right."

She picked up the file and followed him out of the vault. He moved swiftly toward the stairs. She had to hurry to keep up with him.

He reached the concrete steps and started up to the ground floor of the big house. He stopped so suddenly that she almost stumbled into him.

"What?" she said, grabbing the handrail to steady herself.

He hit the light switch, dumping the basement into deep night. He closed and locked the door, spun around and aimed a small flashlight at the steps.

"Under the steps," he said. "Hurry."

Clinging to the rail with her free hand, she bounded back down the stairs to the floor of the basement. Slater was right behind her.

Heavy footsteps echoed in the hall at the top of the stairs. Two men.

"We've got 'em," one man said.

There was a series of dull thuds, followed by a grinding noise and a sudden crack of sound. A couple of seconds later the door crashed open.

Slater leaned out from the shelter of the concrete stairs and fired two shots in crisp succession.

"Fuck," one of the men yelped. "Nobody said he was armed. Use the damned fog."

Slater fired another round at the doorway and ducked back under the staircase.

The lights came on just in time to reveal two glass objects that looked like snow globes sailing through the air. But whatever was inside didn't look like snow. It looked like fog.

The glass balls shattered on the floor of the gallery. The heavy door at the top of the steps slammed shut.

Slater reached out and grabbed Catalina's hand.

"Whatever you do, don't let go," he said.

She was trying to comprehend his meaning when the tsunami of fog engulfed her senses. The hallucinations struck an instant later. She was plunged into the kaleidoscope from hell.

CHAPTER 19

Blinded.

Panic splashed through her, acid-hot. All her senses roared into the red zone, mental sirens screaming. Gray fog formed in the gallery. The hallucinations rapidly worsened. Paranormal flames leaped. Visions of the dead and dying that she had conjured at old crime scenes descended upon her in a storm of nightmares.

"Just hallucinations," she whispered.

"Yes." Slater tightened his grip on her hand. "We've got this."

"Good to know," she gasped. "For a minute there I was a little worried."

The hallucinations got more intense. Now she could have sworn she felt the heat of the flames that surrounded them.

"I think this fog is acting like a stimulant to our senses," Slater said. "It's throwing us into overdrive. Go dark. Now."

Shutting down her other vision while she was under assault went against all her survival instincts. It was like closing her eyes when confronted by a snake or a tiger. Her mind and body were both screaming at her to call on all available weapons, telling her she needed everything she had to do battle with her attacker.

But the harder she fought the hallucinations, the worse they got. She sensed that Slater was shutting down. It was worth a try. She pulled on all her control and managed to lower her sparking, snapping, flaring senses a couple degrees. The hallucinations did not vanish, but they faded. She thought the fog had thinned a little, too. She was able to make out Slater standing beside her.

Encouraged, she dampened her senses a little more. Some of the hallucinations retreated. The fog continued to thin. She could see a nearby row of shelves now.

"You're right," she said. "But we can't just walk out of here. They'll be waiting for us."

"We're not leaving the way we came in. We're going into the vault."

"Okay, I understand it can function as a safe room, but we'll still be trapped. For all we know, those two will wait us out."

"Collectors are well aware that their safe rooms can become traps, so they make sure they've got an exit."

"Huh. You do know a lot about collectors."

"I am one, remember?"

"Oh, yeah. Right."

They made their way back through the fog and moved into the vault. Slater released her hand at last to pull the thick steel door shut. He slid the massive bolt into place.

Next he began a careful scrutiny of the glass walls. It did not take him long to find what he was looking for.

"Here we go," he said.

She watched a panel slide open, revealing a narrow, unlit tunnel. When Slater aimed the flashlight into the darkness, she saw the gleam of tiles. The passage was just barely large enough to accommodate one person.

"I'll go first," Slater said. "Here, take the phone. I'll need one hand for the flashlight and the other for my weapon."

She realized she was still clutching the card file. She gripped the phone in her free hand. "You're expecting trouble at the other end?"

"I no longer know what to expect in this screwy case."

"I doubt if anyone heard those shots you fired a few minutes ago, because there are no close neighbors, and the concrete in here will have muffled the noise. But if we come out of this tunnel above-ground and you start shooting at those clones, we're going to attract attention. The police will be here before we know it, and by the time we finish explaining what happened, it will be too late to drive to Fogg Lake."

"I promise not to shoot anyone unless there is no other option."

"Well, okay, I guess."

Compromise. She reminded herself that good relationships were founded on such things.

Slater moved into the tiled passageway—the very narrow, very dark tiled passageway. Clutching the phone and the contacts file, she took a deep breath and followed. Memories of the nightmarish flight through the Fogg Lake cave complex fifteen years earlier rose up in a choking wave. The claustrophobia hit hard and fast.

You will drown in the lake . . .

She could do this. She had to do this. The other option was to retreat back into Royston's gallery and wait for the clones from hell to take her. That was no option at all.

Desperate not to succumb to full-blown panic, she cautiously jacked up her senses. Doing so helped suppress the panic. Up ahead she could see Slater's fierce aura. She found the sight reassuring.

She was also relieved to discover that the hallucinations did not return. The atmosphere might be stale, but it was free of the fog.

"I see the exit up ahead," Slater said.

"Thank goodness."

Something in her voice must have alerted him.

"Are you okay?" he asked.

"Yeah, sure. Peachy. I have a little problem with tight, enclosed spaces. Just get us out of here."

Slater came to a halt in front of a steel panel. He switched off the flashlight and slid the door aside.

More darkness spilled in through the opening, bringing with it a stale, musty odor.

"I think we're in the basement of the house next door," Slater said. "I noticed that it was vacant. I'll bet Royston owned it as well as the one he lived in. No surprise. Collectors like their privacy."

He led the way out of the tunnel and swept the flashlight around the room. Catalina took in the damp concrete floor and walls.

"You're right," she said "Another basement."

She was amazed to discover that she was still clutching the file tray and the phone. Slater went quickly toward a flight of steps.

A brilliant light flashed on, pinning Slater in its glare. A voice boomed out of the shadows. Catalina's senses were still heightened. She could not see the full aura of the man, because he was standing to one side of the open door. But his head and shoulders were exposed in the opening, revealing enough of his energy field for her to identify him as the identical twin of the runner who had come so close to her that morning. She knew Slater could see him, too.

"Drop the gun, Arganbright," the twin said. "Or I'll drop you where you stand."

"Take it easy," Slater said. "We're all businesspeople here. Why don't you tell us what you're looking for? Maybe we can work out a deal."

"I said get rid of the gun. Then we'll talk."

"Sure." Slater crouched and set the pistol down very slowly. The bright flashlight followed his every move. "Where's your clone?"

"What the hell are you talking about?"

"Your twin," Slater said.

"How the hell did you figure that out? Never mind. Tony is watching the other house. We knew about Royston's escape route. We figured there was a chance you might find it. Where's the woman?"

"Right here," Catalina said.

She walked forward. Very deliberately she stepped in front of Slater.

"Catalina," Slater said quietly. "Don't do this."

She ignored him, concentrating on the vision that was coalescing out of the shadows. She could read the intention of the killer as clearly as if he had spelled it out for her. The only way to keep him from shooting Slater was to use herself as a human shield.

"Get out of the way," the twin ordered. His already hot aura spiked in frustrated anger.

"You'll have to shoot through me to kill him, and we both know you need me in reasonably good shape, so let's make a deal," she said. "Here's my offer. I'll come with you, but in return you have to let my friend here go unharmed."

The twin was clearly caught off guard. She could literally sense him turning over alternatives. At last he seized on what probably looked like the easiest solution to his problem.

"All right," he said. "I don't give a damn about Arganbright. You're the one I need. Come on up here. Arganbright can stay down there in the basement. There's a lock on this door. It will take him a while to get through it. That will give you and me plenty of time."

"Spoken like any self-respecting sociopath," she said cheerfully. "Do you have a lot of luck with lines like that?"

"What the fuck?" The twin's aura radiated confusion. "Get up here."

"On my way," she said.

She went up the steps very quickly, taking them two at a time. She never took her eyes off his aura. When she reached the top he had to move out of the way. As soon as she went through the doorway he leaned around the opening, intending to take the shot.

But she had seen his intent in the vision that had flashed across her senses a few seconds earlier. She was already in motion. The twin's attention was on Slater. Catalina slammed the heavy base of the vintage phone against the side of his head.

The twin was blindsided. He dropped the flashlight and the gun and reeled back. Blood saturated his blond hair and ran down the side of his face.

"You crazy bitch," he yelled.

He reached out to grab her, but she was already backing away, giving Slater a clear path.

He came up the steps very fast. Dark energy flared in his aura.

Catalina dropped the phone and grabbed the flashlight. She swept the beam around the floor and saw the glint of metal. The twin saw his gun, too. He lurched toward it.

But Slater hit him like a heat-seeking missile, slamming the clone hard against the wall.

The twin grunted and sagged slowly downward until he was sitting on the floor.

Slater studied the clone's bloody face as he patted down the man's clothes.

"They don't make telephones like they used to," he said.

The twin groaned.

"The other one will be here soon," Catalina said.

"No ID," Slater said. "These guys are pros." He gripped the twin's shoulder and shook him.

The twin stirred and opened bleary eyes. He managed to focus on Slater.

"They said you wouldn't be a problem," he mumbled.

Slater ignored that. "Where did you take Olivia LeClair?"

"Don't know what you're talking about."

"I don't have time to be polite about this," Slater said. "I know you're expecting your twin to show up soon, so we're going to have to hurry things along. Where did you take Olivia LeClair?"

"Fuck you. If you're smart, you'll get out of here while you still can. I'm not working alone. My brother will be here any minute."

"Where did you take Olivia LeClair?" Slater repeated.

He made no threatening moves, but a tide of glacial energy surged in the atmosphere. Catalina realized it was coming from Slater's aura. She had never experienced anything like it. Confusion turned to shock, and then a strange excitement sparked across all her senses, normal and paranormal.

She did not know whether to be terrified or thrilled. Maybe both. Power in any form never failed to grab a person's attention.

Slater tightened his grip on the twin's shoulder. "Where did you take Olivia LeClair?"

The twin convulsed as if he was having a seizure. His face twisted in a mask of horror.

"Wh . . . what are you doing to me?" he gasped.

"Answer my question," Slater said.

"Just a job. Nothing personal, okay? Client said pick 'em up and leave them at the old motel. Got one. Supposed to grab the other woman but you got in the way."

"Where is the motel?" Slater asked.

"I'm cold. Too cold. What are you doing to me?"

"Where is the motel?"

The words were spoken in a terrifyingly neutral tone of voice. It wasn't just the twin's aura that was getting cold. The temperature in the hallway was dropping, too.

The twin stared at Slater. "You're a fucking icer. You're not real."

"Where is the motel?" Slater said.

The room got a little colder. So did the twin.

"Slater," Catalina said, "be careful. We need him alive."

Slater glanced at her, frowning a little, as if she had spoken in another language and he was having trouble translating.

The twin started speaking in a thin, panicky voice.

"Frontier Lodge. Outside Hinley. We didn't hurt her, I swear it. Instructions said undamaged goods. That's what we delivered. You gotta help me. You can't kill me."

"Probably best if you don't give me the incentive to try," Slater said. "Catalina, use your phone to take a picture of this guy."

She was trembling in reaction to the violence but she managed to dig her phone out of the pocket of her trench coat. She took a couple of shots of the twin, who stared at her, dazed.

A draft of air swept down the hallway just as she dropped the phone back into her pocket. She realized a door had opened somewhere in the house. Footsteps sounded in the shadows.

"Deke? Where are you? They found Royston's safe room and the damned tunnel. Did you get them?"

Deke jerked violently and tried to lever himself into a sitting position. "Tony. Tony, help me. He's an icer. Gonna kill me—"

Slater tightened his grip on Deke. The cold in the atmosphere intensified. Deke twitched again and then slumped on the floor.

Slater rose and started down the hall. A storm of midnight ice swirled around him.

But Deke's desperate cry for help had sounded the alarm. The thud-thud-thud of rapidly retreating footsteps told Catalina that Tony was on his way back out of the house. Evidently one violent sociopath saw no reason to stick around to try to save another violent sociopath, even if they were twins.

The footsteps faded quickly. Catalina heard the muffled rumble of a motorcycle engine.

Slater reappeared. "He got away, but we've got one."

"I don't think Deke is going to be able to answer any more questions for a while," Catalina said.

"Why not? Is he dead? Damn. He's no use to me dead." Slater moved closer to the man on the floor. "Good. He's got an aura. He's alive."

Catalina decided not to point out that the fact that Deke was still breathing was something of a happy accident.

"He's alive," she said. "But he's in a very deep state of sleep. Unconscious. Maybe in a coma. There's no way to know when he'll wake up, but assuming he does, I don't think it will be anytime soon."

"In that case, we'll leave him in the basement. I'll contact Victor and have him send someone out to collect this piece of garbage. You and I can't waste any more time."

"We have to check that motel before we go to Fogg Lake," Catalina said. "Olivia might still be there."

"Waste of time," Slater said. "We have to get to Fogg Lake."

"I'm not going to argue about this. You are free to leave for Fogg Lake. I'm going to find that motel. It's our first solid lead. I can't ignore it."

Slater fixed her with a considering look.

"Don't even think about it," she warned.

"What?"

"You're wondering if you can grab me, stuff me into the car and take me to Fogg Lake. Forget it."

He sighed. "Did you see all that in a vision?"

"I didn't need one to figure out what you were thinking. Some things are pretty damn obvious."

"All right, we'll find the motel and then we'll head for Fogg Lake. But first we have to stop at your office or your apartment, someplace where we can print out that photo of the clone."

"Why?"

"We may need it to show to people in Fogg Lake. Cell phones and computers don't work there, remember?"

"All right," Catalina said. "We can print out the photo at my office and then we'll find that motel. I'll drive."

"Fine. Let's get going."

His easy acquiescence worried her.

"Are you okay?" she asked.

"I don't know. I need to think about it."

She glanced at the unconscious Deke and remembered his words. *You're a fucking icer. You're not real.*

———————

The Frontier Lodge was on an old road outside a tiny farm town in the foothills of the Cascades. It was clear that the motel had been closed for a very long time. Most of the doors and windows were boarded up, but one door stood open. The room, with its sagging bed and stained carpet, was empty.

The electricity had been cut off. Slater swept his flashlight around the small space. An object glittered beneath the bed. Catalina got down on her hands and knees and pulled out the bracelet.

"This is Olivia's," she said. "I was with her when she bought it. That creep Deke was telling the truth. She was here."

"Can you tell how many people besides Olivia were in this room recently?"

Catalina prowled the musty space, forcing herself to concentrate. A murky vision appeared. She turned to look at the bed.

"Three," she said, aware that she was sliding into her other voice. "Three people in addition to Olivia were in this room."

"Two of them would have been the twins. That leaves us with one unknown individual."

"The clones left. Someone else arrived." Catalina stepped into the prints of the third individual. They seethed with anticipation.

"He is excited," she whispered. "Thrilled."

"Sexually?"

"No. But he is close, so close, to something he wants very badly."

"Are you sure it's a man?"

She hesitated and then shook her head. "No. I can't be sure. But the person is strong enough to carry Olivia outside. I suppose a strong woman could manage that. Just seems more likely it was a man."

"How do you know she was carried outside?"

Catalina shook off the vision and looked at him. "Because I can't see any sign of her footprints on the floor between the door and the bed. I think she was carried in here. Someone arrived a short time later to pick her up and carry her outside."

"Anything else?"

Catalina walked around to the other side of the bed and stopped cold. Once again she jacked up her senses.

"Olivia," she whispered.

Footsteps blazed on the floor.

"She wakes up. She's dazed and disoriented and scared. But she has an objective. A goal. She's frantic."

Catalina followed the hot prints to the door of the dingy bathroom and stopped. She snapped out of the vision.

"She needed to use the facilities after the long drive from Seattle," Slater said. "Makes sense that the kidnappers would allow her to go in there."

Catalina gazed into the small room. "She left us a message, Slater."

He moved quickly to stand behind her.

"So she did," he said very softly.

The tip of a finger had been used to inscribe one word on the thick dust that coated the mirror.

VORTEX

CHAPTER 20

I t's starting to look like your uncles may be right," Catalina said. "Maybe Vortex is not a legend after all."

Slater watched the narrow mountain highway unwind in the headlights of Catalina's tough little SUV. Catalina was at the wheel. She was clearly an expert on bad mountain roads, and this was one hell of a bad mountain road. He was in good hands. That was excellent news, because he probably should not be sitting behind the wheel just now. It was all he could do to battle the strange lethargy that was stealing through him.

Catalina deserved answers, but he hadn't had time to give her the few that he possessed. He had gotten on the phone with Victor as soon as he and Catalina had left the Frontier Lodge, and he had ended the call a moment ago. A Foundation team was already on the way to Seattle. They would pick up the twin who had been left bound and gagged in the basement of Royston's safe house and transport him back to Las Vegas for questioning. Assuming he ever came out of his coma. *You're an icer. You're not real.*

Slater pushed the memory of the twin's accusation aside. The matter of what he had become would have to wait. He had other problems, not least of which was the issue of communication. The phone call to headquarters would be the last phone call he would be able to make for some time. The rural mountain area through which they were driving made GPS and phones increasingly unreliable. The situation would become even more untenable when they arrived in Fogg Lake. A hot radiation environment of any kind played havoc with computers and cell phones.

"One of the things you learn early on in my line is that a powerful legend can do just as much damage as the real thing," he said.

"Because people want to believe it's true and they'll do whatever it takes to chase after it?" Catalina asked.

"Exactly. In the case of the Vortex lab, there are just enough clues out there to make Victor and Lucas and several of the Foundation experts believe that it really did exist and that a rogue scientist took control of the research. If they believe it, you can bet there are others who are convinced that it existed."

"Let me guess. This rogue scientist who ran Vortex wanted to conquer the world using weaponized paranormal energy?"

"Probably not. This was a rogue scientist, remember, not some dictator or warlord. It's more likely he wanted to discover the full potential of paranormal energy so that it could be used to cure disease, prolong the human life span, discover new worlds, et cetera, et cetera. But to do that he needed access to money, power and unlimited resources. If the legend is true, he was willing to kill to get them."

"So he was no better than the average dictator or warlord."

"He was potentially more dangerous, because he was smarter than the average power-hungry dictator or warlord."

"Does this rogue scientist have a name?" Catalina asked.

"I'm sure he did, but that was one of the most closely guarded secrets of the Bluestone Project."

"What this comes down to is that Olivia was probably taken by some creep or multiple creeps who believe in the legend of the Vortex lab."

"Someone evidently thinks she knows something about Vortex," he said.

The lethargy was getting heavier. He drank some of the bad coffee they had picked up at a gas station.

Catalina tightened her grip on the steering wheel. "She left that message on the mirror for you or someone else from the Foundation. She knew that I would call Victor once I discovered she was kidnapped, and she knew that whoever showed up from Las Vegas would understand the significance of 'Vortex.'"

"She was right."

"At least we've got one of the kidnappers now. If Deke ever wakes up, Victor's team may be able to get some useful information out of him."

"Maybe, but I doubt it. I think the twins are hired muscle. Smart people do not confide in guys like that."

"That leaves us with the one unknown individual in the motel room," Catalina said.

"You're sure it was just one individual?"

"Almost positive. I never go with a hundred percent when it comes to crime scenes, though. Too many pools of energy around to be absolutely certain of anything. That motel room wasn't hot the way a murder scene is hot, thank heavens, but there was a lot of intense emotion in that space."

"Victor has a team on the way to Seattle. They'll pursue the investigation from that end. If the twin we left in the basement has any useful information, the cleaners will get it out of him."

"That's it?" Catalina said. "That's all good old Uncle Victor is going to do? Question the damned clone?"

"Trust me, Victor is taking this case very seriously."

"How do we know that?" Catalina asked.

"He is sending the team to Seattle on the Foundation's private jet."

"So?"

"He sent me commercial," Slater said.

"You mean he went cheap where you were concerned?"

"He would have had me booked economy class, but luckily Uncle Lucas intervened and told the travel department I had to fly first class."

"Yeah?" Catalina glanced at him. "Because you're special?"

"No, because I have a little problem with claustrophobia."

Catalina stared straight ahead at the road. "You're not the only one."

"The night in the cave incident?"

"Uh-huh. You?"

"The month I spent locked up in the attic."

Catalina went quiet for a while.

"You'll be okay," she said finally.

"What?"

"You're worried that maybe you really have become what Deke called you," she said. "An icer."

"Did you see that in a vision?"

"I didn't need a vision to figure out what you were thinking," she said.

"How can you be sure of that?"

"Mostly because you haven't brought up the subject."

"Let me get this straight. The fact that I haven't talked about it made you realize I was thinking about it?"

"Naturally."

He closed his eyes for a few seconds and then forced himself to open them again. Sleep summoned him with a Siren's call but he did not dare give in to the lure. He might wake up in a room full of hallucinations.

"Icers are supposed to be the stuff of paranormal legend," he said quietly.

Catalina smiled. "Like Vortex?"

"I could have iced Deke's aura."

"But you didn't."

"I could have killed him."

"You had a gun. You could have used that to kill him, too. But you didn't. You're not a blank, and you're not one of the crazies. I'm assuming from the way you're dealing with this issue that until now you didn't know you could use your talent to cool someone's aura?"

"I knew that I was . . . changing. I just didn't know how."

"Now you know."

"I'm an icer. One of the monsters."

"No, you are not one of the monsters." Catalina's voice sharpened. "Monsters do evil things because they can. You've got a new talent, but you are the same man you have been all along."

"You've only known me since this morning."

"Your aura is strong, but it's stable, and you are in full control."

"You can really see all that?"

"Yes," she said. "I can also see that you are in desperate need of sleep. You burned a lot of energy today, and from what you told me earlier you didn't get any sleep last night. You need to rest."

"It might not be a good idea for me to sleep."

"Are you afraid you'll wake up in the attic?"

"I'm serious, damn it."

"Go to sleep, partner," Catalina said. "I'll wake you when we get to Fogg Lake."

"You've still got that auto-injector?"

"Yes, but I won't need it."

"Keep it handy."

"Okay."

He gave up trying to fight the exhaustion. He bunched up his jacket, wedged it into the corner created by the door and the headrest of the seat, and closed his eyes.

He was out between one breath and the next.

He fell straight into the locked-up-in-the-attic dream.

"What did you put in the food this time?" he asks.

"Just a little something to ease the visions," Uncle Victor says.

"How long are you going to keep me locked up?"

"Until you have recovered," Uncle Lucas says. "Eat the soup. You'll feel better afterward."

"I don't want any more drugs. They might make me sleep, but the nightmares are worse than the hallucinations."

"You need to sleep," Uncle Lucas says. "Eat the soup. If you don't you're going to end up in Halcyon Manor."

He picks up a spoon and starts to eat the sedative-laden soup . . .

"Wake up, Slater," Catalina said. "We're almost there. Just in time, too. It's getting dark. Night comes early in these mountains. Another half hour and we wouldn't have been able to make it into town."

He opened his eyes, braced for four walls and a room full of nightmares. But all he saw were tendrils of fog creeping out of the heavy woods that bordered the narrow road.

A battered sign came up in the headlights of the SUV.

WELCOME TO FOGG LAKE.
NOTHING TO SEE HERE.

CHAPTER 21

The sharp raps on the front door sounded just as Catalina was studying the limited selection of canned goods in the kitchen cupboard and trying to decide whether to heat up beans or chicken soup for breakfast.

"It's Bev Atkins, Catalina, dear. Heard you arrived in town late last night. Figured you might need some basics for breakfast. I've got eggs and a fresh loaf of bread for you."

Catalina closed the cupboard. She walked quickly out of the old kitchen and across the small, cozy living room. She opened the door and smiled at the cheerful middle-aged woman on the front step.

"Good morning, Ms. Atkins," she said.

"It's Bev, dear. You're not a little girl anymore. No need to be so polite." Bev held out a picnic hamper. "Here you go. Everything you need for breakfast. Enough for two people. I heard you had a friend with you."

By now it was a good bet that everyone in Fogg Lake knew she had brought a *friend* with her. It would be interesting to see if the welcome baskets continued to arrive after word went out that the friend was an Arganbright and that he was from the Foundation.

Catalina took the basket. "Thank you so much. I really appreciate this. I didn't think to do some grocery shopping before leaving Seattle. Mom keeps some canned goods on hand, but it would have been beans and chicken soup for breakfast if you hadn't dropped by."

"Euclid will have the general store open later this morning, so you'll be able to stock up." Bev peered past Catalina's shoulder. "Is your friend up and about yet?"

Slater spoke before Catalina could say anything.

"I am up and hungry," he said. He crossed the room and came to a halt just behind Catalina. "Slater Arganbright." He glanced at the contents of the picnic hamper. "That looks great."

Bev's eyes widened. "Arganbright?"

"Yes, ma'am. One of Victor Arganbright's nephews. I don't think I caught your name."

Catalina decided she was under no obligation to explain or defend Slater's presence. He was an Arganbright. He could fend for himself. She gave him a bland smile.

"This is Beverly Atkins," she said. "She lives just down the road."

Slater ducked his head in polite acknowledgment of the introduction. "Ms. Atkins."

"We don't get a lot of visitors from the Foundation," Bev said, her tone turning sharp. "Generally speaking, we don't have the sort of problems that tend to attract the attention of that bunch in Las Vegas, thank goodness."

"I know," Slater said. "Nice, quiet little town you've got here. But sometimes stuff happens, even in places like Fogg Lake."

Bev ignored him to focus on Catalina. "What brings you and your friend to Fogg Lake?"

There was no point in trying to conceal the reasons she and

Slater were in town, Catalina thought. There were few, if any, secrets in the small, closely knit community.

"Something has happened to Olivia LeClair," she said.

"What?" Bev looked appropriately shocked. "Is she ill? Hurt?"

"We have reason to believe that she's been kidnapped," Catalina said. "I've asked Slater to help me investigate."

"This is horrible news," Bev said. She darted a quick glance at Slater. "I suppose that does explain why you're here."

Slater slanted a veiled glance at Catalina. "Yes, ma'am."

Bev turned back to Catalina. "Olivia doesn't have any family left here in town. She's not rich. Why on earth would someone kidnap her?"

Slater rested one hand on Catalina's shoulder. "This looks like it goes back to that murder Olivia and Catalina witnessed in the caves."

Bev stared at him. "But that makes no sense. There was no murder. Everyone agreed that the girls experienced some sort of hallucination. All that old energy in the caves, you know. People who spend a lot of time in there often see and experience strange things."

"We are going to try to verify whether or not someone died in the cave fifteen years ago," Slater said. "If we can come up with a lead, it may help us find Olivia."

"This is just so awful," Bev said, stricken. "We never have any crime here in Fogg Lake. Are you absolutely certain Olivia was kidnapped?"

"Yes," Catalina said.

"Has there been a ransom demand?" Bev asked.

"No," Slater said.

"Then how can you be sure?" Bev shot back.

"We're sure," Slater said. "Now, if you don't mind, Catalina and I need to get to work. Time is critical in a kidnapping case."

"Yes, I understand," Bev said. "Will you be going into the caves?"

"That's one of the reasons we're here," Catalina said.

Bev started to retreat back down the front steps. She paused, glancing from Catalina to Slater and back again.

"Then the two of you are not . . . a couple?" she asked.

It was clear she was trying to be diplomatic, but a blunt question was a blunt question.

"We are a couple," Catalina said. She did not have to be psychic to know that Slater had gone very still. She smiled at Bev. "A couple of investigators working a case together."

"A couple of investigators?" Bev nodded quickly. "I see. Well, then, I'd better let you two get to work."

Bev hurried down the steps and walked briskly toward the center of town, a few short blocks away.

Slater closed the door and looked at Catalina.

"A couple of investigators?" he said.

"It was the best I could come up with on the spur of the moment. It has the benefit of being true, not that it matters."

"It doesn't?"

"Nope."

"You don't think they'll believe we're just colleagues working a case?"

"Oh, I'm sure they'll believe that part." Catalina hefted the picnic hamper and turned to go back to the kitchen. "But they'll leap to other conclusions about our relationship."

Slater followed her into the kitchen. "What kind of conclusions?"

"In small towns, two people sharing space in the same house equals a couple."

"Is that a problem for you?"

"No. What happens in Fogg Lake stays in Fogg Lake. Unlike, say, Las Vegas."

"About yesterday."

She froze for a split second and then very deliberately took an egg out of the hamper and cracked it into a bowl.

"Nothing happened yesterday," she said. "Aside from the fact that someone tried to kill you and kidnap me, that is."

"Something very important did happen for me," he said evenly. "I've spent the past several months wondering what that radiation had done to me. Yesterday in Royston's safe house I got the answer."

She picked up another egg. "This is about the icer thing?"

Slater crossed the small space to stand directly in front of her. "A lot of people who understand just what that means would panic if they knew exactly what I have become."

She cracked the egg into the bowl. "Maybe later. I'm a little busy at the moment."

Energy whispered in the atmosphere.

"I'm trying to thank you for taking my new talent in stride," he said. "For acting as if I'm normal, or as close to normal as people like us get. You are making this a lot harder than it should be."

She turned to face him. "Neither one of us qualifies as normal, but neither one of us is crazy. Neither one of us is a blank. Neither one of us is a monster. What's more, we are both in control of our talents. There is no need to thank me for affirming that state of affairs. I'm sure that in time you would have figured it out on your own."

Slater was starting to look wary. "This was supposed to be a simple case of me thanking you. But I get the feeling I'm missing something here."

"All right, fine, I'll spell it out. I do not want you to kiss me because you're grateful to me."

"Huh?"

"Did I misread the situation?"

Slater narrowed his eyes a little. The heat in the atmosphere got more intense.

"Yeah," he said. "You did misread it. I do want to kiss you, but not because I'm grateful."

"Why, then?"

He caged her, his hands gripping the edge of the counter on either side of her. He leaned in close but he did not touch her.

"I would like very much to kiss you because I think you are so damn hot that you could single-handedly set this house on fire, to say nothing of setting me on fire. I've been burning since I ran into you on the street in Seattle yesterday morning."

The shock of his words hit first. Men did not generally talk to her like that. Actually, they *never* talked to her like that. Previous conversations with men about sex tended to fall into one of three distinct categories. The first group of males said things like *I need discipline*. Those in the second group told her she was a control freak. Last but certainly not least were the guys who advised her to talk to a sex therapist about her inability to have an orgasm.

Slater wanted her; really wanted her. He wanted her the way a man was supposed to want a woman. But the real shock was the realization that she wanted him.

She put the egg down on the counter with exquisite care, because the shivery thrills snapping through her made her feel a little unsteady. She finally understood the true nature of the strange tension—the bone-deep sense of awareness—that she had been experiencing ever since she and Slater had collided on the street.

So this is it. This is what passion feels like. You've been waiting for a man who would climb the tower wall to get to you. Now here you are about to jump straight into his arms.

Wrong time. Wrong place. Wrong man.

Maybe not the wrong man. Maybe this is the only man you'll ever meet who can make you feel like this.

She put her hands on his shoulders to anchor herself, because she knew that whatever happened next, it would shatter the walls of her fortress.

"Do it, then," she said. "Kiss me."

The sensual heat in his eyes went up a couple of degrees.

"Sure," he said. "But here's the deal. You have to kiss me, too."

She was breathless now. "You've got a deal."

She kissed him, hard and fast and with a sense of desperation. He wrapped his arms around her and took her mouth with a fierce intensity that was unlike anything she had ever experienced. But it was her own response that truly blindsided her.

It thrilled her to know he was rock-hard because of her. His scent compelled her. He was strong enough to handle her if she lost control. She would not frighten him or damage his ego or make him wonder about her sanity. In his arms there was no need to hold back.

She could have sworn she felt a storm of energy swirling in the kitchen. She would not have been surprised if they did start a fire.

When she finally surfaced for air, the compelling heat in the atmosphere threatened to draw her back down into the depths. For a few beats she stood there in his arms, struggling to steady her senses. The fire in his eyes made it clear that he was fighting his own inner battle.

"Wrong time," he finally said.

"Right." She got her breathing under control and turned around to pick up the egg that she had set down on the counter. "Wrong time."

"But there will come a right time," Slater said.

It was a vow.

CHAPTER 22

If you go inside you will go mad. You will throw yourself into the lake and drown.

Catalina stopped in front of the deceptively narrow entrance to the cave complex. She could do this. She had to do this. For Olivia's sake.

Slater studied the opening in the rocks.

They were both wearing day packs filled with the usual things sensible people took on a hike—spare flashlights, bottles of water, first aid kits and some energy bars. Slater had added a couple of additional items to his pack—the vintage telephone and the card file that he had taken from Royston's vault.

She had been offended when she saw him stuff the phone and the file into the pack.

"You don't trust my neighbors?" she had said. "You think they're going to rifle through your things while we're gone?"

"When I'm working a case involving hot artifacts, I don't trust anyone," he had said.

She had not made any more comments about trust or the lack thereof. She had other things to worry about, things like incipient panic.

"That's it," she said. "That's the entrance to the cavern. Once you get inside there's a short tunnel that leads to the big chamber where the murder went down."

Slater glanced at her, frowning a little. "Are you okay?"

"Yes."

I can do this.

Slater took out his flashlight.

"You're the expert here," he said. "Do you want to take the lead?"

And suddenly she knew that she had been fooling herself all along. She could not do this.

"I can't," she whispered, sliding into her vision voice. "Can't go in there."

She could hardly breathe. Her heart started to pound. The vision coalesced. She saw herself falling, falling, falling forever into the bottomless depths of the ice-cold water.

No. You can't go in there. The nightmares will overwhelm you. You'll go mad. You will throw yourself into Fogg Lake and drown.

"Catalina?"

Slater's voice came to her from another dimension. She stared at him.

"What are you doing to me?" she asked in her vision voice.

"Catalina, wake up."

Slater moved forward, clamped his hands around her arms and pulled her hard against his chest. His aura flared, enveloping hers. He was an icer, one of the monsters. She should be going cold, freezing to death. Instead there was heat. A lot of heat. Her own aura welcomed it as if it were a lifeline.

"Catalina," he said. "Talk to me."

She wrapped her arms around him and let him pull her back to the surface. To safety. She could breathe again.

With an effort of will she managed to drag herself out of the last vestiges of the vision of herself drowning in Fogg Lake. She took a deep breath. Her senses steadied. So did her nerves.

"Sorry," she said. "Had a bad flashback. An old nightmare that I've had for years. It just welled up out of nowhere."

"You don't have to tell me about nightmares. I'm familiar with the subject."

She managed a shaky smile. "I know."

"Will it be easier if we keep physical contact on the way in?"

"Two auras are stronger than one," she said. "Yes, I think that might help. I've developed a phobia about going back into the caves. So did Olivia. I feel that if I can just get past the entrance I'll be okay. More or less. If I try to fight it, I want you to force me through it."

"Not sure that's a good idea."

"This is for Olivia. Promise me you'll do it."

Slater studied her for a moment and then nodded once. "All right, let's give the two-are-stronger-than-one theory a shot."

He held out his hand. She took it. His fingers gripped hers very tightly. He started to take the lead.

"No," she said. "I need to go first."

Clutching his hand, she cranked up every ounce of raw willpower that she possessed and broke into a run. If she could just crash through . . .

Slater ran with her. She shot through the opening in the rocks at full speed. *Icy water closed over her head. She was going down, drowning . . .*

She would not give in to the cold darkness. She was not alone. She fought her way back to the surface.

She flew past the entrance, Slater's hand in hers. His flashlight blazed, lighting up the stone walls of the cave tunnel.

And then it was over. They were safely on the other side. She was not going mad and she was not about to throw herself into the lake.

She scrambled to a halt and discovered that she could still breathe. Encouraged, she clamped down on her frazzled senses. Back in control.

Exhilaration shot through her. Memories returned in a disorienting flood. Not nightmares. Not hallucinations. Real memories.

"I'm okay," she said, still a little amazed.

"Let's go take a look at the crime scene," Slater said.

CHAPTER 23

Slater set a battery-operated camping lamp on a rocky outcropping and aimed his flashlight at the jumble of rocks in the center of the big cavern.

"That's where the murder took place?" he asked.

"Yes," Catalina said. She pointed at a boulder near the deeply shadowed entrance of a side tunnel. "Olivia and I were hiding over there."

He was about to ask if she could still sense the energy of the crime scene, but the tension in her shoulders and the shadows in her eyes rendered the question unnecessary. He knew it had taken a lot of raw nerve for her to get past the entrance of the cave complex. She needed a little time to steady herself.

"Walk me through it," he said. "Just as you would any other crime scene."

She slanted him a quick, searching glance. "I'll try, but it's been fifteen years. Also, keep in mind that I was a witness. I saw it all happen."

"That makes a difference?"

"Of course it does. My memories were not all that clear afterward, and neither were my senses. It was the same for Olivia. The combination of our panic and the hallucinations and, later, the nightmares really did a number on us. We both had trouble sleeping. We frequently woke up in the middle of the night with screaming nightmares. Scared our parents, and us, too. Eventually we recovered from the trauma, but Olivia and I both have throwback dreams occasionally."

"I understand, believe me."

Catalina slanted him an unreadable look. "That kind of thing can really complicate a romantic relationship."

"No shit."

Catalina's brows rose. "I thought that was my line."

"I borrowed it because it seemed appropriate."

"Right." She straightened her shoulders, raised her chin and walked to a large rock. "All these years, every time I tried to think about the details of that night I got an anxiety attack. But now I remember very clearly that this is where the short man with the glasses was standing."

"If Uncle Victor is right, the guy with the glasses was John Morrissey."

"If you say so. He took a clunky-looking instrument out of a black case and set it up here."

She was standing several feet away from him, but he could sense the energy rising in the atmosphere. The powerful currents of her aura were as distinctive as her scent and just as addictive. He would always know if she was nearby, he realized. He had already figured out that he wanted her, but the electrifying kiss in the kitchen had sealed his fate. No matter what happened, whether they made it into bed or not, he would never forget her.

But they would make it into bed, he promised himself.

"Can you be a little more specific about the device Morrissey brought with him?" he said.

"It looked like something you would see in a laboratory," Catalina said. "But it didn't have the appearance of an instrument or a piece of equipment that had come off a production line. I think it might have been handmade."

"It probably was. I'll bet Morrissey built it himself."

"I remember that he told the other man the thing had to be properly tuned. It was clear Morrissey was having a problem doing that. Even a lot of low-tech gadgets don't work well in the caves, or anywhere else around Fogg Lake. Flashlights and a few other old-fashioned battery-powered devices are about it."

"The paranormal radiation is too strong," Slater said absently. He thought about that for a moment. "It sounds like the two men came in here with a clear objective. They were planning to search for something. They were hoping that the gadget Morrissey had brought along would help them locate whatever it was they expected to find."

"That makes sense." Catalina went still. "But I think . . . I think the killer screwed up."

Slater knew from the change in her gaze and in her voice that she was sliding into her other vision. But she wasn't being overwhelmed by whatever it was she perceived. She was in control this time.

He waited.

"Morrissey is very intent on what he is doing," Catalina said, speaking in an eerie, dreamlike cadence. "He is excited. Impatient. He is concentrating very hard. But he is suddenly distracted. He is . . . bewildered. Then he realizes something is wrong. He's . . . sinking into himself. He can't breathe. He knows now that he is dying. You stupid bastard. You'll never find what you're looking for without me."

The last bit sounded like a direct quote, but Slater refrained from verifying that because he did not want to interrupt the vision.

Catalina backed away from the rock where the man had been killed. She clasped her hands very tightly together.

"The killer is excited, too," she continued in the dream voice. "He is thrilled. But suddenly he is alarmed. Furious. He runs toward one of the side caves. There are witnesses. He cannot allow them to live."

Catalina snapped out of the trance. She was damp with perspiration and she was breathing quickly.

"Are you all right?" Slater asked.

"Yes," she said, once again in her normal voice. "I can tell you what alerted him. He spotted a camp lantern that we left behind. He realized there might be someone else around. We knew he would find us so we fled down that tunnel. He called out to us. Told us he was an undercover cop. We didn't believe him. We just kept going. Eventually he gave up, but we couldn't be sure he was gone."

"So you spent the night in the caves."

"We were afraid he might be waiting for us out here. We stayed put until we were sure it was morning. We knew that people would be out looking for us."

"Any idea why the killer gave up trying to find you?"

"Sure." Catalina unlocked her hands and gestured toward one of the side tunnels. "He wasn't from around here. He didn't know how to navigate the caves. He must have realized that if he went too far into the complex he would get hopelessly lost. It's not just that the tunnels are a maze—there's also the paranormal radiation. It's very disorienting. You start seeing things. The deeper you go, the worse it gets."

"Hallucinations?"

Catalina looked at him. "Oh, yeah."

"How did you and Olivia keep from getting lost?"

"We followed the currents of a hot paranormal river going in. Followed the same currents out the next morning."

"But the killer wasn't able to follow you, at least not very far."

Catalina raised her brows. "A lot of the locals can't navigate the energy rivers in these caves. Olivia and I are both pretty strong, but even working together it was all we could do to sort them out."

"I don't doubt it. There's a considerable amount of disorienting energy here near the entrance. It's bound to get really hot in the side tunnels." Slater swept the flashlight around the cavern. "Back to Morrissey and the killer. According to the records, no body was ever found."

"Olivia and I saw the killer dump the body into the underground river." Catalina turned to look at the stream of deep water that emerged from a cave on one side of the cavern and vanished into a flooded tunnel a short distance away. "The current is very strong. If you throw something into that water it disappears very quickly."

Slater walked to the river and stopped a safe distance from the edge. He aimed the flashlight down into the depths. The water was incredibly clear.

"Does anyone know where this river ends up?" he asked.

"No. Some of the locals have tried putting a coloring agent into it to see if the dye shows up in any of the local springs or lakes, but so far no one has been able to locate an exit point."

Slater aimed the light at the mouth of the flooded tunnel where the water disappeared.

"The killer knew it was unlikely that the body would ever be recovered," he said.

"Or else he just thought the river was as good a way as any to get rid of the evidence of the crime."

Slater thought about that and then shook his head. "No, I think he knew it was a safe way to dump Morrissey's body."

"What makes you so sure of that?" Catalina asked. "I told you he wasn't from around here. Neither was Morrissey."

"Trust me, if Morrissey and the killer were able to find the entrance to this cave complex on a fog-bound night, they knew about the river. At least, the killer knew about it. What about his prints? Can you see where he exited the cavern?"

Catalina concentrated for a moment. "He left the same way he came in. There isn't any other exit, at least none that I know of. But on the way out his prints are very hot and a little unstable. He's in a murderous rage."

"If we go back outside will you be able to see where he went after he left this place?"

"No. I can track prints on hard surfaces like stone, but out in the woods the raw earth absorbs paranormal radiation very quickly. After fifteen years it would be impossible to find the killer's prints."

"Any idea of where he might have headed when he left this place?"

Catalina hesitated. "There are only three options. The first is that he went into town, but that would have been extremely risky because he was a stranger."

"And strangers get noticed in a hurry around these parts."

"Yes," Catalina said. "The second option is that he went into the woods. But at night in heavy fog he would have gotten disoriented in a hurry. You can't even trust an old-fashioned compass here. The third possibility is that he took a boat out on the lake."

"Is that a viable option?"

"At night? In the fog? It would have been extremely risky, even for someone who was familiar with the terrain. The thing about the lake is that the only way to navigate it is by keeping within eyesight of the shoreline. The fog makes that extremely difficult at night. Over the years Olivia and I have tried to convince ourselves that if we really did witness a murder, the killer must have died out there on Fogg Lake."

"But you didn't believe that," Slater said.

"We didn't know what to believe. Our memories were so jumbled. As time went by we became more and more certain that we had seen a murder and that we did find a place to hide that night. But all of the details were hazy. Until now."

"Did any boats go missing around the time of the murder?"

"No, I don't think so," Catalina said. "There aren't very many boats here, so if one had disappeared it would have been noticed."

"Given that the killer probably left by way of the lake and the fact that no one reported a stolen boat, there is only one logical conclusion," Slater said.

"The killer drowned in the lake while trying to get away?"

"No," Slater said. "The conclusion is that the killer wasn't alone that night."

"Well, Morrissey was with him, but he was a stranger, too."

Slater looked at her. "The reason the killer was able to come and go from this place without leaving a trace is because he had an accomplice here in Fogg Lake."

CHAPTER 24

It took a moment for the shock of Slater's explanation to wear off. Catalina pulled her scattered thoughts together with an effort.

"But that would mean someone in town was involved," she said at last.

"Is that so hard to believe?"

Catalina widened her hands. "Yes, it is hard to believe. It means that a person my parents considered a friend was involved in the murder and the cover-up."

"Not necessarily. You said your family moved here when you were a little girl. The individual who assisted the killer might have left town long before that."

Catalina's spirits rose. "Right. People move away from Fogg Lake all the time. Most leave right after high school. That's what Olivia and I did. Our parents left at the same time we did."

"Still, the implication is that someone who was once a member of the community is connected to the murder."

"That is very . . . depressing, to be honest."

"Got news for you, Catalina. Not everyone who has a connection to Fogg Lake is a good guy just because he hails from your hometown. That's one of the reasons the Foundation employs the cleaners, and it's the primary reason for the existence of Halcyon Manor."

"Yeah, yeah, I know. All right, moving along, I'll warn you up front that if you start questioning the locals about a possible accomplice to a murder that no one believes actually occurred, you're going to run into a brick wall."

"Because I'm from the Foundation. That is why I will let you handle that end of the investigation."

Catalina suppressed a groan. "I doubt if I will have any more luck than you would." She looked around the cavern. "I got past the phobia about entering this place, but it still creeps me out. Are we finished here?"

"One more thing. Do you think you could find the cavern where you and Olivia hid from the killer that night?"

"Why? Is it important?"

"Something about your memories of the place makes me think it might be very important."

"The mirrors and the chandeliers?"

"Yes," Slater said.

"I'm sure they were just the products of our hallucinations. Like you thinking you were locked in an attic."

"Maybe. But I'd like to take a look."

"All right."

Flashlight in hand, she led the way across the cavern to the entrance to the tunnel where she and Olivia had hidden on the night of the murder. Slater picked up the camp lantern he'd brought and followed her.

The hot energy flowing down the tunnel quickly became a stream, and then a river.

"You're right," Slater said. "There is a strong current in here."

"It gets heavier the deeper you go," she said. She turned a corner and paused in a small cavern. "This is where the killer gave up the chase. Even after all this time I can sense panic in his prints. He's frustrated and angry but mostly he's afraid of getting lost."

"But you and Olivia kept going."

"If he had managed to follow us I don't think he would have found us."

"Why not?"

She followed the powerful river around a few more twists and turns and stopped. "That's why not."

The storm of paranormal energy that had been the stuff of her nightmares still barred the entrance to the Devil's Ballroom. The currents were so fierce and so powerful that in places they crossed over into the normal spectrum. Here and there currents of cobalt blue and fiery red could be seen with just her normal vision.

The atmosphere in the tunnel sparked and flashed, lifting her hair, exciting all her senses. When she looked at Slater she saw that he was studying the storm with intense fascination. His eyes were hot.

"This is . . . amazing," he said. "It looks like a miniature category five hurricane. How the hell did you and Olivia get through it?"

"The raw power of flat-out panic, I think. We just held hands and aimed for the eye of the storm. Woke up on the other side."

"You woke up?"

"The storm knocked us out for a while. Not long."

"Did you get out the same way?"

"I remember now that we had no problem getting back out. It was going in that was tough. Like running through a storm of nightmares and hallucinations."

"Think you're up for another try?"

"If you're sure it's important. I'm older now and I've got much better control over my senses. It may not be as bad."

"We'll do it the way you and I got into the outer cavern. To-gether."

He threaded his fingers through hers.

"On the count of three," he said.

She braced herself and heightened her talent. "Right."

"One—"

He plunged forward, hauling her with him. They slammed into the eye of the storm. For an instant she was back in the kaleidoscope. Chaos reigned. The world shattered into a million glittering pieces . . .

And then they were on the other side. Her senses were skittering wildly, but at least she was awake. She hadn't passed out this time. She realized that Slater's hand was still locked around hers.

"What happened to two and three?" she asked.

"I was in a hurry," Slater said.

He studied the reverse side of the paranormal storm for a moment and then he turned on his heel, taking in the broken stalactites; the jagged shards of grimy mirrors that lined the walls, floor and ceiling; and the jumble of fractured crystals that littered the floor.

"Incredible," he said softly.

"Welcome to the Devil's Ballroom," Catalina said.

"Good name for it," he said.

He began to prowl the chamber but he kept his grip on her hand. The physical contact made it easier to combine forces to suppress the hallucinations.

"Do you have any idea what this place was?" she asked.

"Yes." Slater stopped to examine a large chunk of yellow-green crystal. "I think we are standing inside what's left of a machine that was designed to generate paranormal energy—a lot of it."

"I didn't know there were machines that could do that."

"Designing and constructing such a device was one of the goals of the Bluestone Project. Looks like the Fogg Lake lab got as far as building this chamber."

"Why the mirrors on the walls and floor and ceiling?"

"Mirrors and glass in general have some unusual and rather complicated physics that make them essential to paranormal research. The same is true of crystals."

"It looks like the researchers got this generator up and running," Catalina said. "But something went wrong."

"There was an explosion," Slater said quietly. "I think we know what the fallout was."

He drew her toward what appeared to be a panel of very thick green glass.

"A window?" Catalina asked.

"Looks like it."

There was so much grime on the thick glass that it was impossible to see what was on the other side.

Cautiously, Slater set down his flashlight and used his palm to wipe off a layer of dust and debris.

Fascinated, Catalina aimed her flashlight through the window. Inside was an array of old-fashioned control panels covered with dials, gauges and switches. There was a metal desk in one corner. Logbooks and drawings were scattered everywhere.

A vintage pinup calendar hung on the wall. Miss July was a long-legged, well-endowed redhead. Her makeup, hairstyle, skimpy negligee and sexy pose were clearly from the middle of the previous century. Someone had drawn a circle on a very familiar date.

"July twenty-fourth," Slater said.

"That's it," Catalina whispered. "The date of the Incident. The annual Fogg Lake Days celebration is held every year on July twenty-fourth."

"The explosion that took place here triggered the release of the paranormal gases that blanketed the town and the surrounding area," Slater said. "Congratulations, Catalina. Fifteen years ago you and Olivia LeClair found one of the lost labs. Whatever is inside that control room and the rooms beyond it is all still a highly classified secret and worth a fortune on the black market."

"Whoever grabbed Olivia must think she can lead them to this place."

"Looks like she hasn't done so yet," Slater said.

"We have to find her."

"We've got a lot more information to work with now—"

He broke off and tilted his head a little, as if trying to hear something that was being said in the distance. He flattened his palm against the thick green glass and went very still.

Catalina watched him, not speaking. She felt the energy heighten in the atmosphere and knew he was going into his zone: hearing voices.

"Fear," he said. "Panic. Something has gone wrong. Disaster. 'Can't shut it down. Out of control. Get out. Get out.'"

Now Catalina could hear a sound, too. She flinched in reaction to the strident, insistent noise.

Not voices.

The retro telephone in Slater's pack was ringing.

CHAPTER 25

"What the hell?" Slater said.

He yanked his hand off the glass and slipped the pack off his shoulders. He set the bag on the floor and quickly unfastened the straps.

The phone rang again, a demanding, discordant summons that was impossible to ignore.

Catalina watched him take the phone out of the bag.

"Please don't tell me we're dealing with a ghost calling from the Other Side," she said.

He studied the phone. "No such thing as ghosts, remember? I think the energy in this chamber activated this device."

"Right. Well? Are you going to answer the phone?"

"Oh, yeah."

Excitement crackled across his senses. Even if he had become one of the monsters, he still lived for moments like this, moments when the past sent shock waves into the present and made it dazzlingly clear that it could not be ignored.

He closed his hand around the receiver, lifted it out of the cradle and cautiously held it to his ear.

He heard a series of high-pitched pings.

"Voices?" Catalina asked.

"No," he said. "Sounds like it's sending out a signal of some kind."

A muffled grinding noise rumbled in the section of mirrored wall adjacent to the control room.

Catalina swung around to stare at the source of the rumbling.

"What's happening?" she asked.

"Gears," Slater said. "Old and rusty but still functional."

Ponderously, the section of paneling slid aside, revealing a portion of the control room.

The pings stopped. Slater crouched to set the receiver back into the cradle. He put the device into his pack and slung the strap over one shoulder. He walked closer to the doorway and aimed the flashlight into the room.

"The phone sends the signal that opens the door of the control room," he said. "It probably closes it, too."

"Why did whoever created it make it look like a standard telephone?"

"I think it's safe to say the engineers who designed it wanted to camouflage the fact that it's a functioning paranormal machine meant to provide access to this chamber."

"In case the thing fell into the wrong hands?"

"Exactly," Slater said.

Catalina moved to stand beside him. She played her light over the space.

"Whoever was in here on the night of the explosion sure left in a hurry," she said.

The evidence of a frantic, chaotic departure was everywhere. In addition to the litter of papers and schematics, chairs were over-turned. Coffee mugs lay in pieces on the floor. One of the drawers in the desk stood open. Slater crossed the space to take a look inside.

"Empty," he said. "When they evacuated this place someone grabbed whatever was in this drawer."

At the rear of the control room a door stood ajar. Catalina moved toward it and aimed her flashlight into the inky darkness beyond.

"A hallway," she said. "Offices on either side. Maybe some labs. The doors are all wide open. There are drawings and papers every-where. They were running for their lives. I wonder if they all made it out safely or if there will be skeletons at the end of that corridor."

Slater moved to stand behind her. He added the beam of his flash-light to hers.

"If there are bodies, there's no rush to find them," he said. "This is the most significant discovery the Foundation has ever made. We need to get a team in here to secure the artifacts and any data that was left behind."

"Good luck with that."

He glanced at her and saw that her eyes were narrowed and her jaw was rigid.

"You think the good citizens of Fogg Lake will have a problem with the idea of the Foundation sending a team to this site?" he asked.

"Yep."

"Look on the bright side. It will give Uncle Victor a chance to sharpen his people skills."

"Uh-huh."

"We'll let him figure it out later. Right now we have to secure this place."

"And find Olivia. Time is running out for her, Slater."

"Now that we know why they grabbed her, we've got what we need to set a trap."

Catalina turned to look at him. "How do we do that?"

"We go back to the beginning of this thing and figure out who in Fogg Lake helped Morrissey's killer get in and out of town unseen."

"What makes you think the person is still in town?"

"I don't know if he or she is still around but I am sure that the individual was here fifteen years ago. This is a small community. It won't be hard to narrow down the list of suspects, and then we can start eliminating them."

"You said earlier that the accomplice might be someone who knew the area but wasn't living here at the time," Catalina reminded him.

"That's still a possibility, but after seeing this place I think it's far more likely that the accomplice was a resident when Morrissey and the killer arrived. What's more, I think that individual was still around the next morning when you and Olivia came out of the caves."

"Why?"

"From an operational point of view, there was a lot of planning involved by someone who was intimately familiar with the area around Fogg Lake. That person had to meet Morrissey and the killer somewhere on the old highway and guide them to the cavern. That individual also had to secure a boat and return it without anyone knowing it had gone missing. The accomplice was still in town the next morning and in a position to learn that you and Olivia had survived but that everyone thought you had hallucinated the murder. That person also may have cleaned up the crime scene, just to make sure there was no evidence left behind."

"I agree that the accomplice was well acquainted with the terrain and the dangers in this area. I just don't understand why you're so sure that the accomplice was someone who was living in town when the murder went down."

"I told you, I can't be absolutely positive," Slater said. "I'm going with what feels like a probable scenario. But there is one more piece of evidence I can offer."

"What is that?"

"You said that when the search party showed up, you and Olivia told everyone about the murder. You also described the ruins of the generator chamber."

"The Devil's Ballroom." Catalina watched him closely. "Right."

"You said you stopped talking about it because people told you it was just a hallucination. But at first you must have provided a lot of details."

"So?"

"As you keep pointing out, it's been fifteen years since you witnessed Morrissey's murder. Now, after all this time, someone has come looking for you and Olivia. I think something happened recently that made the accomplice realize you and your friend didn't hallucinate the Devil's Ballroom. I think that person has figured out that you and Olivia LeClair actually did find a critical part of the Fogg Lake lab."

Catalina took a breath. "You believe that only someone who was in town immediately after Olivia and I got out of the caves would have heard our detailed description."

"Yes. You said the two of you stopped talking about what you had seen when your parents and the other adults in the community told you it was all a vivid hallucination."

"Olivia and I were all about passing for normal in those days— about showing that we had control. But that doesn't mean that someone who heard us describe the chamber at the time didn't tell someone else later, someone who recognized the description when they came across some evidence fifteen years later."

"That's a stretch," Slater said. "Not an impossibility, but a stretch. The logical assumption is that the accomplice was here the morning you and Olivia got out of the caves. Whoever it was heard every detail and remembered it."

She nodded. "Where do we go with that information?"

"Nowhere," Slater said. "We stay in Fogg Lake."

Catalina eyed him with grim determination. "How are we going to find Olivia if we hide out here?"

"Think about it, Catalina. If the kidnappers expect Olivia to lead them to the Devil's Ballroom, they will have to bring her here. Best guess? They've got her stashed somewhere nearby in the caves."

Catalina stared at him, stunned. "The cave system has never been mapped. They could hide a hundred captives indefinitely in these tunnels."

"Not if they want to find the Devil's Ballroom. Sooner or later the kidnappers will have to make their move."

"We can't just sit and wait."

"No," Slater said. "We're going to make our move first."

"Are we going to tell everyone in town that we found this place?"

"No, for now this is our secret. But we are going to rattle some-one's cage."

CHAPTER 26

S later believes Olivia's kidnapping is connected to the murder that occurred in the caves fifteen years ago," Catalina said. "After concluding our investigation today I have to tell you that I agree with him."

She and Slater were sitting in a red vinyl booth in the Lake View Café, the only restaurant in town that was open in the evenings. They were talking to Euclid Oaks, the heavily built, bearded owner of the Fogg Lake general store. Euclid was also the mayor. He had stopped by the table to find out what was going on.

Catalina was well aware that they had an audience. Most of the town's population had managed to crowd into the establishment that evening. The restaurant and bar had gone silent when Euclid arrived. Everyone knew why he was there. Everyone was listening to the conversation.

"What murder?" Euclid Oaks said.

Outsiders might be excused for thinking the mayor was not very bright. They would have been very wrong. Euclid had been born and raised in Fogg Lake. He had left in his teens to go off to college to study mathematics. He had ended up teaching the subject at the graduate level. Later he had used his talent for probability theory to make a fortune in casinos around the world before returning to Fogg Lake to work on a theory involving something he called the duality of paranormal energy waves.

Catalina put down her fork. "The murder Olivia and I witnessed, Euclid. I'm sure you remember. You were one of the people who came looking for Olivia and me the morning after we spent the night in the caves."

Euclid's thick brows bunched. "But there was no murder. Your folks and everyone else agreed that you and Olivia had hallucinated the whole thing."

Slater looked at him. "Turns out I was able to collect some evidence at the scene."

"Well, I'll be damned," Euclid said. He eyed Slater with undisguised skepticism. "What kind of evidence?"

"At the moment I'm not at liberty to discuss it."

"Is that a fact?" Euclid's scowl got tighter. He folded his arms across his broad chest. "Who got murdered?"

"A Foundation researcher named John Morrissey," Slater said.

"What was he doing in our caves?" Euclid asked.

"Good question," Catalina said. "The Foundation thinks he was probably looking for hot artifacts."

Euclid eyed her and then shifted his attention to Slater. "You're sure he got killed?"

"As sure as I can be without a body," Slater said. "Now that I've had a chance to examine the scene, I'm convinced the killer dumped Morrissey into the river."

"Huh." Euclid pondered briefly. "Any idea who killed your guy?"

"No, but we do have a lead on the people who grabbed Olivia," Slater said.

A breathless silence gripped the restaurant and the bar. No one moved.

"What have you got?" Euclid asked.

"The kidnappers hired some muscle to pick up Olivia," Slater said. "Catalina and I caught one of them. By now he will be enjoying the hospitality of the Foundation. Currently, however, he is not of much use."

"Why not?" Euclid asked.

"He's not talking," Slater said. "He will eventually. For obvious reasons, we don't have time to wait for him to wake up. But he has a twin brother who helped him pull off the kidnapping. If I can find him I might be able to get the answers we need."

"You expect to find this twin around here?" Euclid said. He waved a hand to indicate the crowd. "Take a look. See anybody who looks like him?"

"No," Slater said. "But we've got a photo."

He pulled the picture out of his pocket and placed it on the table. Suddenly everyone in the room was crowding around the booth.

"What happened to his face?" Euclid said.

"I hit him with an old telephone," Catalina explained.

Euclid nodded. "Looks like you did some damage. They don't build phones like they used to."

Slater looked briefly amused but he did not say anything.

The photo was passed from hand to hand.

"Nope, never seen anyone who looks like him," someone said.

"No one I know," a woman declared.

"Nice-looking young fella," Euclid said. "Except for the blood, of course. You sure he's a bad guy?"

"Trust me, he's a blank," Catalina said.

Euclid nodded in a sage manner. "Those damned blanks can fool you every time. People fall for their cons even when they can see the empty places in their auras. Amazing."

"Their ability to pass for normal is their camouflage," Catalina said.

The door of the café opened. Damp night air swept into the room. Catalina turned to look. So did everyone else. Nyla Trevelyan, wrapped in a puffy down coat, her feet clad in worn leather hiking boots, walked into the room. The crowd parted, creating a path to the booth. Nyla came forward quickly, unfastening her coat.

"Catalina, dear," she said. She smiled her warm, gentle smile. "I heard you were in town. So good to see you again. It's been too long."

It seemed to Catalina that Nyla had scarcely aged in the past fifteen years. True, there were a few more lines in her face, but she had been gifted with the kind of good bones that guaranteed an elegant beauty that would last through the years. Her long hair was shot with silver now, but she wore it the same way she always had, secured at the back of her neck so it fell in a long ponytail to her waist. There was a delicate, fragile quality about her that some said was due to her long-standing heart condition.

By the time she reached the booth her coat was open, revealing the flannel shirt and jeans underneath, the same uniform that she had worn for as long as Catalina could remember.

"Hi, Nyla." Catalina slipped out of the booth, exchanged a quick hug with the older woman, and then stepped back to introduce Slater, who was on his feet. "This is Slater Arganbright. He's with the Foundation."

"Yes, I know," Nyla said. "Word gets around fast here in Fogg Lake." Her tone was dry but her smile was genuine and her eyes were shadowed with concern. "I would say welcome to town, but I understand that you are here because you're investigating the disappearance of Olivia LeClair. Is that true?"

"Olivia LeClair did not disappear," Slater said. "She was kidnapped the day before yesterday."

Nyla's smile gave way to an expression of shock and dismay. "This is almost unbelievable. Why would anyone kidnap Olivia? It's not as if the family has any money."

"We don't think this is about a ransom payment," Slater said. "It seems to be connected to the murder that took place in the caves fifteen years ago."

Nyla turned to Catalina. "So it's true? You really did witness a murder?"

"Yes," Catalina said. "We think someone grabbed Olivia because she was also a witness."

Nyla turned back to Slater. "But why now? After all this time?"

"We don't know," Slater said. "All we know for sure is that Olivia has been taken. I've got a photo of one of the two kidnappers. He's in the custody of the Foundation. Last we heard he was in a coma, but he's expected to recover soon. Meanwhile we're looking for his partner, who happens to be his twin."

Someone handed Nyla the photo. She examined it closely, frowning a little.

"He's injured," she said. "Was he in an accident?"

"Sort of," Catalina said.

"No wonder he's in a coma." Nyla shook her head. "I don't recognize him. Are you here because you think these twins have a Fogg Lake connection?"

"What we know," Slater said, "is that they have a connection to the hot artifacts trade. We think they murdered a collector named Royston in Seattle. They ambushed Catalina and me in Royston's gallery. They were armed with some sort of gas that affected our senses. A heavy hallucinogen."

Alarmed, Nyla looked at Catalina. "Are you all right?"

"Yes, I'm fine," Catalina said.

"Thank goodness." Nyla glanced at the photo again. "I'm sorry I can't be more helpful. You say he's in a coma?"

"Unfortunately, yes," Slater said.

Euclid frowned. "How the hell did that happen?"

"He was probably affected by the same gas he and his twin used on us," Catalina said. "Hallucinogens can be very problematic."

Slater's brows rose in acknowledgment of her smooth response to the question, but he kept quiet.

The door of the café opened again. Catalina and the others turned to look at the newcomer. Harmony—as far as anyone knew she had no last name—did not go out of her way to make dramatic entrances. The ability came naturally to her. She was almost six feet tall with a mane of white hair, a statuesque body and the eyes of an Old Soul.

She strode into the restaurant with the long wings of a full-length black wool cloak swirling around her knee-high leather boots.

She halted just inside the door and went very still. An expectant hush fell over the crowd.

"The energy of the past has been disturbed," she declared in the rich voice of a Shakespearean actor. "A great darkness is gathering deep in the fog. Lock your doors and stay close to your hearths to-night."

There was a stark silence. No one snickered. There was no eye-rolling. If you grew up in Fogg Lake, you knew that when Harmony spoke in that particular voice it was a good idea to pay attention.

"Got anything more specific for us, Harmony?" Euclid asked.

"No." Harmony's voice was normal now. It was still a strong voice befitting her size and build, but the drama was gone. "Sorry. That's all I've got. There's just a vibe in the fog tonight that reminds me— Never mind. I heard Catalina was in town."

Catalina got to her feet again. "Right here, Harmony."

Harmony brightened and started forward. Once again the crowd parted.

"There you are," she said. She enveloped Catalina in a warm hug. "So good to see you again. What's this I hear about Olivia being kidnapped and you bringing a Foundation cleaner here to investigate?"

"Long story, but that is the short version," Catalina said. She stepped back and indicated Slater. "This is Slater Arganbright, the investigator. Slater, this is Harmony."

Slater rose politely. "Harmony."

Harmony studied him for a long moment with her deep eyes. Catalina sensed a shiver of energy in the atmosphere. She held her breath, because she knew that Harmony was trying to view Slater's aura. Harmony had a strong talent, but no one knew exactly what it was. If she could perceive the icy energy in Slater's field she might decide he was dangerous and warn everyone to stay away from him.

"Well, well, well," Harmony said finally. "You're an Arganbright all right."

Catalina breathed a small sigh of relief. She plucked the photo from Euclid's fingers and handed it to Harmony.

"This is one of the kidnappers," she said. "We're searching for his twin."

"Hmm." Harmony allowed herself to be distracted. She took the photo and studied it. "What happened to him?"

"I hit him with a phone because he was going to shoot Slater."

Harmony glanced up in surprise. "A little cell phone did that much damage?"

"An old phone," Catalina said. "Maybe from the late nineteen fifties."

"I see," Harmony said. "That explains it. I'm sorry, I've never met this man or his twin, but there's something about him that reminds me of someone I may have come across in the archives. He looks to be around thirty years old, don't you think?"

"I would say that's about right," Slater said.

"I'll tell you what," Harmony said. "I'll take a look at the ancestry files and see if I can find any male twins who would be that age."

Slater's gaze sharpened. "You keep ancestry records of people who have a connection to Fogg Lake?"

"Part of my job," Harmony said. "The files go all the way back to the night of the Incident. I can't guarantee they're complete. We've lost contact with a lot of people who have moved away. But I'm pretty good at tracking down the descendants of the people who were living here at the time of the Incident. I'll go back to my place and start the search."

"Thanks," Slater said. "I would appreciate it if you would contact me immediately if you find anything tonight. Don't wait until morning."

"Olivia's life is at stake," Catalina said.

"I understand," Harmony said.

She turned on her booted heel and strode toward the door. A man rushed to open it for her. She paused long enough to pull up the hood of her cloak, and then she disappeared into the fog-bound night.

When the door closed behind her, an uneasy hush fell over the crowd. Euclid looked around.

"You heard Harmony," he said. "Best to make an early night of it. I know we don't usually lock our doors around here, but do it tonight. There might be some bad people out there in the woods."

Chairs scraped as people got to their feet and began pulling on coats and caps. The waiters got very busy clearing the tables. Within a very short period of time the café and the bar were nearly empty.

Slater looked at Catalina. "Does Harmony have a last name?"

"Probably," Catalina said. She got to her feet and took her coat down off the hook. "I'm sure there is one in the ancestry books, but she has always made it clear that she wants to be addressed only as Harmony."

Slater stood and reached for his wallet. "Gotta tell you, she sent a chill through me when she walked in here and delivered that comment about the bad vibe in the fog tonight."

"She does that kind of thing once in a while. You get used to it."

Slater put a few bills on the table and slid his wallet back into the pocket of his trousers. "I noticed people paid attention to her."

"Well, sure. She's the current Oracle of Fogg Lake."

"Seriously?"

"Yes. But there's no money in that line, at least not here in Fogg Lake. She has a day job."

Slater pulled on his jacket. "What is it?"

"She's the town librarian."

CHAPTER 27

*The dreamer raced through a hall of mirrors, searching for Olivia.
Visions seethed in each looking glass she passed, taunting her. She
knew that if she could find the right mirror she would find Olivia.
But the corridor was endless and time was running out. The visions were growing more ominous.*

*She ran faster, desperate to identify the mirror that concealed
Olivia.*

"Catalina. Wake up. You're dreaming."

Slater's voice brought her out of the nightmare on the wings of an
anxiety attack. She sat up abruptly, trying to orient herself. It took
her a moment to realize she was in her old bed in her parents' Fogg
Lake home. A night-light plugged into a wall outlet illuminated the
space in a faint bluish glow.

Slater stood beside the bed, not touching her; giving her space. In
the faint light she could see that he was wearing the dark trousers

he'd had on earlier and a crew-neck T-shirt. Her senses were a little fried by the anxiety, so they were flashing and sparking. She could see enough of Slater's midnight aura to know he was cranked up, too.

"Sorry," she said. "Bad dream." Embarrassed, she swung her legs over the side of the bed. She was wearing the ancient flannel pajamas that she kept in a drawer of the dresser, so she wasn't concerned about modesty. She got to her feet and raked her hair back behind her ears. "Didn't mean to wake you."

"I wasn't asleep," Slater said.

Catalina went to the window and looked out into the gently glowing fog. The residents of Fogg Lake were not the only living things affected by the events of the night of the explosion. The local vegetation had also been changed in some ways. At night many of the plants emitted a pale, eerie light. Tonight the energy-infused mist seemed ominous.

"Harmony was right about the bad vibe in the atmosphere tonight," she said.

Slater moved to stand behind her. "You don't really believe in oracles and prophecies, do you?"

"No, but I do believe there is such a thing as evil and that it has power. Whoever took Olivia is responsible for the bad energy out there tonight."

"I agree," Slater said.

"Do you really think the kidnappers have Olivia hidden somewhere in the caves?"

"I can't be certain but the logic works for me. This case has had a local angle from the beginning."

"Maybe we should give up trying to identify the kidnappers and organize a search party in the morning. We should be looking for her, Slater."

"That would be worse than useless at this point." Slater put his arms around her. "You said those caves are a maze. We could search for years and never find her. We need a starting point. Give me a few more hours. We're getting close. The pieces of the puzzle are starting to come together."

"Really? You're not just saying that? Because I've done too much crime scene work. I'm a little jaded when it comes to false hopes."

Slater turned her in his arms and caught her head between his hands. In the shadows his eyes burned. So did his aura.

"I give you my word that I'm telling you the truth," he said. "I can't see the future. No one can. But I do know the vibe I get when an investigation starts to yield an answer. I swear to you, that's the sensation I've got now."

She wrapped her arms around him and pressed herself against him, taking comfort in his heat and strength, indulging in the sensual intimacy that quickened in the atmosphere around them.

Since their collision on the street she had been telling herself that the attraction between them was superficial, nothing more than the natural connection between two people who were sharing risks and dangers together in pursuit of the same goal. But the kiss that morning had confirmed that whatever the cause of the attraction, it was powerful and deep.

I am never going to forget this man.

"Catalina," Slater whispered into her hair, "this isn't the time or the place, and it's probably too soon to ask, but I need to know if you think that, when this is over, we might have a future—"

She put her fingers against his mouth, stopping the question before he could finish it.

"I don't know," she said. "But I would like to find out."

His eyes darkened with the heat of masculine need and then his mouth closed over hers.

The kiss scorched her senses. Hot. All-consuming. It was laced with the fire of desperation and the thrill of the unknown. The shock waves of passion that had arced between them that morning had been little more than a prelude to what was happening now.

With an urgent groan, Slater deepened the kiss and moved his hands to the front of her pajamas. She could feel the faint tremor in his fingers when he started to undo the buttons. The realization that he was shivering with need sent a rush of delight through her. It told her that, like her, he was unfamiliar with this level of intensity.

He got the top open. When his palms closed gently over her breasts it was her turn to shudder. She was so exquisitely sensitive now that she didn't think she could stand a more intimate touch. Along with that realization came the knowledge that she did not have to hold back tonight. There was no need for control, not with this man.

She eased her hands up under the edge of his T-shirt. His body was a furnace. She savored the feel of muscle beneath warm skin.

He drew the pads of his thumbs across her nipples and then he slid his fingers down her ribs to the curve of her hips. He peeled off the pajama bottoms and let the garment fall to her ankles.

The next thing she knew he was lifting her out of the puddle of flannel and carrying her across the room. She braced her hands on his shoulders to steady herself.

He lowered her onto the tumbled bed. She knelt there and watched as he yanked off the T-shirt and undid the front of his trousers.

His briefs disappeared next. She was fascinated by the thick, rigid length of his erection. She watched as he sheathed himself in a condom. When he was ready she reached out and encircled him with her fingers. A shudder went through him. His aura ignited with the energy of his desire.

Her senses rose to the challenge. She had never been free to let herself go with a lover. She had learned the hard way that abandoning herself to the moment was a surefire way to kill a perfectly good relationship. The three categories of bedroom disasters whispered in the atmosphere. *I need discipline. You're a real control freak, aren't you?* And last, but the most chilling of all: *Maybe you should see a therapist about your inability to have an orgasm.*

"I told you this morning you are so damn hot you could probably set the house on fire," Slater said. "I was wrong."

"Were you?" she asked.

"We'll be lucky if the whole damn town doesn't go up in flames tonight."

She laughed and tightened her grip on him. He gave a low growl and came down on top of her, flattening her onto her back and pinning her to the bed. He took her mouth again, insisting on a response. She dug her nails into the skin of his back.

He stroked one hand down the length of her to the inside of her thigh. She knew she was melting. When he clamped his hand around her core she closed her eyes and lifted her hips off the bed.

"So wet," he said against her throat. "For me."

She was beyond speech now so she twisted against his hand, demanding ever more intimate contact. He stroked her until she would have screamed had she been able to draw enough breath. The tension built rapidly deep inside her. She clutched at him, demanding more.

When he slid two fingers deep inside her she convulsed. The climax rolled through her in waves.

He guided himself into her before she had finished, sinking deep. It was too much. She was sure that she would shatter. A second wave rippled through her.

He surged into her again and again. The muscles of his back were granite hard. She wrapped her legs around him. His release slammed through him. She heard his muffled roar and realized that he had buried his face in the pillow beside her to quiet the sound.

They collapsed together into the sweat-dampened sheets.

Catalina opened her eyes and looked up at the shadowed ceiling. They had not set the house or the town on fire, but it had been a very close call.

CHAPTER 28

He lay quietly, aware of the satisfying warmth and softness of Catalina's curves, the primal scents of lovemaking in the atmosphere and the utter relaxation that was flooding his body. It occurred to him that he could not remember the last time he had felt this Zen-like sense of inner balance. The more he thought about it, the more certain he was that he had never experienced it, not even before the disaster six months earlier.

"Oomph." Catalina's voice was muffled.

"What?"

"You have to move," Catalina said. "This is a very small bed and you are taking up most of it."

He realized she was wriggling underneath him.

"Sorry," he said.

Reluctantly he rolled off her.

. . . And slid off the edge of the narrow mattress. He landed on the floor.

"Slater." Catalina sat up quickly, holding the sheet to her throat. "Are you okay?"

"Yes and no." He got to his feet. "I am definitely awake. You're right. That is a very narrow bed. Be back in a minute."

He wandered into the tiny bathroom and spent a few minutes inside. When he returned to the bedroom he saw that Catalina was on her feet, pulling on her pajamas. A wave of regret welled up inside him.

"I take it you're not into enjoying the postcoital glow thing?" he said.

She flashed him a smile that lit up the shadows. "Is that what you call it?"

"For want of a more eloquent phrase."

"Just so you know, I am enjoying it." She slid her feet into some fluffy slippers. "Enormously. How long does it last?"

"What?"

"It's the first time I've experienced it," she said. She headed for the door. "I'm not sure what to expect."

She went out into the hall. He gathered up his clothes and went after her.

"Where are you going?" he asked.

"To your bed. It's a double. Much bigger than mine."

His mood abruptly reversed course. Once again he was in his new happy place, the territory that he had just discovered and could not wait to explore.

"Well, why didn't you say so?" he said.

She glanced back at him over her shoulder, eyes sultry, mysterious and inviting.

"I just did," she said.

She went into the darkened bedroom she had given him earlier, kicked off her slippers, removed her pajamas and burrowed under the sheet and the heavy quilt.

His night was getting better by the minute.

He dumped his clothes onto the nearest chair and climbed into bed. He pulled her into his arms so that she sprawled on top of him.

"What did you mean when you said you hadn't ever experienced a postcoital glow?" he asked.

She folded her arms on top of his chest and watched him with her witchy eyes.

"I've always had a problem in this department," she said. "No, that's not right. Men usually have a problem with me when it comes to this kind of thing."

"Yeah?"

"Some of them are convinced that I'm in the dominatrix business, which, while it certainly has some novelty appeal, gets awfully boring after a while, at least from my end. Then there are those who think I should get counseling to help me learn how to have an orgasm. But I actually do know how to do that."

"Because you're smart."

"Right. All it took was a little research online and a small battery-powered appliance. But I think it's safe to say that the most common reason I've had a problem in this department is because a lot of men decide I'm just flat-out scary in bed. They decide I'm a control freak, but that's not really the issue."

"Your aura?"

"Yep. If it gets a little too hot, men who don't understand what's going on tend to freak out."

"And the ones who do understand get nervous."

"Not you."

He slid his palm down her back to the curve of her hip.

"No," he said. "Not me."

"Well, there you have it, the history of my sex life. It's why I've been learning to enjoy the pleasures of celibacy for the past six months."

"Since you and that consultant Gossard ended things?"

"Yes."

"Funny you should mention the joys of celibacy. I've been exploring that option myself. Ever since my uncles let me out of the attic."

"Was there anyone special before your talent changed?" Catalina asked.

"I thought so. Her name was Roanna Powell. She works in one of the research labs at the Foundation."

"Ah. So the two of you had a lot in common?"

"Yes. Seemed like a good match. Our families all approved. But after I spent that month in the attic she changed her mind."

"Did she visit you while you were locked up?" Catalina asked.

"One time. There were a lot of rumors flying around the Foundation. People were saying that something terrible had happened on my last case and that I was going to end up in Halcyon Manor. Roanna had every reason to be worried, not just about me but about her own future with me. She demanded to see me. My uncles agreed to a short visit."

"I take it the visit didn't go well."

"I managed to hold it together while she was there but she could tell something had changed, and the change scared her. When she found out I was being treated for uncontrolled hallucinations, she decided I was too much of a risk."

"I'm sorry," Catalina said. "Breakups are tough."

"They happen."

"True."

"How serious was your relationship with Gossard?"

"I thought things were going well," Catalina said. "Roger didn't beg me to dress up in leather. He didn't accuse me of being a control freak. The best part was that I think he has just enough natural talent himself to realize that I'm not a fraud. I didn't have to hide my psychic side from him. He was okay with it. More than okay. I think he got a bit of a thrill out of it."

"In bed?"

"We never got quite that far. My fault, not Roger's. I'm a little risk-averse in that department. Present circumstances excepted."

"The present circumstances are definitely exceptional. I've been damn risk-averse myself for the past six months."

"I was getting ready to take the next step in the relationship," Catalina said. "But your uncle showed up. After I was outed as a psychic, albeit a fake one, I became a professional liability, a threat to Roger's precious brand. His consulting firm is all about doing state-of-the-art forensic consulting. He would have lost a lot of credibility if word spread that he relied on a woman who claimed to be psychic. So of course he had to end our relationship."

"And of course you had every right to be pissed."

"I was angry and hurt at first, but afterward I realized I was mostly annoyed with myself. I should have realized right from the start that he didn't really care for me. He was just using me. He knew I didn't like the work so he figured out real fast that he could persuade me to do more of it if I was involved in a relationship with him. I helped him solve a couple of high-profile cases."

"In other words, you helped him establish his brand in the world of law enforcement."

"Yes. I think I knew, deep down, that what Roger and I had probably wouldn't last forever, but I wanted to believe we had as much going for us as other couples."

"You leaped to that insightful conclusion because he didn't want you to play the part of a dominatrix, didn't call you a control freak and was able to accept your talent? That's it? That's all you had?"

"What can I tell you? It seemed like a reasonably good foundation for a relationship."

Slater caught her head between his palms.

"Guess what?" he said. "We've got all that and more going for us."

"More?"

"The really hot sex."

"Oh," she said. "Right. I forgot about that."

"Allow me to remind you."

He eased her onto her back. Bracing himself on his elbows, he lowered his mouth to hers. When she opened her senses he felt the energy rise in the atmosphere. His own senses surged in response.

"Catalina," he said.

"Yes," she said.

It was enough, he told himself. For tonight.

———————

The pounding on the front door brought Slater out of the drowsy aftermath of the lovemaking. Next to him, Catalina sat up quickly.

"The door," she said.

"I'll get it."

Slater rolled to his feet and reached for his trousers and his gun.

The pounding sounded again. This time a muffled voice accompanied it.

"Catalina, it's me, Harmony."

"Maybe she found the twins," Catalina said.

He went out into the front room, twitched the curtains aside and checked the front porch. Harmony must have sensed him, because she pushed back the hood of her cloak so he could see her face in the porch light. She looked straight at him. Her gaze was unnerving, as if she saw things no one else could see. *Oracle.*

He dropped the curtain and opened the front door. Harmony swept into the room, the long cloak whipping around her high boots. She glanced pointedly at the gun.

"You won't be needing that," she said coldly. "Didn't Catalina tell you Fogg Lake is a crime-free zone?"

"Except for the occasional vanishing act," Slater said.

"About that," Harmony said. "I may have found something interesting."

"The twins?" Catalina hurried out of the bedroom, tying the sash of her robe. "Were you able to identify them?"

"I found some interesting descendants of a man named Harkins who was living here in Fogg Lake at the time of the Incident. He moved away a few years later and died decades ago. But according to the ancestry charts, one of his offspring gave birth to identical triplets about thirty years ago."

"Triplets?" Slater said.

"Did not see that coming," Catalina said.

"Got a photo?" Slater said.

"Yes, but only because one of the triplets did time," Harmony said. "My predecessor in this job was good. She made a copy of the mug shot and stuck it in the file."

Harmony brought an envelope out from under her cloak.

Slater opened the envelope. Catalina hurried across the room to see the photo. The image of a young man of about twenty gazed back at them with soulless eyes.

"Add about a decade and he looks exactly like one of the guys who tried to grab Catalina in Seattle," Slater said. "What did he do time for?"

"Drugs," Harmony said. "According to the file he was selling some kind of designer crap."

"Thanks," Catalina said. "This is very helpful."

Slater looked at Harmony. "Why didn't you call?"

Harmony shrugged. "Phones are down. Even with landlines it's tough to keep them working in this town. Euclid and the others will take care of things in the morning. Well, if that's all you need, I'll be on my way."

"I'll walk you back to your place," Slater said.

"No, you won't," Harmony said. "You need to get to work. Don't worry about me. I live at the other end of the street."

She strode to the door and opened it before Slater could reach it. She switched on a flashlight and went down the front steps.

Slater moved out onto the front porch. Catalina followed. Together they watched the beam of Harmony's flashlight move through the fog-bound street until it disappeared into a building at the far end. A short time later a light glowed in an upstairs window.

"That's the library," Catalina said.

"She lives in the town library?" Slater asked.

"The Oracle always lives in the rooms above the library," Catalina said. "There aren't a lot of perks for someone in that position. It's often a rather depressing job. So for as long as anyone can remember the town has provided the free apartment."

They went back inside, then closed and locked the door.

"Triplets," Slater said. "Damn. That means there are two more of those blanks out there."

"The third one may not be a blank," Catalina pointed out.

"Are you kidding? With the way our luck has been running lately?"

"Those of us with a strong psychic vibe do not believe in luck, remember?"

"Speak for yourself," Slater said.

He went into the bedroom and returned with his pack. He put the gun on the counter, within easy reach, and took a notebook and a pen out of the pack.

"Got a sheet of paper?" he asked. "Or, better yet, a map of the Fogg Lake area?"

"There are no maps of Fogg Lake," Catalina said. "It's against the town council's rules."

"Why?"

"A, because no one around here needs one. B, there is a prevailing belief that maps might fall into the wrong hands and encourage tourism. The lake. The caves. The woods. It's all stuff that campers and hikers love."

"No maps," Slater said. "All right, we'll have to draw our own. That means we'll need the sheet of paper."

"My mom always keeps a sketchbook here. She likes to draw. I'll see what I can find."

Catalina went down the hall and opened a closet door. When she returned to the kitchen a moment later she held out a sketchbook.

"Will this do?" she asked.

Slater flipped through a few of the pages. A frisson of certainty flashed across his senses.

"These are all scenes of the Fogg Lake area?" he asked.

"Yes."

"This is better than a map. The drawings are superior to photographs in many ways. Your mother has a great eye for detail."

"Why do you need a map or those sketches?" Catalina asked.

"Because I've had what we in the psychic investigation business like to call a blinding flash of the obvious."

"And?"

"I should have seen it earlier," Slater said. "In fact, I think I did see it earlier, in a dream that I had on the way here. But I was too exhausted to pay attention to what my intuition was trying to tell me."

"What are you talking about?"

He looked at her. The whispers got louder.

"Drugs," he said.

"What about them?"

"They keep showing up in this case. Specifically high-tech drugs, the kind that come out of a sophisticated lab. We need to focus on them. They are the key to identifying the person who is behind everything that has happened."

CHAPTER 29

Catalina sat down on the stool next to him and watched him page through the sketchbook. She could feel the hot energy in the atmosphere around him and recognized the sensation. She had experienced it herself on a few occasions. Slater was a hunter closing in on prey.

"Tell me where you're going with this new theory of yours," she said.

"Exotic drugs have been involved from the start," he said. "Someone supplied the killer with whatever was in that syringe that was used to murder Morrissey."

"Right. But so what? There are any number of drugs that can kill a person."

"Yes, but it's not a typical method of committing murder. Most killers go with the tried-and-true options: A gun. A knife. A blunt object. Why fool around with some exotic drug unless you're afraid the body might be found? But in this case whoever murdered

Morrissey didn't seem to be worried about that. He planned all along to dump the body in the river."

"Maybe the killer had a medical background and felt comfortable using some toxic drug."

"Or else he had connections to the illicit drug–dealing business. Needles are often used to inject dangerous substances."

"Huh," Catalina said. "Now fifteen years later it looks like Ingram and Royston were murdered with drugs, and Olivia is kidnapped and also injected with some unknown drug—presumably not a lethal one, because whoever grabbed her wanted her alive."

"Then you and I start to investigate and we are attacked with a gas that causes violent hallucinations. But it isn't lethal, either."

"Because they didn't want to kill me. They wanted to take me alive."

"Tonight we find out that one of the triplets from hell did time for selling drugs," Slater continued. "Not just the standard street shit. Designer drugs."

A feverish chill crackled across Catalina's senses. It came straight from her nightmares. *You don't want to go back there. That way lies madness. You will throw yourself into the lake and drown.*

She met Slater's eyes. "You're going with the theory that the many drug connections in this case are not a coincidence."

"I'm not big on coincidences, but even if I was okay with that possibility, there is another factor that has to be taken into account."

"I'm listening."

"Whatever was in that fog the kidnappers used on us in Royston's cellar did not simply knock us out," Slater said. "It played havoc with our paranormal senses."

"There are a lot of drugs that can produce hallucinations. LSD, for example. There must be dozens more."

"Yes, but *weaponizing* them, making them into a potent gas that can swamp the senses of a couple of strong talents in a matter of seconds, isn't that simple. It would take the skill set of an experienced individual with a sophisticated lab and a working knowledge of how various drugs affect people with talent."

You don't want to go back there.

Catalina sat quietly for a moment, processing what Slater had just said.

"My turn to get hit with a blinding flash of the obvious," she said. "Maybe."

"What?"

"If the appearance of drugs is not a coincidence in this case, if you're on the right track here, then we shouldn't overlook the one other time they showed up."

"When was that?"

"Back at the start," Catalina said.

She told him about the possibility that had just occurred to her. When she was finished, Slater nodded, satisfied.

"That fits," he said. "And your theory has one other thing going for it. I knew there had to be a local connection. This is it."

CHAPTER 30

consider myself a naturally suspicious person," Catalina said. "I'm an investigator, after all. But I have to tell you that until you insisted that the accomplice had to be local and that there was a high probability of a drug connection, Nyla Trevelyan would not have been at the top of my list of suspects. I mean, she's the local *healer*. A lot of people in this town are very grateful for her skills."

They were standing outside Nyla Trevelyan's small vine-covered cottage. Fog cloaked the scene, but it was possible to make out the small SUV that Nyla used to transport her homeopathic medicines and herbal tonics to craft fairs. The only electric light was the one that glowed above the door on the front porch. It illuminated the pots of thriving herbs and the spectacular ferns that crammed the space and bordered the steps.

But electricity wasn't the only source of illumination around the cottage. The lush gardens sparkled faintly with what looked like fairy lights. Nyla had planted several varieties of the local foliage that gave off a faint glow after dark.

"I remember my parents saying Nyla was trained as a botanist," Catalina said.

"That explains a lot," Slater said.

While the gardens around the cottage emitted an eerie, otherworldly light, the windows of the house were dark. If Nyla was inside, she was asleep like most of the other inhabitants of Fogg Lake.

"With her extensive knowledge of local herbs and her experience treating people with talent, she would have known exactly what to put in that tisane you and Olivia were given after you came out of the cave," Slater said.

"She administered the first couple of doses to both of us personally," Catalina said. "I think she tried to plant a strong hypnotic suggestion at the same time: *You don't want to go back there. That way lies madness. If you try to go back you will fall into the lake and drown.* Olivia and I have often wondered why our dreams of that night were so similar."

"The tisane must have had hypnotic properties," Slater said.

"Nyla left packets of the herbs with our parents and instructed them to give us two doses a day for at least ten days. Afterward Olivia and I became increasingly confused by our memories. Eventually we tried to convince ourselves that maybe the adults were right. Maybe we had imagined everything that happened that night. But as we got older we compared our memories and our dreams. There were so many similarities that we decided we really had witnessed the murder. We were never entirely certain about the Devil's Ballroom, though."

"Did you ever try to convince your parents or the people of Fogg Lake that you were right about what happened that night?" Slater asked.

"No. There didn't seem to be any point. They would have wanted some proof, and we had none. So Olivia and I kept our secrets. After we left town, neither of us came back here very often. We never went back into the caves."

"That is probably what saved your lives," Slater said. "Until now you were not a threat."

"That's just it," Catalina said. "We haven't ever been a threat, because no one here believed us."

"What's changed is that someone has figured out that you and Olivia found the old Fogg Lake lab that night."

"How?"

"That is one of the questions Trevelyan is going to answer for us," Slater said.

"What makes you think she'll tell us anything?" Catalina asked. "It would mean admitting she was involved in a murder and a kidnapping."

"I think she'll talk to us," Slater said.

"Because of your new talent?"

"If that doesn't work, there's always the staff at Halcyon Manor."

Catalina realized she was gritting her teeth. "And you and your uncles wonder why the citizens of our fair town don't invite the Foundation authorities to the annual Fogg Lake Days celebration."

"I think Uncle Victor would settle for a little cooperation from time to time, especially when murder is involved," Slater said.

"I tried the cooperation thing six months ago. It didn't go well for me."

"We can talk about that later. At the moment we've got other priorities."

They went up the front steps of the cottage. Slater rapped sharply on the door.

There was no response. Slater knocked again.

A deep silence echoed inside the cottage. Slater tried the door-knob. It turned easily in his hand.

"She didn't lock her door," Slater said. "Guess she didn't pay attention to the Oracle tonight."

Flattening his back against the wall, Slater pushed open the door. Catalina was braced for gunfire or some other unpleasant surprise, but there was only silence. She heightened her senses and knew that Slater had done the same. He risked a quick glance inside. If there was someone concealed in the shadows inside the cottage, the individual's aura would be visible.

"I don't see anyone," he said. "Stay here. I'll take a look around inside."

"I'm coming with you. Nyla is probably asleep. The last thing you want to do is walk into her bedroom and scare her. She may be innocent. We still don't have any proof that she's the one behind this."

Slater hesitated. "All right. But no more high-risk moves like the one you made at Royston's place."

"It worked, didn't it?"

"Don't remind me."

Slater reached around the corner and groped for and found a switch. A lamp came on in the small living room and kitchen area. No one jumped out of a closet with a gun. No one sprayed them with toxic fog. The silence just got deeper.

"She's gone," Catalina said. "You can feel the emptiness."

"We need to be sure."

They went down the short hall, pausing to check the tiny bathroom. In the bedroom Slater hit another switch. This time an overhead fixture came on, revealing a neatly made-up bed.

"There's one other place we can check," Catalina said. "Nyla has an old-fashioned stillroom off the kitchen. It's where she concocts her herbal products."

They went back down the hall and through the small kitchen and opened the door. What had once been the back porch of the cottage had been closed in with glass to create a quaint little stillroom. The scents of lavender, roses and peppermint drifted in the atmosphere. The room shivered with a gentle paranormal vibe. Bundles of dried herbs dangled upside down from the low roof. Empty jars sat on a shelf, waiting to be filled with creams and lotions.

Slater moved to a workbench and examined the burner and the simple equipment that Nyla used to process herbs into essential oils, tisanes and other concoctions.

"This is all pretty low-tech," he said. "Hard to imagine that she could produce the sophisticated stuff used on us with this basic equipment."

"Maybe we're wrong about her."

"You said Trevelyan made periodic trips out of town to sell her products. It would be easy for her to purchase lab equipment while she was away."

"Sure, but I'm telling you, if she had a more sophisticated lab anywhere around Fogg Lake, everyone in town would know about it."

"Not," Slater said, "if it was hidden in the caves."

Icy fingers touched the back of Catalina's neck. "If you're right, maybe that's where she's hiding Olivia."

Slater did not respond. He was opening and closing drawers, checking out the contents.

"Receipts, notebooks filled with data about the local plants, flyers about upcoming craft fairs." Slater tossed several papers aside. He picked up a booklet and flipped through it. "Here we go."

"What?" Catalina said.

"It's a catalog of lab equipment. Some of the items are circled." Slater looked up briefly, taking in the glass beakers and the simple burner on the workbench. "I don't see any of these things here. She's got another lab, Catalina. That's the only explanation that fits the facts."

"How are we going to find it?"

"With your mother's sketches and the map we are going to draw," Slater said.

CHAPTER 31

They made their way back to the Lark house to embark on the creation of a map. The process went quickly. Less than an hour later Catalina sat beside Slater at the dining bar and watched Slater study the rough sketch of Fogg Lake and the surrounding countryside. Her memories combined with her mother's drawings had provided a remarkably accurate rendering of the area, but it only served to illustrate just how daunting the task of locating Nyla Trevelyan's lab—assuming it existed—would be.

"Talk about a needle in a haystack." Catalina looked at the map. "It would be easy to conceal a drug lab anywhere inside the caves."

"We've got a few facts to work with," Slater said. "We know that the lab has to be within a reasonably short walking distance." He looked up. "Unless Trevelyan is in the habit of disappearing overnight?"

"Not that I know of, except when she goes down the mountain to the craft fairs," Catalina said. "But she only does that a few times a year."

Slater tapped the tip of the pen against the map, thinking about it. "You said she has lived here for years?"

"Yes. I think she moved here about five years before Olivia and I witnessed the murder."

"She's had a couple of decades to get to know the caves and the woods."

"She's probably quite familiar with the woods, but I very much doubt that she's gone deep into the caves. No one does. The radiation is just too intense."

"A lot of heat would probably have unpredictable effects on any drugs that she might be producing. That tells us her lab is probably well hidden, but not far inside the cave complex."

"Even if you allow for a relatively short hike to one of the entrances to the caves, you're not talking about a stroll in the park," Catalina said. "It's more of a trek. The terrain is very rugged. There is a decent trail from town to the lake and another that leads to the entrance of what we call the Freak Zone complex, where the murder occurred, but that's about it. This area is riddled with caves."

"If we're right about any of this, Trevelyan needs a cave entrance large enough to allow her to come and go with her lab equipment."

"That still leaves a lot of options for her," Catalina warned.

"It's a good bet that she's been running her drug operation for years," Slater continued. "You don't invent exotic street pharmaceuticals and hallucinogenic gases over the course of a long weekend."

"What are you getting at?"

"There will be a trail," Slater said. "And I think it will be very, very hot, because tonight she realized we are closing in on her. That's why she ran. She's probably in a state of high anxiety or maybe outright panic. She'll head for the one place she feels safe."

Catalina hopped off the stool and began pulling on her trench coat. "If there is a hot trail, it will start at her cottage. If she used the path tonight, the tracks will probably still be fresh enough for me to identify them. We have to hurry."

She grabbed her day pack and a flashlight and headed for the door.

"Not so fast," Slater said. But he was on his feet, too, shrugging into his jacket. He grabbed his pack with the vintage phone and the contacts file and picked up the gun he had placed on the counter. "If we do find her, she may have a couple of Marge's clones with her. We need backup."

"We'll wake up Euclid Oaks and some of the others," Catalina said. "They've all got guns and they know how to use them. They will help us if we convince them that we may have a lead on Olivia's whereabouts."

The lights inside the house and the lamp on the porch winked out just as Catalina opened the front door. The sudden fall of darkness and the blinding glare of a powerful flashlight had a brief but disorienting effect on her heightened senses. It took her a beat to realize there was a figure standing on the front porch.

"I've been waiting for you, Catalina," Nyla Trevelyan said.

CHAPTER 32

As far as Catalina could tell, Nyla Trevelyan was not armed with anything other than a flashlight, but she was not alone. Two auras, each with the signature pale wavelengths of true blanks, blazed in the shadows on either side of the door.

One of them aimed his weapon at Slater.

The auras of the two triplets were strikingly similar but there were some small, subtle differences. No two people were ever exactly the same individuals, after all.

"Which one of you is Tony?" Slater asked in a disturbingly casual voice.

"That would be me," Tony said. "I hear the cleaners got Deke. You're gonna pay for that."

"Nothing like a little brotherly solidarity," Slater said. He glanced at the second man. "So you're Clone C."

"What the fuck are you talking about? I'm Jared. Want me to do him now, Nyla?"

"Not yet, you idiot," Nyla snapped. "And not with a gun. Are you crazy? You'll wake the entire town."

"I told you we might need another dose of the drug," Tony grumbled.

"Even if we had brought it with us, we couldn't use it here," Nyla said. "We don't have time to get rid of the body. We'll deal with Arganbright later."

"Where is Olivia?" Catalina asked.

"Don't worry, you'll see her soon," Nyla said. "Let's go."

"This is working out nicely," Slater said. "We won't have to waste time stumbling around in the woods trying to follow your trail."

"What trail?" Tony demanded.

"Ignore him," Nyla said. "Can't you see he's just trying to rattle you so that you'll get careless? Speaking of careless, one of you search him for a gun. Hurry."

"Hands on top of your head," Jared said.

Slater raised his hands. "Under my jacket."

Jared found the pistol and took it. Catalina felt a new chill in the atmosphere and knew that Slater had raised his talent. But he made no move to try to ice Jared.

"Let's get going," Tony muttered. "It's fucking cold out here. Feels like the temperature dropped about twenty degrees."

"Follow me," Nyla said. "Keep a close eye on both of them. And try not to lose sight of me, all right? If you do you'll get lost within about thirty seconds in this fog. I do not have time to look for you."

"Yeah, yeah," Jared said. "Let's get going before it gets any colder."

Nyla took off, setting a brisk pace. Catalina and Slater followed. The two triplets brought up the rear, guns and flashlights firmly fixed on their captives.

The fog was very heavy now, but it was infused with the ambient glow of some of the foliage in the woods. Here and there fluorescing creepers and vines climbed trees and rocks, providing Fogg Lake's version of streetlights.

Catalina kept her senses only partially elevated, trying not to waste energy that she might need later. But she could feel the heat, old and new, on the path they were walking.

"You've come this way many times, Nyla," she said quietly.

"For more than fifteen years," Nyla said. "Ever since I found the infirmary."

"What infirmary?" Catalina asked.

"You'll see. I realized at the time that I had discovered a small chamber that originally had been connected to the main facility of the Fogg Lake lab. I have been searching for the rest of the lab ever since."

"You thought John Morrissey could find it for you," Slater said.

"Morrissey worked for the Foundation, but he had a nice little drug operation going on the side. He used to purchase specimens from me."

"Are you trying to tell us you and Morrissey were business colleagues?" Catalina said.

"More like competitors," Slater said. "Right, Trevelyan?"

"Yes," Nyla said. "But for a time our interests were aligned."

"You became allies?" Catalina said.

"Morrissey certainly thought so," Nyla said. "But it would be more accurate to say that I found him useful. Morrissey wasn't a botanist. He got into the drug business to finance his private research. He was convinced he had found a way to tune a kind of paranormal compass so that it could be used to navigate the caves. He was sure he could find the main lab facility here in Fogg Lake with it."

"But unfortunately the person who accompanied him that night fifteen years ago acted too quickly," Catalina said. "He murdered Morrissey and then he realized there were witnesses."

"You and Olivia," Nyla agreed. "I should have gone into the caves myself that night, but I didn't want to take any chances. I stayed with the boat."

"You did not want to leave a hot trail behind inside the caves in case someone from the Foundation showed up to investigate," Slater said. "I knew there had to be a local connection."

"For nearly two decades I've been trapped here in Fogg Lake," Nyla said. "I've been afraid to leave for more than a few days at a time because I've been terrified the bastards at the Foundation would realize I didn't die in that lab fire that killed my bastard of a husband and his girlfriend."

"Well, damn," Slater said softly. "You're Alma York, aren't you? The chemist who murdered her husband and two women in one of the Foundation labs twenty years ago."

"He was fucking that bitch," Nyla said, her voice tight with fury. "I trusted both of them. Helen made me believe that she was my best friend. I actually thought Greg loved me. The three of us had a nice little drug business going."

"You're in this for the *money*?" Catalina said, shocked. "You're a *scientist*."

Nyla reacted with genuine outrage. "The street drugs were supposed to finance our real work after the three of us left the Foundation. We knew we had to get out while we could because the Rancourts had found out about the drug business and wanted a cut. Helen and Greg and I had a plan. We were going to disappear and set up a lab on a private island. We would do brilliant research in the field of paranormal drugs. Then I found Greg and Helen in bed together. They were planning to set me up. They said they didn't need me. I acted first. Self-defense."

"But you botched the job," Slater said. "I'm told the explosion in the lab was impressive, and so was the fire that followed. You even made sure the remains of three bodies were found in the wreckage, one male and two females. Who was the other woman, by the way?

Uncle Victor and Uncle Lucas opened an investigation after they took over the Foundation, but they were never able to identify her."

"She was just an addict who had been living on the streets for years," Nyla said. "She was about my size and age. I didn't think your uncles would go to the trouble of running a DNA test. The Rancourts certainly didn't give a damn."

"You don't know Victor and Lucas very well," Slater said. "They told me they were suspicious from the start. But the case had gone very cold by the time Victor became director. He and Lucas didn't have a lot to go on."

"I thought I could just disappear," Nyla said. "I had cosmetic surgery to change my face. I got a new identity. But I never felt safe. All these years I've been looking over my shoulder, watching for those damn cleaners."

"So you sought refuge in Fogg Lake," Catalina said. "The one place you assumed the Foundation would probably never think to look for you."

"And even if they did send someone, you would have plenty of warning," Slater added. "Because this is a close-knit community. Everyone knows everyone else, and the community as a whole regards the Foundation with deep suspicion."

"You created the perfect cover for yourself," Catalina said. "You became the local healer."

"I hate this town," Nyla said.

"What was in that tisane you made for Olivia and me?" Catalina asked.

"A hallucinogen that had the benefit of making users confuse their memories with dreams," Nyla said. "I tried to add a hypnotic suggestion, too. But there was no way to know how long the effects would last."

Catalina sensed the strange stillness that signaled the fog-bound lake. She was very glad Nyla was in the lead, because walking along the water's edge was dangerous enough in the daytime. At night it was foolhardy.

Nyla stopped in front of a mass of vines that glowed with a faint blue sheen. She pulled the greenery aside as if it were a curtain. Catalina saw the rowboat.

"Be careful when you get in," Nyla said. "If you go overboard it's very unlikely that you'll come out alive. In fact, they probably won't even find your body."

She made sure Catalina, Slater and the two clones were seated before she carefully got aboard herself. She untied the rope that secured the craft to the trunk of a tree. She sat down in the back of the boat and picked up a long pole.

Catalina held her breath as Nyla used the pole to guide the rowboat toward the entrance of a partially flooded cave.

The boat glided silently into the deep darkness of a cavern. Tony switched on a flashlight, revealing the tunnel walls. In several places, large stalactites and rocky outcroppings loomed dangerously low over the water.

"Keep your heads down," Nyla advised. "It's a little tight in places."

Catalina shivered. Even though it was cold, she was sweating. It helped that the boat was moving, but the unrelenting darkness all around combined with the unknown depths of the cave river was unnerving. She focused on the thought that she would see Olivia soon. Unless Nyla was lying.

"When did you realize Catalina and Olivia had discovered the main lab facility on the night Morrissey was murdered?" Slater asked.

"Not until a few days ago," Nyla said. "I finally tracked down one of the old logbooks from the Fogg Lake facility. It described the generator chamber the lab had constructed. I could not believe that all those years ago I had come so close to what I'd been looking for. But at the time I thought the girls really were hallucinating when they described what they called a ballroom."

"You looked for the logbook first in Ingram's collection, didn't you?" Catalina said.

"There were rumors that he had just acquired a cache of valuable Fogg Lake lab artifacts," Nyla said. "There were several interesting items in his vault, but nothing that described the generator chamber or anything else that was useful."

"But six months later you heard more rumors," Slater said. "This time it was about Royston's collection. You talked him into showing you the items in his vault. When you saw the logbook you knew it was what you were looking for."

"Everyone in the artifacts world knew that Royston was a very careful man. He wouldn't let someone he did not know into his vault. So I sent another collector to see him, someone he considered a rival. Royston was only too happy to show off the latest additions to his vault."

"That person murdered Royston and stole the logbook," Slater said, "and probably several other artifacts as well."

"The only thing I cared about was the logbook," Nyla said. "It recorded the results of several experiments conducted in a special power-generating chamber developed in the Fogg Lake lab."

"It was the description of the chamber that made you realize Catalina and Olivia had found it fifteen years ago," Slater said.

"Fifteen years *wasted*."

"You sent the clones to grab Olivia and me in Seattle," Catalina said.

"What's with the clone shit?" Jared demanded.

Catalina ignored him. "They succeeded in kidnapping Olivia, but by the time they came for me, Slater had arrived on the scene."

"I swear, it seems that everything that could have gone wrong with this project has gone wrong," Nyla said. "But now I've got you and Olivia, who, I'm sorry to say, hasn't been of much help."

"Maybe because you shot her full of drugs?" Catalina asked.

"Conducting experiments on human subjects is something of a challenge around here," Nyla admitted. "I may have had the team use a little too much of the drug on Olivia. It's been two days and she's still groggy and delusional. Now that I've got you I won't have to take the risk of making a similar mistake."

"Why should either of us help you find the main lab facility?" Catalina asked. "You'll just murder us afterward."

"No," Nyla said. "I will give you a dose of the drug that I gave you fifteen years ago. You'll get the two-point-oh version. I've perfected it. You won't remember anything this time."

It didn't take paranormal-grade intuition to know that Nyla was lying, but Catalina kept her mouth shut. The atmosphere got a little colder. Slater had jacked up his talent again.

They rounded a bend in the underground river. Artificial light glowed inside the entrance of what looked like a man-made tunnel.

"There's the infirmary," Jared said. "About time."

He sounded hugely relieved. *He isn't the only one,* Catalina thought.

Seconds later the boat bumped gently against an old wooden dock.

Nyla got out first and dealt with the ropes. Catalina stood and stepped carefully onto the dock. Jared and Tony followed. When they were safely out of the boat they ordered Slater to stand and step onto the dock.

Catalina followed Nyla through the opening and stopped at the sight of the large chamber inside. It was furnished with a lot of metal and glass cabinets and workbenches that all appeared to be the same vintage as the items in the ruins of the old power generator control room. The chemistry apparatus on the workbenches, however, looked modern and sophisticated.

On one side of the room a figure huddled under a thin blanket on an old-fashioned hospital gurney.

"Olivia." Catalina started toward her.

"Stop," Nyla said. "Or I will give her a dose of the same thing that was used on Royston and Ingram."

Catalina halted.

Olivia sat up suddenly. "Cat. I was afraid she would get you, too. Meet the mad scientist of Fogg Lake. All these years we thought she was such a nice person. You'd think a town full of people with good intuition could have figured it out sooner."

"Shut up," Nyla ordered.

Catalina rounded on her. "How could you do this, Nyla? You've known Olivia and me since we were kids. You know our parents. You're a *healer*. How can you betray your friends like this? Fogg Lake took you in and sheltered you."

"Only because the people in this town desperately needed someone who didn't think they were all crazy, someone who knew how to treat their parapsych problems. They thought it was safe to let me live here because I was alone. I wasn't a threat."

"Any way you look at it, Fogg Lake has been a refuge for you," Catalina said. "This is how you repay the town?"

"I said *shut up*." Nyla's voice rose in a shriek that sounded precariously unstable. She regained control and glared at Olivia. "Congratulations on your remarkable recovery. You're a very good actress, I'll give you that. But now that I have Catalina, I no longer have any reason to keep you alive. If you want to live through this, you will do exactly as you're told."

CHAPTER 33

Slater stood quietly absorbing the heavy vibes of the various artifacts in the chamber. It was not unlike the sensation he got when
he was inside the vault of a collector or when he went down into
the basement of Gwendolyn Swan's antiques shop. But everything in
this room was a whole lot hotter. He was trying to figure out why.

It made sense that there would be some strong energy in the atmosphere. The infirmary was, after all, part of the Fogg Lake lab. In
addition, Nyla had been using the chamber to conduct experiments
involving chemicals with paranormal properties for years. That
meant everything in the room had been exposed to a lot of ambient
radiation.

But there was a current of unstable energy just under the surface.
His paranormal senses reacted to it the same way his normal senses
would have if he had entered a room and caught the scent of smoke.
He heightened his talent a little more and looked around, trying to
identify the artifact that was giving off the ominous vibe. It took

him a moment to realize that it was coming from a pile of plastic packets that were filled with some white powder. The products of Nyla's drug lab, no doubt.

Tony shifted uneasily.

"Can't you turn up the heat in here?" he said to Nyla.

Slater spoke before Nyla could respond.

"Mind explaining how you got the clones in and out of Fogg Lake without anyone noticing?" he asked. "In fact, how did you get Ms. LeClair here?"

Nyla flashed him an impatient look. "Why do you keep calling Tony and Jared clones?"

"It's not important," Slater said. "But I will admit I'm damned curious about how you were able to operate this lab and bring people in and out of the area without drawing the attention of the locals."

Nyla's mouth curved in an icy smile. "The partially flooded tunnel we used to get here continues for quite some distance underground. It's navigable the entire way in a small boat. The exit point is concealed inside another cavern on the far side of the lake. There's an abandoned logging road there that eventually connects to the old road down the mountain."

"What changed?" Slater asked. "I assume something happened to convince you that it was worth taking the risk of kidnapping Olivia and Catalina."

Nyla's face lit with triumph. "I was contacted by a representative of an organization that recognizes my talent."

"Vortex," Slater said.

Nyla rounded on him. "I know what you're going to say. That Vortex is just a legend, a myth attached to the stories of the lost labs. But I've got news for you. It was real all those years ago, and it will be real again."

"Bullshit," Slater said. "Someone is playing you."

240

"That's not true," Nyla shouted.

"I don't doubt that someone contacted you and claimed to represent Vortex, but the truth is, someone just wants to use you to take all the risks."

"You haven't got a clue," Nyla said. "And neither does the Foundation. And that's the way it needs to be, at least for now. But the truth is that Vortex is rising from the ashes and I have been offered a position as the director of a lab that will conduct the kind of cutting-edge paranormal research the Foundation refuses to do."

"If you've got an offer like that, why didn't you disappear again and set up shop in a Vortex facility?" Slater asked.

"Because there is a price to pay to be admitted into the inner circles of Vortex," Nyla said. "In my case, that price is the Fogg Lake laboratory complex."

"I would have thought this one chamber would have been more than enough to buy your way into Vortex," Slater said. "There must have been a fortune in artifacts in this room when you found it."

"Unfortunately someone else found it first," Nyla said, disgusted. "Raiders, most likely. Or maybe someone in Fogg Lake discovered it and quietly sold off the artifacts. This chamber was almost empty when I arrived. The only things left were some workbenches and a few beakers. But it did provide me with the space and privacy that I needed for a halfway decent lab."

Slater looked around. "So the people claiming to be from Vortex are using you to find the Fogg Lake lab. You take all the risks. They stay in the shadows. Sweet. You do realize that as soon as you give them what they want, they will figure out that they don't need you anymore, don't you?"

Nyla turned to Tony. "Get rid of him."

"About fucking time," Tony said. He raised the gun.

"No," Catalina said. She stared at Nyla. "You can't do this. You have to stop now. You can't keep killing people."

Nyla did not take her attention off Tony. "Not in here. Do it out on the dock and dump the body in the river."

"That's how you instructed the killer to get rid of Morrissey's body," Slater said. "You know, it's a mistake to do things the same way twice. Points to a pattern. The Foundation cleaners are really, really good when it comes to identifying patterns."

"Get him out of here," Nyla said.

"No," Catalina said. "Please. I'll do what you want. I'll take you to the old power generator chamber."

"You don't need to kill him," Olivia said. "Why risk having the Foundation launch an investigation? You can give him some of that drug you're going to use on Catalina and me."

"You mustn't do this, Nyla," Catalina said.

The plea for mercy sounded authentic, but Catalina's voice had taken on the familiar eerie note. Slater recognized the haunted look that indicated she was having a vision. He knew she sensed what he planned to do.

"I said get rid of Arganbright," Nyla snapped.

"Let's go," Tony said.

Slater did not move.

"I said *move.*"

Tony grabbed Slater's shoulder, jerked him around and propelled him outside and onto the dock.

The physical contact provided the connection that allowed Slater to use his talent like a dagger. When they reached the end of the dock he struck hard and fast, using everything he had to overwhelm the triplet's aura. This time he had full control.

Tony convulsed, wheezing as he tried to take a breath. But his lungs were locked up by the sudden cold. He collapsed and toppled forward. He squeezed off a shot but it was a reflexive move. The round went into the water. Unfortunately, his gun did, too.

Okay, so not everything was going according to plan, Slater

thought. But the plan, such as it was, had been shaky from the start. Sometimes you had to improvise.

He flattened his back against the stone wall beside the doorway. Sooner or later someone would venture outside to see what had delayed Tony. Odds were good that it would be Jared who stuck his head through the doorway.

Catalina and Olivia were screaming now. Their anguish sounded genuine. Their fury and despair reverberated off the stone walls of the lab.

"Shut up," Nyla shouted. "Shut up, both of you, or Olivia will be next."

Both women went suddenly quiet.

Finally, *finally*, Jared realized something had gone wrong outside. He yelled through the doorway. "Tony? What's happening?"

When he got no response, he did the smart thing and got nervous.

"Something's wrong," he announced to Nyla.

"The boat," Nyla said, alarmed. "If Arganbright gets into it, he'll get away. Stop him."

Jared hesitated and then fired several shots randomly through the doorway. Evidently satisfied that he had provided sufficient cover for himself, he stuck his head and the gun through the opening to survey the scene.

Slater grabbed the arm holding the gun and hauled the triplet through the doorway. Jared grunted and pulled the trigger a couple more times. The shots thudded into the wooden boards of the dock.

Inside the lab the screaming started up again. Nyla this time. Howling in rage and panic and pain. Glass shattered.

"You're crazy," Nyla screeched. "What have you done?"

Another surge of adrenaline gave Slater the energy he needed to send currents of ice into Jared. The triplet landed heavily on the boards. He looked up at Slater, his face twisted in horror and disbelief.

"What are you?" he gasped.

"Really pissed off," Slater said.

The triplet collapsed, unconscious.

Slater grabbed the gun and lunged through the doorway. He slammed to a halt when he saw that Nyla was clinging to the end of one of the old workbenches. As he watched, she lost her grip and sagged to her knees. Her mouth opened and closed. Her eyes rolled back in her head.

"Not like this," she whispered. "Can't end like this."

She crumpled to the floor and did not move.

Catalina looked at Slater.

"Finally found a use for that auto-injector you gave me," she said.

CHAPTER 34

understand that the Foundation authorities are not popular here in Fogg Lake," Slater said.

"Damn right," Euclid Oaks muttered. "Nothing but trouble."

A chorus of affirming responses rippled across the crowded room. Unlike the informal gathering that had taken place in the restaurant, this was an official town hall meeting. The venue was the library. It was still early morning, but the place was packed. Catalina was sure the entire population of Fogg Lake had turned out for the event. The future of the community was at stake.

Catalina and Olivia sat in the front row. All eyes were on Slater, who was standing at the front of the room. Euclid, in his role as mayor, stood nearby.

"Your opinion of the Foundation was formed when the Rancourts were in charge," Slater continued. "It was another time. I'm asking you to give Victor Arganbright and his people a chance to prove to you that things have changed."

A lot of snorting and murmurs of disbelief greeted that statement.

"Tough crowd," Catalina whispered to Olivia.

"Small towns," Olivia observed in equally low tones. "They don't change easily. One of the reasons we left, remember?"

At the front of the room, Slater continued. "My uncles are working to bring attitudes and policies into the modern era, but the legacy of the Bluestone Project is complicated. There are those in high places who are willing to do whatever they think is required to keep the past buried."

Jake Crabtree, a thin, intense man of about forty, shot to his feet. "Why is anyone worried about having the truth come out? Everyone who was affiliated with the project is either dead or too old to care."

"The people who want the program hushed up aren't concerned with the embarrassment factor," Slater said. "You're right. These days no one really gives a damn that, back in the day, the government spent a fortune on paranormal research. Certain clandestine agencies have a long history of investigating psychic phenomena. Most people know that. But the Bluestone Project was different because it produced some results. Everyone in this room is proof of that."

"Damn it, man, are you talking about us?" Jake said. "The folks here in Fogg Lake?"

Slater looked at him. "I'm talking about all of us who have some genetic connection to the Bluestone Project. That includes my family, the Arganbrights, as well as Lucas Pine's people. It's true the Arganbrights and the Pines don't hail from Fogg Lake. None of our relatives were here on the night of the Incident in the caves. But we do have a connection to Bluestone and we were affected by some of the experiments that were carried out in other Bluestone facilities."

Euclid's eyes narrowed. "Are you saying there were accidents in some of the other labs?"

"Trust me when I tell you that we have plenty of evidence to indicate the other labs were engaged in equally dangerous research,"

Slater said. "Some of the experiments were conducted on volunteers. Others resulted in serious accidents. In every case there was a cover-up. That means that today we don't have the information we need to locate everyone who was affected. My point is that, one way or another, we are all dealing with the fallout from the Bluestone Project."

"Go on," Euclid said. He was paying close attention now.

"You know as well as I do that most people on the outside assume that anyone claiming to have a little talent is either an entertainer or a con artist," Slater continued. "But there are those who do take the paranormal seriously, and they can be dangerous. Catalina, for example, had to deal with a stalker after the media announced that she had helped solve a murder in Seattle."

A round of uneasy muttering followed that statement.

"The Foundation's mission is to protect the descendants of Fogg Lake, as well as the others who were affected by the experiments carried out in the course of the Bluestone Project." Slater paused a beat. "It is also our job to take care of the bad guys. As Uncle Victor likes to say, it takes a psychic to catch a psychic."

A sturdily built woman with a short mop of gray hair leaped to her feet.

"The Foundation cleaners are nothing more than a bunch of private security cops who think they've got the right to arrest people like us and lock us up in that so-called asylum they operate," she declared.

"All right, Tabitha, we know where you're coming from," Euclid said, his tone soothing. He turned to Slater. "Tabitha has a son who is being treated at some private clinic run by the Foundation."

"Imprisoned, you mean," Tabitha shouted. "Those damn cleaners came to his apartment in Portland one night and took him away."

"In fairness to the Foundation," Euclid said, "there's a bit more to the story. Tabitha's son got ahold of some bad street drugs. The shit did things to his head and had a real destabilizing effect on his aura. He became a danger to himself and, uh, probably others as well."

"I understand," Slater said. He looked at Tabitha. "Sounds like your son is at Halcyon Manor. You are not the only mother dealing with the damage that is done every day by drugs in this country. But I have to ask you if you would rather have had your son end up in the prison population, where he wouldn't have gotten any medical treatment? Or maybe in a rehab center, where the so-called experts would have concluded that he really was crazy because he claimed to see auras?"

Tabitha sniffed and started to cry quietly. She blotted her eyes with the hem of her shirt and sank back into her seat. The people sitting next to her patted her on the shoulder.

Euclid nodded at Slater. "Go on, Arganbright."

"Just a couple more points I'd like to make," Slater said. "One is that, although we have every right to be concerned with how the rest of the population would deal with us if they realized what happened to us because of the Bluestone Project, we also have a responsibility to protect outsiders from the bad guys in our community."

"Yeah, we've all heard that argument," Euclid announced. "Regular law enforcement isn't well equipped to handle bad dudes who have a lot of talent. If we don't police ourselves, who will? Blah, blah, blah. Rancourt used that excuse whenever he wanted to get rid of someone who was standing in his way."

"My uncles are aware of that," Slater said. "They have put some safeguards in place to prevent abuse of the system. There's something else I want you to consider. There's a fortune in hot artifacts in the Fogg Lake lab. We all know that now that it's been found, there's no putting the toothpaste back in the tube. Too many people are aware of the discovery. The rumors will soon start to circulate throughout the hot artifacts market. You can barricade the road into Fogg Lake, but you won't be able to stop the raiders. Once they get wind of this lab, your town is going to be crawling with a lot of ruthless people, some of whom will be willing to kill to get their hands on just a single valuable artifact."

Euclid gripped his suspenders and rocked on his heels. "You're going to tell us that we'd be better off if the Foundation folks set up an on-site operation here in town than we would be if those damn raider crews came around looking for the lab."

"I believe so," Slater said. "But this is your community. You will have to make that decision. I will give you my word that the Foundation authorities will make every effort to keep the work as low profile as possible. I would suggest you make the decision quickly, though. Fogg Lake is good at keeping its secrets, but no community can keep this kind of secret for long."

Euclid grunted and turned to the audience. "You've all heard what he has to say. I think it's time for Harmony to speak."

Harmony rose from behind the desk. Although the library was warm, she was wearing her long black cloak and knee-high boots. Her mane of silver hair was brushed back behind her ears. An expectant, respectful hush fell over the crowd.

For a few seconds she was silent. Her eyes got an otherworldly look. Then she blinked a couple of times, gave a small sigh and looked out over the crowd.

"Sorry," she said. "I've got nothing."

There was a gasp of dismay.

"But if you will recall, I am a librarian and the keeper of this town's archives," Harmony continued in brisk tones. "I am well acquainted with the history of this place. I will give you my professional and personal opinion. I am convinced that we will be better off inviting the Foundation into town. If we try to keep them out we're going to end up dealing with a bunch of low-rent raider crews. We all know those guys are dangerous. It's not like we have our own police force to handle that kind of trouble. The Foundation can provide some security."

Harmony sat down behind the desk.

Euclid looked out at the throng. "All right, people, talk amongst yourselves for a while. When you're ready, we'll take a vote."

Conversations started up immediately. Neighbor turned to neighbor and launched into earnest discussions.

Catalina and Olivia got to their feet and joined Slater. The three of them stood quietly. Catalina knew they were exhausted. Following the violent scene in Nyla Trevelyan's lab, they had left the two triplets and Nyla, all three of whom were still unconscious, in the chamber while they used the boat to return to Fogg Lake.

Slater had roused Euclid, who, in turn, woke up a few more people who had boats and guns. They had made their way back into the flooded caves and retrieved the two triplets and Nyla. The three were now secured in the basement of the library. Euclid had sent out a team to get the old landline telephone system up and running. The two repair people had reported that the line had been cut, presumably by Nyla and her clones. The problem had been fixed but Slater had not yet contacted Las Vegas. He was waiting for the community to make its decision.

A short time later the crowd became quiet. Euclid picked up the wooden gavel and banged it on a desk.

"Ready to vote?" he asked.

Murmurs of agreement went around the room.

"All in favor of letting the Foundation take charge of cleaning out the Fogg Lake lab say aye," Euclid intoned.

There was a loud chorus of ayes.

"All opposed?" Euclid said.

There were a handful of sullen nays.

"The ayes have it," Euclid declared. "Looks like there will be a few changes here in town."

There was a short pause. Harmony got to her feet. Once again the room fell silent. Everyone looked at her. Catalina felt energy shift in the atmosphere. A hush gripped the room for the second time.

"We have made the right decision," Harmony said. She did not raise her voice, but now her words reverberated throughout the library with the power of a great bell. "A storm is brewing. Past and present will collide. A vortex of evil will threaten this town and all who are connected to it. We must protect our own. To do that we will need allies. The Foundation has the resources that will be required."

Everyone in the room held their breath.

Harmony blinked a couple of times and then sat down.

"That's it," she said. "That's all I've got."

CHAPTER 35

Catalina was with Olivia and Slater at the bar of the Lake View Café when the three big SUVs rumbled into Fogg Lake. She and Olivia each had a glass of wine. Slater was drinking a beer. There were a couple dozen other people seated at tables and on nearby stools. It was early evening. There was still a little light left in the sky, but the fog was starting to pool in the streets.

Everyone put down their drinks and turned to get a look at the newcomers. Several people got up and moved to the windows for a better look.

"Guess who's here," Catalina said. She took a sip of wine. "Not exactly a subtle, low-profile arrival."

"There is no subtle, low-profile way to arrive in Fogg Lake," Olivia said. "As soon as you cross the bridge over the river, half the town knows you're coming. The rest figure it out when you drive past the general store."

Outside on the main street people emerged from houses, cabins and small shops to get a better view.

The caravan of SUVs halted. The doors of the lead vehicle opened. Catalina nearly fell off her bar stool when she saw Victor Argan-bright climb out from the passenger side.

"Will you look at that," she said. "Victor himself decided to honor our fair town with his gracious presence."

Olivia chuckled. "Now, play nice, Cat. You heard what the Oracle said. We need the Foundation's resources to help us deal with whatever is coming down the pike."

Slater put down his beer and got to his feet. "Besides, you can bet Uncle Victor is damn curious. The Fogg Lake lab is the biggest, most important discovery the Foundation has made to date."

Catalina sniffed. "The Foundation did not make the discovery. Olivia and I did."

Slater inclined his head. "I stand corrected."

A handsome, elegant-looking man got out from behind the wheel of the lead SUV.

"Your other uncle?" Catalina asked.

"Lucas Pine." Slater got to his feet. "And I will just say that we can all be grateful he accompanied Victor here today."

"Why?" Catalina asked.

"Uncle Lucas is the diplomat in the family," Slater said. "If you ladies will excuse me, I'd better go take charge of things out there before Victor accidentally says something to offend the locals."

Catalina waved him off. "Good luck."

Slater walked through the restaurant and went outside to greet his uncles. He was joined by Euclid Oaks and the members of the town council. They all went forward to meet Victor and Lucas.

Olivia smiled when the handshaking began.

"Maybe this new alliance between the Fogg Lake community and the Foundation will actually work out," she said.

"Don't be too sure of that," Catalina said. She watched Slater and Euclid lead Victor and Lucas toward the library. "Could be one of those the-enemy-of-my-enemy-is-my-friend things."

Olivia raised her brows. "Why am I getting the feeling that this situation is personal?"

"Because it is."

Olivia watched Slater and the others disappear through the front door of the library. "How personal is it?"

Catalina glanced at her watch and did the calculation. "Slater and I have known each other for less than three days."

"So?"

Catalina drank some wine and lowered the glass. "It's been a very intense few days."

"Well, damn. This is serious."

"Who knows? Three days is not a long time. I think the odds are that Slater will go back to Foundation headquarters and good old Uncle Victor will send him out on another case. Slater will forget about me and whatever we have—whatever we *had*—together."

Olivia got a thoughtful expression. "For what it's worth, I've only known Slater Arganbright for a few hours, but I can tell you one thing."

Catalina tried to suppress the little spark of hope that kept refusing to be extinguished.

"What's that?" she asked.

"Slater is no Roger Gossard," Olivia said. "He wouldn't dump a lover just because she became a liability to his brand."

Catalina felt her spirits lift a little. "No, Slater wouldn't do that."

"Enough about you. Let's talk about me. Does Emerson know what happened?"

"He knows some of it. I called him first thing when I realized that you were missing. He was really pissed and also hurt, of course, because he assumed you were a no-show on that last date. I let him know that you had vanished and that I was really worried about you."

"What did he say to that?"

"He insisted that when I found you I was to call him immediately."

Olivia sighed. "That's all he said? You were supposed to let him know when you found me?"

"Immediately," Catalina said, trying for emphasis.

"In other words, he didn't charge through the front door of Lark and LeClair demanding to help you look for me?"

Catalina cleared her throat. "He's not a trained investigator, Olivia. There really wasn't anything he could have done. He was worried, though. Seriously worried."

"Not worried enough." Olivia swirled the wine in her glass. "If you went missing, Slater Arganbright would look for you until he found you."

Catalina's spirits rose a little higher. Once again she tried to squash them flat. "Well, he is a trained investigator."

"That has nothing to do with it. I've got damn good intuition, remember? It may have let me down when it came to Emerson Ferris, but that doesn't mean I can't get a solid fix on Slater Arganbright. I don't know if he loves you, but I know that you can trust him. If you ever went missing, he'd walk into hell to find you."

Catalina took a deep, steadying breath. "Yes, he would do that."

CHAPTER 36

This is an interesting little community," Lucas said, clearly amused. "I don't know of any other town that houses its dangerous prisoners in the basement of the public library."

"It's not like we've ever had a need to build a jail," Catalina pointed out. She gave Lucas her brightest smile. "Not until this little problem involving a former Foundation employee and some clones from out of town."

They were sitting at a table in the Lake View Café. Olivia, Victor and Slater were there, too. She and Olivia had each ordered another glass of wine. Victor, Lucas and Slater were drinking whiskey. Some of the Foundation cleaners who had arrived with Lucas and Victor were eating at other tables. The rest were guarding the two triplets and Nyla Trevelyan. Victor had reported that the three were starting to wake up but that they were still groggy and confused. Regardless of their condition, they were scheduled to be taken away from Fogg Lake first thing in the morning, as soon as the fog dissipated.

Victor looked deeply hurt by Catalina's small slice of sarcasm.

"We are aware that the situation here in Fogg Lake was provoked by a former Foundation employee," he said. "It was an unfortunate development—"

"No shit," Catalina said.

Slater gave his uncles a benign smile. "She usually goes with 'oh, shit.' Regardless, that particular turn of phrase should be interpreted as a sign that she's annoyed."

Olivia raised her brows. "Catalina isn't the only one who is irritated. We do realize that the Foundation can't keep track of every former employee, but really, how can you explain the fact that Nyla Trevelyan was able to set herself up here in Fogg Lake a couple of decades ago and run a successful drug ring for years without drawing the attention of your ever-vigilant cleaners?"

Victor grunted. "My cleaners weren't even around until five years ago. Rancourt's crowd was in charge before that, and they bought the story that York, or maybe I should say Trevelyan, had died along with her husband and best friend in the lab fire. As long as we're asking questions, how do you explain the fact that a drug lord like Trevelyan was able to operate right under the noses of everyone in a town full of people endowed with psychic abilities?"

"'Drug lord' may be a bit of a stretch," Lucas said.

"Just because a lot of people in this town can detect various kinds of paranormal energy and see auras doesn't mean we can read minds," Catalina said. "It's not as if Nyla Trevelyan is a simple con artist. She was a very good herbalist. A lot of the locals benefited from her remedies. None of us had any reason not to trust her."

"You certainly can't claim the Foundation has a better track record," Olivia pointed out.

Victor snorted. "You know what they say—it takes a psychic to fool a psychic." He paused for emphasis. "And it takes a psychic to catch a psychic. Which is why the Foundation exists, Ms. Lark."

Catalina opened her mouth to respond. Slater moved fast to redirect the discussion.

"Olivia, we got your message about Vortex," he said.

"Did you?" Olivia nodded. "Good. I wasn't sure what it meant and I was still groggy from the drug. But I thought I heard one of the clones say the client thought I was her ticket into Vortex. They let me use the bathroom. I took a chance and left the note on the mirror."

Slater looked at Victor and Lucas. "Speaking of the clones, what do you know about them?"

Victor frowned. "Clones?"

"Just a figure of speech," Catalina said. "That's how the woman who witnessed the kidnapping in Seattle described them. We thought she was talking about twins. It wasn't until the Oracle found a record of triplets who were born to a woman with a Fogg Lake connection that we realized the truth."

Victor put down his whiskey. A great stillness came over him.

"What's this about an oracle?" he repeated.

"That's what we call the librarian," Olivia explained. "It's a tradition around here."

"I see." Victor looked intrigued but he did not ask any more questions.

"About the triplets," Slater said.

"Right." Victor hoisted his whiskey glass again. "The family name is Harkins. The one we picked up in Seattle is Deke Harkins. He finally woke up and started talking. From what we can tell, he and his brothers have been running cons and working the hot artifacts market for years. They did a fair amount of drug dealing on the side. They also did odd jobs as enforcers. Muscle for hire."

"They obviously have some talent," Slater said. "At least enough to sense the vibes in paranormal artifacts. People who can't pick up the energy infused in hot relics don't last long in that business. Pretty sure the Harkinses are low-level aura readers, too. That's probably why they were successful as con artists and drug dealers."

"Aura reading makes it easier to identify the marks and potential addicts," Lucas said.

Catalina caught Slater's eye. She knew they were both thinking the same thing. There was one other piece of evidence that indicated that the Harkinses had a measure of talent. They had understood immediately what an icer could do to an aura.

"The question is, how did Nyla Trevelyan get involved with the triplets?" Slater continued. "She's been more or less stuck here in Fogg Lake for a couple of decades. She left town only occasionally. How did she find them?"

Lucas swirled the whiskey in his glass. "Good question. We're still working that angle."

Olivia paused her glass in midair. "I may be able to help you with that aspect of the investigation, but I'll warn you up front that my memories are fuzzy because of the drug."

"Go on," Lucas said.

"At some point I heard one of the triplets tell Nyla, 'We missed her. Don't worry, we'll get her.'"

"Meaning me, no doubt," Catalina said.

"Yes." Olivia looked at Victor and Lucas. "Nyla really lost it then. She screamed at the triplet. She said, 'This is what I get for trying to keep it in the family.'"

Victor and Lucas exchanged glances.

"Well, now," Lucas said softly. "Isn't that interesting? We have no record of Nyla Trevelyan, or rather Alma York, having any family— certainly no close blood relatives."

Victor sat back in his chair. "Doesn't mean there aren't some. Our ancestry records are pathetic."

"For reasons of which we are all well aware," Catalina said, using her most polite voice, "no one in Fogg Lake wants to wind up in the Foundation's files."

Slater cleared his throat. "Let's save that discussion for another time and place."

Olivia's eyes sparked with amusement. "Sure. Take all the fun out of the evening. Personally, I rather enjoy watching Catalina take on the director of the Foundation."

Slater nodded thoughtfully. "I'll admit that there is some entertainment value."

Victor glared at him. Lucas intervened swiftly.

"The good news about our current situation," he said, "is that once we're finished questioning Trevelyan and the triplets—"

"Sounds like a rock band," Olivia said.

Lucas ignored her. "Once we are done with them, we can turn them over to regular law enforcement. We've got more than enough evidence of kidnapping, drug dealing, attempted murder and conspiracy to commit murder to put them away for a while. Unfortunately, I doubt we'll be able to prove that they murdered Royston and Ingram."

"I suppose Olivia and I will have to testify," Catalina said. "Just what I need—more media coverage of my fake psychic powers."

"Not this time," Victor said. "It's safe to say there won't be a trial. Trevelyan and those clones will confess, trust me."

"Uh-huh." Catalina took a sip of her wine. "What makes you so sure of that?"

Victor smiled a wolfish smile. "Because it will be made clear to them that if they don't, they will be declared insane. They will end up at Halcyon Manor."

Olivia looked thoughtful. "Maybe they will prefer to take their chances in an asylum."

"Maybe, but I doubt it," Lucas said. "At Halcyon Manor they will be guarded by people who know exactly what they are and how to deal with them. I think they'd rather risk the regular criminal justice system. Besides, the manor has enough problems dealing with people with some very dangerous parapsych disorders. We don't want to fill up our limited facilities with a bunch of run-of-the-mill bad guys. But the Foundation will create detailed files and track them."

"I know the discovery of the Fogg Lake lab is a big deal," Slater said, "but I'm surprised you both accompanied the team this afternoon."

"Professional courtesy," Lucas explained. "We wanted to show some respect to the community. Let them know we appreciate the cooperation."

"Not sure our cunning plan is working," Victor muttered. He looked around the sparsely filled restaurant. "Not a real friendly bunch, are they?"

Catalina smiled. "Don't worry, Victor. I'm sure that once they get to know you, they'll warm up to you and realize what a swell person you really are."

CHAPTER 37

Catalina waited until she was sure Olivia had finally fallen asleep before she got out of bed. The two of them were sharing the big bed in the master bedroom. Olivia had looked amused when Catalina had insisted on changing the sheets, but she had not made any comments about the rather obvious implications. Slater had been relegated to the narrow bed in Catalina's old room.

Most of the members of the Foundation team had brought sleeping bags and had been provided temporary quarters in the library. Euclid had announced that in the morning the town council would open up some of the old cabins that were rarely used.

For one extremely disconcerting moment Catalina had been afraid she would be left with no option but to allow Victor and Lucas to unroll their sleeping bags in her parents' house. Luckily Euclid had made it clear that protocol dictated that the director of the Foundation and his husband should be guests of the mayor and his wife.

Catalina pulled on her robe, slid her bare feet into slippers and paused to adjust the covers over Olivia.

"I'm asleep," Olivia mumbled. "You can go now. He's in the front room."

"Are you psychic or something?"

"Something."

"Get some sleep, pal."

Olivia squeezed Catalina's hand. "I will."

Catalina went out the door and down the short hall. Slater was standing at the window looking out into the glowing fog.

"Can't sleep?" he asked softly.

"Not yet," she said. She walked across the room and stopped at his side, close but not quite touching. "Think you'll be able to get some sleep tonight?"

"Maybe. Eventually."

He reached for her hand. She gave it to him. They stood quietly.

"Do you think it's over?" she asked after a while.

"Almost. We still don't know who committed the murder that you and Olivia witnessed fifteen years ago."

"It wasn't one of the triplets, we can be sure of that much. They look nothing like the man who killed Morrissey. In any event, they would have been too young. The murderer was in his twenties at the time."

"We've got a lot to go on now," Slater said. "Sooner or later we'll identify him. Victor and Lucas are right. Trevelyan and the clones will talk. Just a matter of time."

"It will be good to get back to normal."

Slater turned her so that she faced him. He put his hands around her waist.

"How do you define *normal*?" he said. "Asking for a friend."

She gripped his shoulders. "Darned if I know. Olivia and I have always figured that as long as we weren't locked up in an institution, we were on the right side of normal."

"This friend, the one who's asking for a definition, he was locked up for a while. It was an attic, not an institution, but you get the picture. Pretty much the same thing."

"But he's out in the world now."

"Still not anywhere close to normal, though. Never will be."

"Tell me why your friend cares about the answer."

Slater framed her face between his hands. "He desperately wants to be able to offer the promise of normal to a certain person. But he knows that he can't do that."

"If the certain person in question is not exactly normal herself, she won't care about a promise like that."

"You're sure?"

"Absolutely positive."

He drew her closer. "I know it's too soon to talk about the possibility of a future together, but I need to tell you that I've been thinking about it since we ran into each other on the street. I can't stop thinking about it. I'm not asking for a commitment. Not yet. But if you could give me some time, I'll do everything in my power to show you that I'm serious about a future together."

She took her hands off his shoulders and wound her arms around his neck.

"How much time do you think you'll need?" she asked.

Energy whispered in the atmosphere.

"Whatever it takes," he said. "I'm all in, here, Catalina. I love you."

She traced the corner of his mouth with the edge of one finger.

"I thought there would be fireworks," she said. "Lots of sizzle and heat and flash-bang energy."

Slater went very still. His aura got a little more intense. In the shadows it was impossible to read his eyes, but she sensed he was steeling himself for grim news.

"When did you expect all that to happen?" he said.

"When I found the man I've been looking for, the one I could love. I just assumed there would be a little lightning in the atmosphere."

"Are you telling me that you don't think you could fall in love with me?"

"No. I'm telling you that I am in love with you."

"But no fireworks? No lightning?"

She smiled. "Oh, there is plenty of both. But there is something even more amazing. What I feel is a sense of certainty. Of rightness. I feel grounded and at the same time I think I could fly."

He threaded his fingers through her hair. "That's how I feel, too. A sense of rightness."

"People are going to tell us that it's too soon," Catalina warned. "That we've been through a lot of drama in recent days and that makes everything more intense."

"Who is going to tell us those things?"

"Our families. Olivia."

"Nope, not me," Olivia said from the doorway. "You two look like a perfect match. On behalf of the staff of Lark and LeClair, I offer my sincere congratulations. Now, would you mind taking it into a bedroom? I'm trying to get a little sleep here."

Slater laughed. The sound burst forth in a roar that seemed to emanate from somewhere deep inside him. Catalina was startled, and then a sense of wonder came over her. It was, she realized, the first time she had heard him laugh. They really did have a lot to learn about each other. The drama of the past few days was mostly over, but their adventure together was just beginning.

Olivia smiled at Catalina and disappeared back down the hallway.

Slater scooped up Catalina and carried her toward her old bedroom.

"Now that we've got the important stuff settled," he said, "let's see about the fireworks and lightning part."

She wrapped her arms around his neck. "That sounds like a very good idea."

He got her into the bedroom and paused long enough to allow her to close and lock the door. He set her on her feet, pulled aside the covers and stripped off her flannel pajamas.

He kissed her with enough intensity to set off the fireworks. The lightning came next. A hungry, urgent, aching tension built within her.

She flattened her palms against his bare chest and drew her hands down to the waistband of his trousers. She unfastened his pants, her fingers shivering a little, but not from the evening chill. Gingerly she lowered the zipper, cautious of the heavy bulge of his erection.

He got a packet out of his pocket, ripped it open and sheathed himself in the condom. When he was ready he hoisted her up into the air. A rush of feminine heat swept through her. She wrapped her legs around his waist and sank her teeth lightly into his earlobe.

He groaned and kissed her neck. She closed her eyes against the giddy heat. She felt him move and assumed he was going to put her down on the bed. Instead her back was suddenly up against the wall. He braced her there, gripped the undersides of her thighs and slid into her, slowly, relentlessly, filling her completely. She tightened her legs around his waist and dug her nails into the muscles of his shoulders.

He retreated a little. She cried out in protest and clutched him close.

In response he eased back into her, going deep once again. She fought to keep him where she needed him to be. But again he pulled back.

She gave a muffled moan of protest. Her nails became claws. She was gasping now, straining to take control of the rhythm and depth of each penetration, but he refused to let her set the pace. Again and again he sank himself into her, only to ease back out.

She was so tense, so tightly wound, so desperate for release she started to get frustrated.

"Damn it," she said.

At that he let go of her right thigh. She was still trapped against the wall and she still had both legs chained around him. He reached down between them and found the taut, swollen bundle of over-stimulated nerve endings. He stroked gently.

It was too much. Too intense. She gave a muffled shriek and came undone. Her climax rippled through her in deep, heavy waves. She could not catch her breath.

He drove into her one last time, his own climax crashing through him, fierce and exultant.

When it was over he somehow got her to the bed. They collapsed together in a damp tangle.

"If we keep doing this," Slater said after a while, "we really are going to set the bed on fire."

Catalina smiled. "Fireworks and lightning."

———————

She came awake to the sound of loud knocking on the bedroom door. When she opened her eyes she saw that the fog was tinted with enough daylight to suggest that morning had arrived, just barely. The question about how she and Slater would manage to fit on the narrow bed had been settled at some point during the night. They had gone to sleep spoon fashion. She was still tucked into Slater's heat. His arm was draped over her hips. She could feel the beginning of his morning erection pushing between her thighs.

"Sorry to interrupt you two," Olivia said through the door, "but Victor Arganbright is here. He's got some news about Nyla Trevelyan. Oh, and in case you're interested, I've got coffee going."

"Coffee sounds good," Slater whispered into Catalina's ear. He stroked her hip. "But I can think of better things to do first."

"Forget it." Catalina got up and reached for her robe. "You heard what Olivia said—your uncle is here with some news."

"Victor has lousy timing," Slater said.

"I think we can agree on that."

Slater rolled out of bed and pulled on his trousers and a T-shirt. "No need for you to rush. I'll go see what is so important that Victor felt he had to wake us up."

He went out into the hall. Catalina took a few minutes to pull on a flannel shirt and jeans. She ran a brush through her hair and hurried out of the bedroom. She found Olivia, Slater and Victor gathered in the kitchen. Olivia was pouring coffee for them. The men looked grim-faced.

"What is it?" she asked. "What's wrong?"

"Nyla Trevelyan is dead," Victor said.

Stunned, Catalina turned to Slater. "That sedative in the auto-injector? Is this my fault?"

"No," Victor said. "It wasn't the sedative. We know because she woke up a few hours ago. She was having chest pains. She asked for her medication. The librarian said everyone in town knew she had a heart condition."

"That's true," Catalina said.

"There was a bottle of prescription meds in her backpack," Victor said. "I let her take a dose. She collapsed and died a short time later."

"Maybe the shock of the failure of her scheme was just too much for her heart," Catalina said.

"Maybe," Victor said. "But I'm going to order an autopsy, and I'm also going to have the meds analyzed as soon as we get back to head-quarters."

Slater gave him a knowing look. "You think someone got to her, don't you?"

"Yes," Victor said. "Whether or not she was successful, I don't think she was supposed to survive this business."

"But why murder her?" Catalina said.

"She obviously knew too much," Victor said. "Now all we have to do is figure out what the hell she knew."

CHAPTER 38

The Fogg Lake operation had ended in disaster. A complete fuckup.

Trey Danson's fingers shook a little as he dropped the phone into his pocket. He wasn't sure if it was rage or incipient panic that was rattling his senses. Probably both.

There was no point hoping that the information was wrong. The Vortex operative who had just texted him had made it clear that nothing could be salvaged from the project. The lost lab had been located, all right, but somehow the Foundation had gotten there first and was now in full control.

The Vortex operative had been quite clear. The recruitment offer had been rescinded. There would be no further contact. No second chances.

Trey Danson got up from behind his desk and went to stand at the window. From his office on the fortieth floor of a gleaming downtown tower he could see a storm coming in over Elliott Bay. It would strike soon.

He jacked up his senses and forced himself to consider the number one priority—his own safety. He was almost positive that Vortex would not make any move against him. The organization had no reason to take the risk of having him killed. The operative had been careful to remain in the shadows. Even if the Foundation arrived on his doorstep this afternoon and shot him full of some sort of truth serum, he could not give them any useful information about Vortex. They wouldn't get anything from his phone, either. He was sure of that because he had tried to trace the Vortex connection himself. The messages had been placed using an anonymous cover provided by a Darknet service.

Vortex had dumped him but he did not think that he had to fear them.

That left the Foundation. According to the Vortex source, the cleaners had picked up all three of the Harkins triplets and Nyla Trevelyan. The triplets were not a problem. They were just hired muscle with a little talent. They were distant cousins from the Harkins side of his family. He had recommended them to York/Trevelyan because they had what it took to sell drugs and run hot artifacts. As far as the three were concerned they had been working for Trevelyan. They knew nothing about him.

Alma York/Nyla Trevelyan knew everything about him, of course. But she was dead. There had been no way she could have been allowed to survive, regardless of the outcome of the project. He had done his research. The last time he had picked up her medication he had substituted the tablets in the bottle with a substance that was guaranteed to be lethal to a person with her particular heart condition.

Mentally he went down his checklist. York/Trevelyan was no

longer a problem. The triplets did not know enough to be dangerous to him. There were only two people who could conceivably cause trouble for him now—the same two people who had been a problem right from the start.

So close. He had been so *close*. He had taken so many risks, and all for nothing. Because of Catalina Lark and Olivia LeClair.

A smart man would walk away now, cut his losses and leave Seattle. He had money stashed in an offshore bank. He could leave town tonight and vanish. There was nothing to link him to the disaster in Fogg Lake.

But the longer he thought about how it had all gone wrong, the hotter the fires of rage burned. Someone needed to pay.

He would start with Catalina Lark.

CHAPTER 39

Catalina pulled into the driveway in front of the old Victorian mansion and parked her car behind an aging Cadillac.

Beatrice Ross had phoned Lark & LeClair that morning and pleaded with Catalina to examine what she was sure was a crime scene. She explained that she was thinking of redoing her will because she suspected her nephew was plotting to murder her to get his inheritance.

"I'm sure now that he murdered my sister," Beatrice had explained in quivering tones. "I'm afraid I might be next."

The sister's death had been attributed to natural causes. A lifelong smoker, she had suffered from a variety of ailments, including lung disease. Beatrice had found the body on the floor of the kitchen one morning a few weeks earlier. There was no obvious reason to suspect murder. Then again, those were often the kinds of cases that convinced people to call in Lark & LeClair.

Catalina grabbed her handbag and slipped out from behind the wheel. Looping the strap of the bag over her shoulder, she walked along a stone path to the front door of the faded mansion.

She pressed the doorbell and surveyed the expansive gardens while she waited for a response. The house sat on a large chunk of property located in an exclusive neighborhood on the shores of Lake Washington. The views of the lake and downtown Seattle made it worth a fortune. Beatrice Ross had been a successful actress. She had made some sound investments over the years and now lived quietly.

Footsteps echoed in the hall. A moment later the door opened and an elegant wisp of a woman peered out. Beatrice was in her early eighties. It was clear that she had been a beautiful woman in her younger days. Her blue eyes glittered with intelligence and a barely concealed excitement.

She was dressed in an expensive knit trouser suit. The jacket was studded with snappy gold buttons. The diamonds in her ears and around her throat looked real. Gold bracelets were stacked on each thin wrist. Rings adorned several fingers.

It was obvious that she had gone out of her way to dress for the meeting. She beamed at Catalina.

"You must be the psychic," she said. "I'm Beatrice Ross."

"I'm Catalina Lark from Lark and LeClair. A pleasure to meet you."

"I've been expecting you. Won't you come in? Let's go into the living room and have tea while I explain my problem. This way, dear."

Beatrice led the way into a heavily shadowed living room. Catalina followed, heightening her senses. Old homes were the most difficult to read accurately. The energy of decades of emotions had seeped into the floors, walls and ceilings. The heavy vibe could confuse her senses. Whatever the cause, she was getting the someone-just-walked-over-my-grave chill that told her something was very wrong in the mansion.

The lack of light was unnerving. There were wall sconces in the hallway and lamps in the living room but none of them were illuminated. The blinds were open, but the woods outside, combined with an overcast sky, filtered out most of the sun.

"Do take off your coat, dear," Beatrice said. "You look as if you're ready to rush out the door."

"I'm a little cold at the moment," Catalina said. "I'll leave my coat on if you don't mind."

"Suit yourself, dear. Please, have a seat." Beatrice indicated a cream-colored sofa. "My lawyer arrived a few minutes ago. I asked him to wait in the solarium at the side of the house. Trey insisted on meeting you because he knows I am prepared to change my will immediately if your investigation confirms my belief that my sister was murdered. He's quite concerned. You know how lawyers are."

"I see."

A man appeared in the doorway.

"You're here, Ms. Lark," he said. "Right on time."

Catalina turned quickly to look at him.

The energy of rage radiated in his aura.

She recognized him immediately. He was fifteen years older and his head was no longer shaved, but she knew she was looking at the man who had murdered John Morrissey. He was not in hiking clothes today. Instead he wore a stylish trench coat not unlike her own. Underneath the coat he had on a pair of tailored trousers and a dark pullover. His right hand rested casually inside one of the deep pockets of the trench.

"There you are, Trey," Beatrice said. "Ms. Lark, allow me to introduce you to my lawyer, Trey Danson."

"I didn't know that there would be a lawyer present today," Catalina said, playing for time.

"There's a great deal at stake, I'm afraid," Trey said. "Ms. Ross is a wealthy woman. If she decides to change her will, there will be some significant ramifications."

"I see."

"Let's go into the solarium," Trey said. "Beatrice, please wait here while I explain the situation to Ms. Lark. We'll be back in a few minutes."

"Very well," Beatrice said. "I suggest you use the library instead. You'll have more privacy. And don't be long about it. Ms. Lark charges by the hour. So do you. I don't want to waste time."

"We won't be long, Beatrice," Trey Danson said.

Catalina walked slowly out into the hall.

"The library is on your right," Danson said. When they were two steps away from the living room and out of Beatrice's sight, he spoke again. "You recognize me, don't you? I was afraid you would."

Catalina glanced over her shoulder. She saw that Danson had taken his right hand out of his pocket. He held a gun.

A wispy vision floated across her senses. He would use the gun if he thought he had no choice, but he preferred to use a more subtle method. A syringe full of some lethal drug, no doubt.

"One thing I'm curious about," she said.

"Only one thing?"

"Why haven't you made a move against Olivia and me for the past fifteen years? You must have known we were in Seattle."

"I didn't think it was necessary to take the risk. Nyla was sure the tea she gave you and Olivia in the days following your escape from the cave would mess with your memories. And even if you did remember bits and pieces, you had no way to identify me. At the time I lived in California. I didn't move to Seattle until about three years ago. It seemed unlikely that our paths would ever cross."

"That's not the only reason you didn't try to kill us, is it? You and Nyla were afraid of drawing the attention of the Foundation."

"Nyla was terrified that if something happened to you and LeClair, your parents would call in the Foundation. Fifteen years ago she was afraid of the Rancourts. Later she was even more worried about Victor Arganbright."

"She wanted to protect her drug business."

"Poor Nyla lived in fear that one day the Foundation would show up at her door and take her away to Halcyon Manor," Trey said. "She always claimed she would rather die than be locked up. But I couldn't be sure that, when the time came, she would actually follow through, so I made certain she got her preferred ending."

"You put something deadly into a bottle of her prescription meds."

"I knew that one day she would probably become a liability, so I kept a bottle of the special meds handy. When I delivered Olivia LeClair to Nyla I took the opportunity to replace Nyla's regular tablets with a medication I knew would be lethal to someone with her heart problems. I must admit I didn't know that she would take the pills so quickly, but it worked out well."

"You poisoned your own sister?"

"Half sister. We weren't close."

"I sort of figured that out. You're the collector who murdered Ingram and Royston, aren't you?"

"Both of them were eager to show off the latest additions to their vaults to someone who would understand the significance of their new acquisitions."

"You didn't find what you wanted in Ingram's vault, but you did discover it in Royston's vault."

"I see you and the Foundation crowd have put most of it together," Trey said. "Yes, I chased the rumors of that logbook for six months before I finally found it in Royston's collection."

"All for nothing."

"The project has come apart, thanks to you and Olivia LeClair. Fortunately, now that Nyla is gone, there is no connection between me and the murders and kidnapping."

"Except for Olivia and me."

"It has become clear that your memories have returned. I can't afford to take any more chances."

"You're going to get rid of me today. But what about Olivia?"

"She is your best friend, remember? She will be devastated by your death. She'll have a few drinks and get into a fatal car crash. There's the library door. Open it."

Catalina turned the knob, pushed open the door and walked into another shadowed room. There were a number of books on the shelves. A home theater, complete with red velvet curtains and gilded chairs, took up one half of the library.

"If you shoot me, Beatrice Ross will hear the shot and call the cops," she said. "You'd have to kill her, too. But you're not planning to do that, are you?"

"No," Danson said.

He reached into his other pocket and took out a syringe.

A man walked out from behind the curtain. He had a gun in one hand, a badge in the other.

"Police," he said. "Drop the gun, Danson. And the needle. Hands on your head. You're under arrest for the murders of Ingram, Royston and John Morrissey. You are also under arrest for the attempted murder of Catalina Lark. And then there's the kidnapping charge."

Danson froze.

The library was suddenly swarming with people in SWAT gear. Danson lowered the gun and let it fall on the carpet. He put the syringe down next to it.

"Be careful with the syringe," Catalina said. "Whatever is inside is poisonous."

An officer wearing thick gloves retrieved the syringe and gently placed it into a special container. Someone else took charge of the gun.

Slater and Olivia emerged from the other room.

"Are you all right?" Olivia asked.

"I still say this was a really stupid idea," Slater said. He wrapped an arm around Catalina. "I swear, if you ever do anything this crazy again I'll . . . Never mind. Are you okay?"

"Yes, but this vest is really hot and uncomfortable," she said. She opened the front of her jacket to reveal the Kevlar vest. "Can I take it off now?"

"I'll help you," Olivia said.

Danson did not take his eyes off Catalina. Rage spiked in his aura.

"How did you figure it out?" he said.

Victor strolled into the room. He was accompanied by Lucas.

"Ms. LeClair overheard Nyla Trevelyan make a rather sarcastic comment about the difficulties of trying to work with family," Victor said. "With that information we sought help from an Oracle."

Danson stared at him. "Oracle? What are you talking about?"

Catalina smiled. There was no need to let Trey Danson or the police know that Harmony, using the Fogg Lake ancestry records, had helped them track down Nyla's half brother.

Lucas looked at Danson. "Once we had a name, we brought in an expert forensic psychologist."

Roger Gossard walked through the doorway. "That would be me."

"The problem was that we had zero evidence linking you to the kidnapping of Ms. LeClair or to the murders of Ingram and Royston," Victor said.

"Because there wasn't any," Danson said.

"Until now," Slater said. "Catalina is wearing a wire."

"Mr. Gossard was very helpful," the detective said. "He advised us that if you were smart you would keep your head down and probably leave town. But he said your sense of self-preservation would probably be overridden by your desire for revenge."

"After talking to Olivia and me and compiling all the evidence, Roger was able to come up with a psychological profile that accurately predicted your behavior," Catalina said. "Evidently you've got some impulse control issues. All we had to do was dangle the bait."

"Oh, my," Beatrice said from the hall doorway. "This has been such an exciting afternoon. I haven't had this much fun since my acting days."

Danson stared at her. "What the fuck?"

Beatrice gave him an icy smile. "I knew you thought I was just a doddering old lady but I put up with it because you actually gave excellent investment advice. My sister and I made a lot of money thanks to your talent."

"We didn't have any hard evidence of your involvement in a serious crime so we took a look at your list of clients," Victor said. "Imagine our surprise when we discovered that one of them was Beatrice Ross, a former actress who retired here."

"Born and raised in Fogg Lake," Beatrice added.

"When I contacted Ms. Ross and told her our suspicions about you, she agreed to assist us," Victor said. "Evidently she really did have a few questions about her sister's death."

"This is bullshit," Danson muttered.

Beatrice smiled but her eyes were as sharp as gemstones. "You murdered my sister, didn't you? You knew that I inherited her estate. As soon as you convinced me to take my nephew out of my will and appoint you as the trustee, you would have murdered me, too."

Danson was stone-faced now. "I'm not saying another word until I talk to my lawyer."

"You've already said enough," the detective said. "And thanks to Ms. Lark we've got a recording of every word." He looked at the team in the flashy SWAT gear. "Get him out of here."

Roger looked at Catalina. "Thanks."

"You called it right," Catalina said. "You said Danson would not be able to resist the opportunity to take revenge."

"He committed several murders and risked everything to find whatever it was he was looking for," Roger said. "But it was all for nothing, thanks to two women who operated a small investigation agency. He couldn't let it go. It was just a matter of time before he went after you."

"Thanks," Catalina said. "I think this case will be very good for your brand."

Roger gave her a considering look. "Lark and LeClair could have taken all the credit for this case. Why would you want to help me build my brand?"

"Let's just say I recently discovered that revenge isn't sweet," Catalina said.

Olivia smiled. "Besides, the last thing our brand needs is another media frenzy focused on a crazy fake psychic who solves murders."

CHAPTER 40

Gwendolyn Swan went to the door and turned the Open sign to Closed. She crossed the salesroom floor to her desk, picked up the receiver of the old landline phone and placed the call to her sister.

Eloisa Swan answered on the first ring. "Well?"

"Bad news, I'm afraid." Gwendolyn leaned against the counter. "The project is a failure. The Fogg Lake lab has been located, but the Foundation is now in control of it."

There was a long silence on the other end.

"What went wrong?" Eloisa asked finally.

"I could list any number of things, but in hindsight it's clear that the biggest mistake was made back at the beginning when the triplets botched the kidnapping. They grabbed Olivia Le Clair without incident, but they missed Catalina Lark that same night."

"You said she wasn't at her apartment when they went to get her."

"She had gone to see a client," Gwendolyn said. "There was an incident at the client's house. A fork was involved. Lark wound up spending half the night with the police. One thing led to another. Reporters showed up at the front door of Lark's apartment building early the next morning. The triplets got nervous and called off the operation. They tried to pick her up on the street a couple of hours later but by then the Foundation had a man in Seattle. Things went downhill from there."

"Any way to know how the Foundation got out ahead of us on this?"

"Victor Arganbright was suspicious of Ingram's and Royston's deaths from the start. He got nowhere investigating the Ingram case, but after Royston died in a similar fashion, he sent his nephew, Slater Arganbright, to Seattle to take a look at the crime scene. Victor suggested that Slater contact Lark and LeClair for assistance. But by then LeClair had vanished. Next thing I know, Arganbright and Catalina are in my shop asking about Royston's collection."

"If both women had simply vanished simultaneously there wouldn't have been any trail for Arganbright to follow," Eloisa mused.

"Maybe or maybe not. We'll never know. Regardless, what's done is done."

"Any loose ends?"

"No. Nyla Trevelyan is deceased. The triplets don't know anything about you or me. Trey Danson is under arrest for murder and attempted murder. He'll talk, of course, but if he tries to explain that he was hoping to join a secret organization named Vortex that is dedicated to paranormal research, all he'll succeed in doing is convincing a judge and jury that he's a member of the tinfoil hat club."

"He knows about you," Eloisa said.

"All he knows is what every collector in Seattle knows. I sell antiques and collectibles and trade gossip. He asked me to let him know if anyone came around to my shop inquiring about Royston's collection. I obliged by informing him Slater Arganbright was in town.

That's not a crime. I doubt if Danson will even mention it to the police, because it will only serve to tie him more closely to Royston's murder."

"Think it will dawn on Danson that he was played?"

"We didn't play him. Vortex made him and his sister a legitimate offer. In exchange for membership in the organization they were required to come up with an entrance fee. They failed. Offer rescinded."

"So, no loose ends," Eloisa said. "One hell of a disappointment, though. Damn it, we were so close to gaining control of one of the lost labs."

"It wasn't the Vortex lab," Gwendolyn pointed out. "That's the one we're after. There will be other opportunities."

"The Foundation will be looking for it, too, now that they have some reason to believe that Vortex is more than a legend. We need an edge, Gwen."

"We have one," Gwendolyn said. "The best possible edge. We've got Aurora Winston's diary."

"Which is only useful if we figure out how to break her private code," Eloisa said.

"We're making progress. We've decoded some of her experimental drug formulas."

"Just the simple ones from the first part of the diary," Eloisa said. "We need to decipher the more heavily encrypted passages toward the end. That was when she started doing her most important experiments in the Vortex lab."

"I'll go back to work on the diary tonight," Gwendolyn said. A muffled thud from the basement interrupted her. "Oh, damn. I've got to go, Eloisa. I'll call you if I get anywhere with the diary."

She put down the phone and went around the end of the counter and into the back room. She opened the door at the top of the basement stairs and hit the light switches. She shut and locked the door and descended the stairs.

Sure enough, there was another rat in the trap that guarded the underground tunnel. You'd think the idiots would learn that it was not wise to try to steal from Swan Antiques.

The trap always caught burglars by surprise, probably because it did not look like a security device. It was a clockwork doll about four feet tall dressed in a vintage nursing costume—a crisp white uniform and a perky white cap. In the shadows the syringe in her hand was almost invisible.

When a would-be thief stepped onto the wooden platform at the entrance of the tunnel, the old-fashioned mechanism swung into action. The nurse's arm moved in a stabbing motion that delivered a stiff dose of the drug to whatever or whoever happened to be in the way.

The formula for the drug had come from one of the early pages of Aurora Winston's diary, a section that was only lightly encrypted.

Gwendolyn assessed the raider and decided he was too heavy for her to move. She went back upstairs, picked up the phone and called the pest control service.

"Another one?" The gravelly voice on the other end of the line sounded amused. "That makes two in the past week."

"It's been a busy week."

———————

Gwendolyn took the diary out of the basement vault and carried it upstairs to her condo, located above her shop. She sat down at her desk, opened her notebook and picked up a pen.

The experiments conducted inside the lab code-named Vortex had produced an array of results ranging from lethal to extraordinary. But by far the most interesting were the offspring of the man who had been placed in charge of the lab, Dr. Alexander Winston. He had conducted some of the experiments on himself and his wife, Aurora. They had produced a daughter.

Unfortunately for him, Alexander Winston had not been shy about scattering his sperm far and wide. Most of the women he had impregnated had been unwitting victims of his experiments. Winston had kept careful records of his offspring right up until his wife had discovered his outside activities.

Aurora had been more than a little irritated. As head of the Vortex lab, Alexander had already taken credit for the results of much of her own brilliant work in the field of paranormal research. Discovering that Alexander was cheating on her had been too much.

Officially Alexander Winston had died in the course of a disastrous lab accident involving radiation and an unknown crystal. But Aurora had made detailed notes of her husband's final hours in her journal. Gwendolyn had been able to decipher that section. There was no doubt in her mind about the cause of death. Aurora Winston had exacted her revenge.

> . . . Alex's delirium grows worse by the hour. He now suffers from extreme anxiety and wild hallucinations. I never leave his bedside. The clinic staff think I am the most devoted of wives. But Alex knows the truth. I see it in his eyes. He has tried to tell the doctors I am responsible for what is happening to him, but they attribute his ravings to the effects of the radiation. Everyone here is convinced that what happened in the lab was a dreadful accident. There is no way I can be blamed. After all, I was in another wing of the lab when the disaster occurred . . .

After Alexander Winston's death, management of the Vortex lab had been handed to Aurora, in part because no one else was qualified for the position, but mostly because it was rapidly becoming apparent that engaging in paranormal research was not a smart career path for ambitious scientists. Times had changed, and so had mainstream attitudes. Those who claimed to be psychic or to possess extrasensory perception were often dismissed as charlatans and frauds.

Nevertheless, Aurora believed in the potential of paranormal research and dedicated herself to it—right up until, with no warning, the entire Bluestone Project was closed down. The order was given to destroy all of the labs, including Vortex.

Afterward Aurora had become reclusive and increasingly paranoid. Eventually she had died under mysterious circumstances. Her daughter, Pandora, was profoundly embarrassed by her mother's mental illness. She did her best to ensure a normal upbringing for her own two daughters, both of whom had become successful in their chosen fields.

Eloisa was a research scientist who currently worked for a pharmaceutical company. After obtaining a degree in archaeology, Gwendolyn had opened Swan's Antiques in Seattle's Pioneer Square.

Pandora had died in a car accident a year ago. Gwendolyn and Eloisa had discovered the diary and, with it, their secret heritage while cleaning out their mother's house.

Nothing would ever be the same for either of them.

CHAPTER 41

Victor and I have a business proposition to put to the two of you," Lucas said. "The discovery of the Fogg Lake lab is going to require a lot of professional assistance. We are hoping that the firm of Lark and LeClair will agree to serve as a liaison between the Las Vegas headquarters of the Foundation and the community of Fogg Lake."

They were gathered in Catalina's apartment. Victor and Lucas occupied the sofa. Olivia was in the reading chair. Slater stood near the window. Catalina had put a plate of cheese and crackers on the coffee table and had just finished pouring the wine.

Lucas's proposal stopped her cold.

"Would you define *liaison*?" she said carefully.

Olivia's gaze sharpened with interest. "Yes, please define."

"We are well aware that the Fogg Lake community is not thrilled to have the Foundation move into town," Lucas said. "Unfortunately the Rancourts left an unfavorable impression."

Catalina took a sip of her wine. "You can say that again."

"We need the cooperation of the locals," Lucas continued. "We're afraid that some of the experts on the Foundation staff will not be sensitive to the nuances of the community's expectations and behavioral norms."

"What Uncle Lucas is trying to say," Slater said, "is that he and Victor are afraid that some of the Foundation people will see Fogg Lake as an interesting biological experiment."

"You mean they'll view the residents as research subjects," Olivia said.

"That will definitely piss off the locals," Catalina warned.

"We're aware of that," Victor said. "Our cunning plan is to establish a satellite office here in Seattle."

Olivia's eyes tightened at the corners. "You want to take over our business?"

"No, no, no," Lucas said quickly. "The Foundation would be a client of Lark and LeClair. The teams from Vegas will be flying through Seattle. We will provide guides to meet them and escort them to Fogg Lake but we want them to stop here first to get some background on the history of the community."

"Lark and LeClair is not a travel agency," Catalina said.

Victor fixed his piercing gaze on Catalina. "Here's the rest of the deal, Ms. Lark. While the Foundation will provide security at the excavation site, it's a given that there will be problems. There always are in situations like this."

"Because the artifacts in that old lab are worth a fortune?" Catalina said.

"Yes. No matter how tight our security is, word of the discovery will leak out and attract the attention of raiders and freelancers. But our primary concern is Vortex."

"Assuming it really did exist and that someone is trying to find it," Catalina said.

Slater looked at her. "After recent incidents we can no longer assume it's just a legend. Someone or some group of people is apparently trying to find that particular lab, and they are willing to kill to do it. There's a high probability that there are some very dangerous secrets inside. It would be best if those secrets did not—"

"Fall into the wrong hands," Catalina said. "I get it. You know, what you really should be doing is searching for whoever is trying to find that old lab."

"Trust me," Victor said. "The Foundation is working on that angle. But in the meantime we need to protect the Fogg Lake lab and we would like your professional assistance."

Catalina thought about that for a beat. "Huh."

Olivia looked at her. "A client is a client, and one thing we know about the Foundation is that it pays its bills."

"There is that," Catalina conceded.

"We could use the money to move into more upscale offices," Olivia continued, enthusiasm sparking in her tone. "We would have the resources to go after that niche market of singles-with-a-paranormal-vibe-seeking-singles-with-a-paranormal-vibe that we've been trying to figure out how to target."

Catalina drank some wine and thought about it some more.

"Huh," she said again.

Slater cleared his throat. "I have suggested that if Lark and LeClair does decide to accept the Foundation as a client, it will need a representative from headquarters stationed here in Seattle."

Catalina looked at him. "Would this representative be here on a temporary basis?"

Slater's eyes heated. "Permanent."

A rush of joy lifted Catalina's senses. The room got a little brighter. She looked at Olivia.

"I think we could add the Foundation to our list of clients," she said.

Olivia cast a benevolent smile on her and on Slater.

"Working together at Lark and LeClair will give the two of you plenty of time to get to know each other," she said.

"Right," Catalina said.

Slater's eyes heated. "Right. Plenty of time."

CHAPTER 42

Las Vegas, one week later...

Y ou know," Slater said, "this isn't bad for a couple of risk-averse people. It doesn't get much more spontaneous than a midnight wedding in Las Vegas."

Catalina stirred, rolled off Slater and fell onto her back. She opened her eyes and regarded the mirrored ceiling overhead. The image of the two of them cuddled close together, naked in a wildly rumpled bed, made her smile.

"Just call us Mr. and Ms. Spontaneous," she said.

Slater folded one arm behind his head and studied the reflection. "You do realize a five-minute ceremony with Elvis officiating is not going to satisfy our families. I predict a lavish reception, lots of useless gifts and a night of dancing under the stars on the roof garden of my uncle's penthouse in our near future."

"That sounds nice. Olivia can take me shopping for a sexy gown and some sparkly high heels."

"I thought you looked terrific in your black jeans and that black trench coat tonight."

"Thank you." She turned on her side and drew her fingertips across Slater's chest. "You looked pretty fabulous yourself, in your cargo pants and that T-shirt and leather jacket."

"We are apparently a couple of fashion icons. Who knew?"

Several hours ago they had been sitting in a coffeehouse in Seattle talking about their future when Slater had looked at her and said, "Can you think of one good reason why we should wait?" She had contemplated the question for about two seconds before she came up with her response: "Nope."

Slater had snagged three seats—economy class because there were no first-class seats available—on a flight to Las Vegas. Olivia had taken the third seat. "You'll need a witness," she explained.

The next thing Catalina knew she was marrying Slater in a wonderfully tacky wedding chapel on the Strip. In addition to Olivia, Victor and Lucas had shown up to act as witnesses and serve as the groom's best men. After the event, Slater's uncles had taken Olivia on a tour of the town's hottest nightclubs. Catalina and Slater had slipped away to an over-the-top honeymoon suite at one of the glitziest hotels on the Strip. The room had been a wedding gift from Victor and Lucas.

"What do you say we try out that whirlpool bath in the other room?" Slater suggested.

"Excellent idea," Catalina said.

Slater got to his feet and reached for her hand. She rolled off the bed, entwined her fingers in his and stood on tiptoe to brush a kiss across his mouth. He caught her head in one hand and held her in place so that he could deepen the kiss.

"You know, they say that no one can predict the future," she said. "But between you and me, ours looks very, very good."

"Yes," Slater said, "it does. Better than good. Perfect. I love you, Catalina."

She touched the edge of his jaw with one fingertip. "I love you, Slater."

"Forever," he said.

"Forever."

He kissed her again, sealing the vow. When he raised his head she could see the heat in his eyes. Energy shivered in the atmosphere.

Catalina smiled. "I always knew there would be fireworks and lightning."

WANT MORE JAYNE ANN KRENTZ?

LOOK OUT FOR . . .

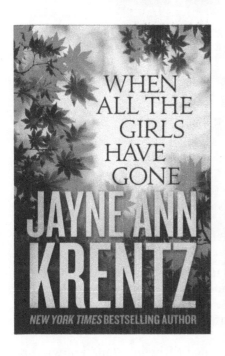 

'Jayne Ann Krentz is one of my favourite
romantic suspense writers'
Meg Tilly

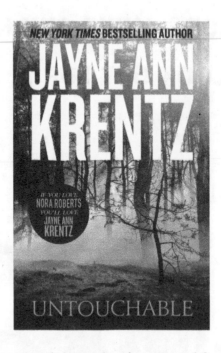

NEW YORK TIMES BESTSELLING AUTHOR

JAYNE ANN
KRENTZ

IF YOU LOVE
NORA ROBERTS
YOU'LL LOVE
JAYNE ANN
KRENTZ

UNTOUCHABLE

Jack Lancaster spends his nights dreaming of fire. After nearly burning to death in his childhood home, he resolved to hunt down the man responsible – the charismatic cult leader known as **Quinton Zane.**

Twenty years later, Jack is a renowned FBI consultant, known for his almost preternatural ability to get inside the killer's head. But the more cases he solves, the deeper he slips into the darkness – and the more his still unresolved past begins to torment him.

His only solace is **Winter Meadows,** a hypnotist who's helping Jack decode his mysterious dreams. But when Winter falls into danger at the hands of an old enemy, they are brought together as more than just therapist and client. Meanwhile, the one man whose dark legacy continues to haunt Jack is nearer than they think – and more powerful than ever.

A feverish, suspenseful read with a smouldering secret at its heart, perfect for fans of Nora Roberts and Melinda Leigh.